DALE LOVES
SOPHIE TO
DEATH

ROBB FORMAN DEW

DALE LOVES
SOPHIE TO
DEATH

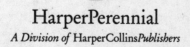

HarperPerennial
A Division of HarperCollins*Publishers*

The first chapter of this book originally appeared, in slightly different form, in *The New Yorker.*

A hardcover edition of this book was published in 1981 by Farrar, Straus & Giroux. It is here reprinted by arrangement with Russell & Voldening, Inc.

HarperCollins books may be purchased for educational, business, or sales promotional use. For information please write: Special Markets Department, HarperCollins Publishers, Inc., 10 East 53rd Street, New York, NY 10022.

First HarperPerennial edition published 1993.

Designed by Jeffrey Schaire

Library of Congress Cataloging-in-Publication Data

Dew, Robb Forman.
  Dale loves Sophie to death / Robb Forman Dew. — 1st HarperPerennial ed.
    p.   cm.
  ISBN 0-06-097539-3 (pbk.)
  I. Title.
PS3554.E9288D3   1993
813'.54—dc20   92-54260

93 94 95 96 97 CW 10 9 8 7 6 5 4 3 2

FOR CHARLES
STEPHEN
& JACK

DALE LOVES SOPHIE TO DEATH

CHAPTER ONE

DALE LOVES SOPHIE TO DEATH

Every summer Dinah was sick in this house she rented. She lay in the double bed alone, amid a jumble of Kleenex and the mail and the morning newspaper, and she did not change the sheets until she felt well. Sometimes two weeks, sometimes three. The light shot into her room in the morning, so that her eyes would ache, and then it shifted and faded as the day wore on, and through all these changes of light she drifted in a fog of sleep and waking and the children's bodies buffeting against her bed. Propped up on pillows, she could see her three children, through the tall branched shrubs beyond the windows, as they ran around playing or fighting. But she would lie dazed and sure that they could get through the day with only her occasional direction. David, the oldest, was always herding the other two, it seemed; when she closed her eyes, the red imprint of his ushering arms in motion shuddered through her mind as her thoughts drifted away from the actual image.

Her mother often stopped by on the way home from her office in nearby Fort Lyman and brought Dinah food from the deli or some other takeout place. Today she brought a barbecued chicken the size of a dove, and Dinah sat in her bed and ate it with her fingers, sucking the knobs of the little drumsticks like candy. Her mother sat on the vanity bench, at an angle not quite facing the bed, and talked desultorily, because the disarray in which Dinah wore out her illness dismayed her. It had always been assumed in Dinah's childhood household that illness was a weakness of character, a burden to the entire family, and, above all else, being ill was considered a sly trick. So Mrs. Briggs pushed her straw-colored hair behind her ears impatiently as she sat there required to hear just how Dinah felt. Dinah said she felt feverish; she said she had a sore throat and aching ears. Her mother sat in the early twilight, covertly eyeing herself in the mirror, and she sighed when she noticed that Dinah had sunk down into her pillows once more, leaving the little chicken carcass stripped bare in its greasy wrapper by her side. She thought she bore up very well under these illnesses of Dinah's.

"I'll take the children on with me, then," Mrs. Briggs said, and she collected the parcel of chicken bones from the bed and went to look through the window to see if the children were in sight. Dinah lay unmoving and with her eyes closed. Mrs. Briggs was not a good cook, so she considered the frozen and canned options for the children's dinner. She also considered scrambled eggs, which were healthful but which no one ever finished at her house. Dinah had told her the reason for this with patient tact, and had advised her about better methods of preparation, but Polly Briggs had never heard all that her daughter said. She still heated butter in a skillet and broke the eggs directly into it, cracking the shells on the aluminum rim of the pan, and then she agitated them as swiftly as possible; they always appeared on the plate as though they had been marbleized, with the yellow and white running separately throughout. Also on the plate she would place one piece of toast with a pat of butter squarely in its middle, to be dealt with however one might wish. These things were gestures: the eggs broken, not just boiled, the toast prebuttered—even the butter itself, rather than margarine. They were quite generous gestures from a woman who cared not at all about food but had a melancholy interest, generally, in the people she fed, and especially in these children to whom she acknowledged a connection.

When the house was empty and there was no sound from the yard, Dinah opened her eyes and regarded the room. This year it was hung with more recent pictures of the family who owned the house. All told, in the past eight years she had spent close to twenty-four months in this house, and although she had never met the owners, she felt that she and they had established a certain intimacy simply by virtue of sharing the same paraphernalia of everyday life. She used up rather than discarded the half-empty jar of mustard in the refrigerator, for instance, and in her view that was a very solemn intimacy; the first summer she would have thrown it out in horror. And, of course, this intimacy in absentia bred its own sort of expectations; Dinah expected to find evidence each summer that life in this house continued during the winter just as she imagined it. She looked with interest at the new photographs hung in the bedroom, because she knew these people—not all their names, but she knew how they were growing up or changing.

This summer there was a new picture of the daughter of the house, whose other photographs, scattered here and there through all the rooms, dated back to her infancy. This current snapshot, enlarged and framed handsomely on the wall opposite the end of the bed, showed a very lovely young woman frozen in the upswing of a jogging step as she ran through a prosperous-looking neighborhood. Dinah studied her drowsily, thinking that she must know her. The girl looked as if she would be interesting to know, with her hair flying around her face and a cast-off sweater tied around her neck by its sleeves. It was possible that they had passed each other at some time or other—at a state park, perhaps, or some restaurant. A public bathroom maybe. Dinah was drenched in her luxurious illness—flu with fever. She felt she glowed inside and out with this lovely, gentle radiance of almost 102 degrees. Her head throbbed independently, so she could objectively consider the shell of pain encasing her mind. She swallowed two aspirin, and when they took effect she allowed herself to sleep until the aching of her head and limbs woke her automatically. When it did, she just lay there in bed, at home, considering her surroundings.

A t the beginning of each summer, Dinah and Martin Howells drove west from the Berkshires, where they lived, with their children in the back seat, and in two days' time they were in the lush farmland outside Enfield, Ohio. When they had first rented a house in Enfield, eight years earlier, they had had only David, then two years old. By now, the children thought it was the only place to spend those long weeks when there was no school. Dinah felt that these modest hills and voluptuous, rolling fields of corn and soybeans were essential to the very stability of her being. She had such a familiarity with this countryside that it didn't occur to her to miss the occasional sweeping view of valleys one happens on at high altitudes in New England. Instead, she hugged herself there in the front seat the moment she became aware of the vast, light-filled landscape proceeding endlessly in every direction. She felt as light-hearted, always, as a claustrophobe must feel upon emerging from an elevator.

On the first morning in their rented house Dinah was always affected with a reckless, thoughtless euphoria. She would make her nostalgic pilgrimage through the rooms, moving dreamily, and she would open all the curtains so that nowhere could there be found a somber corner. "Oh, my God! It's so good to be somewhere where I can pull up all the shades!" She would insist that everyone agree with her. "Isn't it? Don't you feel good?" She would not acknowledge the hesitation with which Martin always embarked upon this summer venture. She didn't think of his saying, "But why do you do this to yourself year after year?"

Dinah had no answer to that. It was only that in West Bradford at Christmas, when a card arrived from the Hortons, the owners of the house in Enfield, she looked out at the winter and began to entertain thoughts of summer. Those thoughts did not run deep but were like photographs flashing through her mind. This winter, on the day the Hortons' card arrived, Dinah and Martin had happened to go to lunch at a pleasant restaurant, decorated with an abundance of greens and a large blue spruce standing in the foyer unadorned except for hundreds of tiny white lights. There were flowers on the tables, and other people's children were being allowed to wander around the room and stretch their legs while their parents lingered over coffee. Everyone was well dressed, even with a certain dash, and the stark landscape—the sky, dense and heavy just overhead, the boundless white ground—only emphasized the singular feeling of goodwill Dinah had toward the other diners. But with all this the atmosphere just brushed over Dinah's senses; it did not permeate her thoughts, because she had tucked the beautiful Caspari card from Adele Horton into her purse; she was thinking of what it said, and her mind had become entangled with images of her summer household. The message was nothing, really: "Wish we could share with you some of this lovely apple chutney I've put up for special friends. Will certainly leave some for you if you take the house again this summer." But Dinah had found such a homely notion—to share some chutney— stupefyingly seductive. She could not help but sit there in a restaurant in New England with her husband and consider the life being led right at that moment in that house in Enfield. Such an intense life—so full that it could not be contained in ordinary spaces and overflowed in little notes and letters and photographs inscribed with cryptic messages that even fluttered from the cookbooks Dinah sometimes pulled down from Mrs. Horton's shelves. More letters were stuffed haphazardly between the books in the living-room cases, and curling photographs and mysterious souvenirs filled every extra drawer. Quaint drawings by children or friends were carefully framed and hung in odd corners. It seemed to Dinah that so much life went on there that her own existence could not compare. She was beginning to think that the five of them—she and Martin and the children—were simply too sparse a group to generate such vitality.

But she knew that Martin loved her and she him. She understood his intentions when he asked her why she put herself through those summers. Well, she could never justify it; she could only raise a hand in a gesture of exhaustion—and exhaustion was all she felt when she thought to examine her motives—to reply halfheartedly, "Oh, you know the children love it. Don't you think it's good for them to get a feeling of family?" She didn't even glance at Martin to see the look of doubt come over his face. He knew the dubious nature of what family feeling there was since Dinah's parents had divorced and her father had moved into his own house, directly across the street from the Hortons'. "Well," she would offer, "things just aren't settled there yet to my satisfaction."

And so summer had come, and here she was once more. But, upon their arrival and her inspection of the familiar rooms, she knew her insistence that Martin share her enthusiasm for this place was unkind. She knew just how unkind, and she lay in bed letting herself be entirely given over to her private admission of guilt. With her head sunk down into her soft pillows, and her whole being made fragile and abject by the mellow, flu-induced ache of her muscles, she acknowledged her cruelty. Perhaps Martin had not felt it. Oh, no. This year, before he had had to leave to go back to teach his summer classes, they had really argued. Dinah tried concentrating on her illness once more. She thought about her various aches, and she pinpointed the fact that the way her ears felt could not really be called pain—more like a sore itching extending down into the base of her throat, so that it hurt to move her tongue. But the thought of the argument stayed in the forefront of her mind despite her, because it was not quite accurate. They had not argued; Dinah had attacked him, and now the thought of it made her flinch.

For the first two weeks of summer Martin and Dinah were always stranded together with the children in the rented house, without many diversions. During the long New England winters, when Dinah reviewed these times together, she said to herself that they were idyllic, but that had never been exactly the case. Their time together had generally been very pleasant, but there was always the stray mosquito or a child's hurt feelings, and there arose a peculiar tension between her and Martin as lovers. She felt a certain chafing at the constraints of being at once a daughter and a wife. But, really, she considered herself to be in great comfort, with her immediate family right there and yet situated so that there were no difficult expectations of herself that she must meet. It was privacy Dinah cherished, and it was the lack of it that she complained so bitterly about in West Bradford. In fact, in Enfield what passed for privacy was the absence of it altogether. So well did all the inhabitants know each other that they had long ago passed the point of pretense. It would have been futile in any case; it would have been absurd. And, therefore, very little was considered scandalous in retrospect—that is, if even just a year had passed since it happened. Very little was even considered remarkable. And so, coming back gave her an ease that she could never experience elsewhere; she understood the place so well.

She and Martin spent the days strolling through the town, eating their dinner at the picnic table under the pin oak in the back yard, and visiting with her family and good friends. They were only three blocks from her mother's house, and only one and a half blocks from the exact place in the sidewalk where Dinah had fallen her first time out on roller skates and chipped her front teeth. They were only a ten-minute walk from Dinah's grammar school, and only a ten-minute ride from her high school in Fort Lyman. As they walked down the shady streets or sat at a meal, Dinah would often point out these remarkable coincidences to Martin and the children, these astounding circumstances of her own childhood. Everyone would walk along the sidewalk with her and regard the tree in which Alan Brooks had built a tree house one summer. "And he's dead now," Dinah would say, bemused. "Buddy wrote me that he died in New Orleans." It was a mystery. But the children wouldn't think of what she was saying, although possibly these words would one day be to them one of those bewildering facts about one's parents that everyone accrues over the space of a childhood. Her children might one day say, "And my mother fell down and chipped her front teeth the first day she ever tried to roller-skate." No doubt they would see in their mind's eye the very spot in that little village where it had happened, and having gained their independence at last, with the usual struggle, they would be overwhelmed by the poignancy of having had so unexpectedly vulnerable a mother.

Or maybe they would never think of it again. Maybe they would think of the day Sarah had been lost, or the morning their grandmother had reached down David's throat to retrieve a piece of candy that would have choked him to death. To think of it! He would not have existed past that moment. They, too, experienced the most crucial turning points of their childhoods here. And how could they not? All winter, when the snow lay around their house in West Bradford, Dinah would urge them, "Wait, just wait until we get back to Enfield this summer." When the children raced up and down the stairs, not holding on to the banister and making too much noise, Dinah would follow after them in great aggravation. "For God's sake, can't you wait until we're in Enfield, where there's no snow? Then you can go outside and run around." And even though the children had seen pictures of their mother when she was a child playing in front of their grandmother's house in the snow, and even though they spoke on the phone to their uncle and grandmother at Christmas, when there was much talk of snow for want of other conversation, David and Toby and Sarah assumed that there never was any snow in Enfield. Enfield was a place of hot sun and light and long summer days.

The trip itself, however, always proved to be a terrible strain on the general good nature of the family. After two endless days on the road, all three children grew edgy and cross. Bribes and diversions no longer pacified them. This year, even Sarah was old enough to join in the melee.

"Toby's looking out my window, Mama! He's looking out *my* window!"

"Toby's sitting in the middle. What can he do?"

"I didn't look out *his* window when I was sitting in the middle!"

If only they were old enough and wise enough to remember to look out for the danger signals. Martin and Dinah recognized the signs forewarning each child's anger or distress—they knew their children so well. And the children knew their parents equally well, but they weren't so versed in the art of survival. From their vantage point, they could only see their mother's hair swing gently from side to side as she shook her head just slightly, in a silent conversation with herself. One corner of her mouth was pulled askew; she crossed her arms and grasped her elbows tightly and stared out the window.

"Oh, Mama, Toby's . . ."

And then Dinah half turned in her seat and stared at them in fury, and all three children were immediately filled with remorse.

"Well, damn it, Martin, stop the car!" she said in deadly, measured calm. "Stop this damned car! There's only one answer to this!" Her voice was so ominously low that the children looked away from her in nervous discomfort. And Dinah herself, with the blood beating in her ears, was not paying attention, either. In her rage she chose not to see the effect of her anger. "We will just put out Toby's eyes! We will just, goddamn it, put his eyes out!" She turned to stare at them more directly, and she gripped the back of the seat with one tense hand. At last, her voice rising, she said, "Will *that* make you happy, Sarah? Then, I swear to God, he will *never* look out of your window again! That should do it . . ."

Martin, of course, had not stopped the car and, in fact, was driving on placidly enough. "For God's sake, Dinah . . ." he finally put in. "Look! We're getting close," he said to the children. "See what landmarks you can find."

The children gladly followed his suggestion. Sarah ground the heels of her hands into her eyes to keep from crying, and the other two observed with relief that their mother turned back to look straight ahead after directing one incensed glare at their father. The children did not take this too much to heart, though. Even Sarah, at age four, had already perceived enough to know that her mother would die—really would die—before she would put out Toby's eyes. She quite rightly absorbed her mother's outburst as a rebuke to herself, and she continued to wipe at her tears furtively, and so she missed the first major landmark.

Toby spotted it, through Sarah's window, and he bounced in his seat. "I see Aunt Betsy's! There's Aunt Betsy's!" They came down the long hill and passed the bizarre diner once known as Aunt Jemima's, which had for years been a towering black mammy whose brick skirt housed a quite ordinary bar-and-grill. Now it was Aunt Betsy's, and the huge head loomed over the highway hideously pink, with gray rather than black hair escaping from the immovable bandanna.

For a while, all their tension was dispelled, and it was Sarah who, having knelt on the seat to repossess her window, shrieked to them all, "Look! 'Dale Loves Sophie to Death'! There it is!" Even though she couldn't read she knew it well. "There it is! 'Dale Loves Sophie to Death!' "

Their station wagon passed beneath the railway bridge on which this legend had been emblazoned ever since they could remember. The children were finally able to believe that they were indeed close to home. And David started up the song:

A hundred bottles of beer on the wall,
A hundred bottles of beer.
If one of those bottles should happen to fall—
Ninety-nine bottles of beer on the wall.

Family theory had it that when the song was done, and
there was only one bottle of beer left on the wall, they
would be home, although this had never yet been the case.
But everyone was relieved, because when the song was done
they would be close enough. Martin drove over the narrow
back roads smiling to himself, and Dinah noticed.

"What?" she asked.

"Oh, I just have always liked all this. It's genuine
Midwestern-tacky. Aunt Betsy's diner. And things written
all over the water tanks and bridges in huge letters." He
glanced at Dinah to smile at her in what he meant to
acknowledge as an admittedly smug conspiracy. Not for a
moment had he imagined that in being so blatantly pro-
vincial he did not also belittle himself. But Dinah was
looking rigidly out the window.

"Well," she said, so that he could hear her but so that
the children in the back seat continued their song, "you
think that 'Dale Loves Sophie to Death' should be typed, I
suppose. And tacked up on a little bulletin board in Jesse
Hall. You know, there's something about real, honest-to-God
emotion—I mean real things that real people go around
feeling—that you just never can understand. I mean, 'Dale
Loves Sophie to Death' is not exactly a lower-case sentiment!
I don't think you know a damned thing about that! You
just go mincing through your life with almost nothing *but*
lower-case sentiments!" She made movements with her
hands and her head, like a person taking small and hesitant
little steps, and she pursed her lips to indicate her immense
disdain.

He had been watching her with a startled expression, and
when he had taken it in, he laughed at the idea of himself,
rather thickset and solid, mincing into his various meetings,
teaching his classes, mincing through his days. And she

laughed, too, but it made her even more angry to find herself amused. She saw as well that Martin was wounded, and it made her so uncomfortable that she returned her gaze to the countryside that swept by outside her window. They both sat there in the front seat bewildered by her fury. They knew that she had been unfair, and Martin was not hurt by what she had said—he couldn't imagine that it applied to him—but he was hurt because she was so angry.

The day after their arrival, Martin and Dinah and the children abandoned their unpacking in the afternoon and walked down through the village to Dinah's mother's house. By now, it had become customary that a party of sorts would come together that evening, and Polly had made a routine of the preparations. She had bought a ham the day before, and Dinah stood at the counter scoring it in a diamond pattern and rubbing it with brown sugar. After she scored it, she would decorate it with rounds of sliced pineapple and maraschino cherries and put it in the oven to glaze. She looked out at the twilight approaching and was struck with sudden petulance.

"This is a little like decorating my own birthday cake," she said to her mother, who was transferring cartons of take-home potato salad to a cut-glass bowl. "Maybe you should line that bowl with lettuce leaves or something first, Mother. Don't you think?" But then Dinah thought of her father leaving the table in a cold rage one evening with a face like ice, saying, "Well, I don't know. Maybe we should just rent out our kitchen or turn it into a spare room, for all the use it gets." Dinah had been aware then that some key element of her parents' alliance was being defined for her when her mother made an eloquent sweep of her arm, palm upward, in a helpless gesture of apology and bewilderment. But her father had already left the room. With that in mind, Dinah turned to look at the potato salad once more. "No, it's fine. We don't know for sure that anyone will be coming by, anyway."

But her mother wasn't really listening. Polly had finished with the cut-glass bowl and had deposited all the little paper cartons in the trash. Dinah did regard that salad with dismay, however, because, as usual, it looked even more gelatinous and unappetizing in the pretty bowl than it had in its own containers, and summer after summer this had perplexed her. Her mother leaned against the counter, resting her weight on one narrow hip, and smoked a cigarette. She gazed through the window with one eyebrow slightly raised, in an attitude of complete indifference to her surroundings. Dinah had come across her mother thus transfixed so often that she no longer perceived it as a mystery. She watched her for a moment in admiration, however, because, caught in the dusky light, her mother—worn out, with her flesh drawn and lined and the skin at her jaw beginning to hang a trifle loosely from the bone—was lovelier than she had been when she was younger. The bare bones of her mother were coming to light, and Dinah thought that Polly was the only woman she knew who could combine a certain brittleness with an air of languid grace. But Dinah no longer puzzled over what her mother might be thinking.

On the porch, the children built card houses with the incomplete and abandoned packs of cards they had ferreted out of obscure drawers here and there around the house. They weren't building with much success, however, because the floorboards were so worn that they didn't afford sufficient purchase, and at crucial moments the bottom cards slipped out from beneath the upper construction. Polly's house resembled her person, by now. Even though her business was interior design, and she was good at it, her own house had been left to its own silent transmutations. The bare bones of the *house* were also coming to light, so that the walls seemed only a thin veil over the basic construction, and the furniture had a delicate look of age.

Martin sat at the other end of the porch with a newspaper resting on the knee of one crossed leg and talked with Dinah's brother, Buddy, and with Lawrence Brooks, who had come across the lawn from next door, where he had lived all his life. Now that house was Lawrence's own house.

He was a lawyer and no longer just a child next door. Lawrence's wife, Pam, idled over with their two-year-old son propped on one hip and sat down next to Dinah, and they began to chat.

As she listened and put in a word now and then, Dinah stared out at the communal lawn shared by the Brookses' and her mother's houses, which sat at right angles to each other. She studied the myriad tiny crosshatched branches of the flowering bushes that grew untended around the stone patio in the center of the yard. She hadn't much to say to Pam. Pam was so young, and her son seemed to take up both of their energies. The two women talked about the little boy, though it was apparent to each of them from the timbre of the other's voice that neither meant to or wanted to.

At the edge of their conversation, Dinah heard David badgering whomever he could find to come and play Monopoly with him, and Martin, who would do almost anything with David, finally got up, and the two of them went to find the board. Buddy and Martin and David and Dinah's mother settled around the card table at last and divided the money while Pam and Dinah went to mix drinks and set out dinner. Lawrence, still seated at the darkening edge of the porch, opened Martin's discarded newspaper and kept a casual eye on the other children.

This was the house in which Dinah had grown up, and her childhood was so fascinating and mysterious to her in retrospect that each room was of great significance. Even the unique and musty scent of the house, a scent like no other, tantalized her with the possibility of an important revelation. So this first night back in her mother's kitchen she could not abide the company of the innocent Pam. Dinah set out food at random and with no show at all of appreciation to Pam, who could only follow her about and try to help. And from the porch the sounds of the Monopoly game being laid out and getting under way made Dinah clench her teeth in apprehension, because David was, to his parents, like a rare gem set between them. He was not necessarily the nicest of their children, nor could it yet be said that he would be the most handsome, but he had been the first. It was not even that they loved him best; of course, he was not always lovable at all. It was just that beneath the surface of their consciousness there was an awareness of David that registered every shadow and nuance of his altering sensibilities. Their curiosity could never be assuaged by anything he might reveal about himself. They yearned after whatever it was that was at the very core of his personality, so puzzling to them was his blossoming independence. Dinah could hear his clear voice babbling above the others, and she noted the effort he made to suppress the keenness he felt for the competition. Listening to the progress of the game was a little like refusing Novocain at the dentist's; it kept her on edge in anticipation of a painful shock.

She turned to Pam and smiled at her. She picked up Pam's little boy, Mark, who was getting into everything, and feigned interest in him. But after a few moments of this she was overtaken by unease, and she realized that she could not be gracious tonight. She thought she felt the beginnings of a cold amassing like clouds behind her brow, and she was anxious. She took her drink out to the patio, though the air had grown chilly, and sat at a distance from her family and friends. Here she was once more, and she sat in a lawn chair expecting the childhood comfort of early evening, with grownups nearby talking over their drinks, to descend upon her. She watched with care to see how the darkness encroached upon the margins of the yard; she impressed upon herself the phenomenon of the intricate tracery of the foliage losing its distinction, so that each tree and each bush became a shaded mass. She evoked all these familiar impressions, but the accompanying sensation of nostalgic pleasure did not surface. No mellowness spread like the warmth of alcohol through her limbs; she found she could not call up the renewed faith that all is well, that all will be well. In fact, all she was feeling was increasing irritation. The image of that ham stuck fast in her mind. There it sat, bedecked like a Christmas tree, waiting to be carved, and only Pam and her baby to attend it. Where were the grownups? So she roused herself and went back to the house to set about the serving of dinner.

A second circle had formed around the card table to see how the game was progressing, and so she, too, stopped to watch. Immediately she was aware of her son's fragile courage hanging so vulnerably in the air when she caught sight of his shining eyes and large gestures of bravado. He made a great show of cavalierly paying a debt. Buddy sat across from him, leaning back in his chair, accepting David's money with a grin and carefully sorting it into the proper piles. "I'm gonna clean up! Oh boy, I'm really gonna clean up!" he said with mock greed. But Dinah watched him as only a younger sibling would, knowing that Buddy didn't play games except to win. He was flicking an imaginary cigar between his fingertips and patting his stomach with the satisfaction of a contented businessman. David relaxed and smiled at him with unassumed pleasure; Buddy's pantomime seemed to assure him that this was only a game. Dinah could scarcely bear it.

Her mother sat with all her bills gathered into a pile that she held in one hand and ruffled absentmindedly with her thumb. She rolled the dice with seeming indifference. Who could tell if it was real? She was looking out into the yard when the dice fell, and she looked around at the numbers on them almost in surprise and reached for her cigarette. She moved her token to St. James Place and completed a monopoly, the first of the game, and David sat up on his knees in excitement to look over the board. "Wow! You got the first one, Polly!"

"Oh, yes, I guess I did," she said, paying out the money for the deed. But she would win as usual, Dinah knew. Polly couldn't lose at games, playing, as she did, with tremendous detachment and no thought given to bribing her luck, while her competitors silently tried to strike up bargains with God or fate. Polly would finally wander away from the game, uninterested even in her own victory. It was maddening.

David rolled the dice and landed on a railroad. He had two already, and now was beside himself with delight. "I'll get you, Uncle Buddy! Now I'll really get you if you land on me! You'll have to pay me a hundred dollars. A hundred dollars!" Buddy covered his face at the grim prospect and sadly shook his head, and Dinah understood with gratitude that her brother was using all his charm to align himself with David, so that David could withstand the suspense of this intolerable game.

But Martin didn't play games, didn't know about games, really; he was so innocent of some things, and he was watching his son with an air of censure. Dinah felt suddenly as though those four people were frozen in the moment: her mother abstracted, Buddy all pretense, Martin the epitome of thought and propriety, and David open to anything, ready to head in any of their directions. And, sure enough, Martin frowned across the table at his son. "Don't be so rude to Buddy, David. You shouldn't gloat. That's one of the first things to learn about playing games. Otherwise, you'll hurt people's feelings."

"Oh, Jesus," Dinah said. "What a pompous ass you are sometimes, Martin. Great God!" And in a frenzy of frustration at them all she glared into their crestfallen little group. "Not one of you—not a single one of you—has any idea how to play this asinine game!" And she stalked from the room while they all stared after her.

"Dinah, you talk like some kind of sailor," her mother said, mildly. Dinah left the room in a fury, going straight to the kitchen, and instead of carving the ham into careful slices, she hacked it savagely into chunks that were scarcely manageable when eaten buffet-style on paper plates.

Two weeks later, when she drove Martin into Columbus to catch his plane back East, she considered various ways of apologizing to him for the foul and dismal temper she had vented at him over the past long days. She looked at his clean head, which she so loved, silhouetted against the car window, and she wanted to weep at the misunderstanding between them. She was sure she was coming down with a flu, and she simply couldn't think. There was no one, no others but the children, to whom she was more tied. But then, as they passed through the familiar fields and the little towns, she could not think how to isolate that misunderstanding; how could she name it?

Now, as she suffered all the physical miseries of the flu, she also ached with a regret at having left a chink uncovered in their carefully constructed foundation of experience and tolerance. She lay in bed staring at the walls, awash in something similar to guilt, only much worse. There was self-loathing, there was fear, and, oh, there was a kind of homesickness she felt at this slight loss of herself, because she might have weakened a profound connection.

She looked at the picture, directly across from her, of that girl running. She was growing more beautiful each summer, and Dinah studied her intently. The girl's endearingly long upper lip was almost ready to smile, but she was clearly giving no thought to the camera. Caught in midstride as she was, she was involved only with herself; she was thinking about her next step. Dinah studied the picture for a long while, so that by the time her fever returned and she began to drift into a light sleep she had become convinced that she did, indeed, know this girl. The girl was Sophie, beloved of Dale, loping steadily toward him, or perhaps away from him, through that neighborhood, to be loved or not to be loved to death.

CHAPTER TWO

SUMMERTIME

For himself, Martin could scarcely bear this leave-taking each summer, always the same, their two weeks in Enfield culminating in an obligatory kiss at the departure gate. He walked away leaving Dinah standing alone and unhappy, but what he thought they both longed to do was to stay—somewhere, in the car, standing on the asphalt, simply stay—just to talk and talk to each other. His vision was of the many words spilling from their mouths and taking a physical shape, all those words entwining them vinelike in what would be the final explanation. They would be enclosed in an arbor that would be the exact definition of themselves. Then they could sigh with relief. They could hold hands and smile. But it never happened, and these summers they parted mute with bewildered misery, feeling at once that they were being forced apart, and yet each anxious to be away from the other. In two days, a week, many times over the summer, they would telephone, and little pieces of apologies, of curiosity and best wishes, would be passed back and forth over the wires, so that at summer's end they had the illusion once more of having made a concrete alignment, a familiar bridge, a bond.

And in the airport with Dinah, and as he took his seat on the plane, Martin was visited with his usual apprehension and fear of death, and also he was plagued by that now familiar but equally unsettling hollowness in his stomach at the prospect of taking up his life alone. That feeling approached sorrow and self-pity, and yet it was also comprised of the few, small lingering doubts about himself and the way he had chosen to live his life. The stretch of solitary time before him seemed shiny and glamorous with possibilities, and yet he did not hunger after change; he didn't like to anticipate the unknown. He had never liked uncertainty, so he buckled his seat belt and sat back in his padded chair in a quandary.

Whenever Martin was in transit, he was more or less a man absolutely free. All the thoughts that tied him either to one place or to another fled his mind; therefore, the trip was a gentle interlude. Once the plane left the ground, his mind went idle; he was fairly undisturbed. But as he glanced at the people in the seats around him and saw the stewardesses at the front of the plane bend to each passenger with some question or instruction, he did, as usual, become preoccupied with his appearance. He could never believe he looked like a man who should be on a plane, because Martin was just old enough, at thirty-eight, so that he could remember airports as exotic places. As a child he had relished his own self-importance when boarding those large passenger planes among the beautifully dressed travelers, and he had stared out the window over the wingspan to see the propellers putt-putt-putt and then become a transparent blur of motion. He could not lose that notion of air travel even now, when he observed that across the aisle a couple in jeans and with backpacks at their feet took it none too seriously. It seemed that it was no more to them than taking the bus.

Still, he considered how he must look to the stewardess. Once, when his mother had come to meet him at the train station where he arrived on a trip home from graduate school, she had been laughing when he had finally made his way through the crowd and reached her. "Oh, Martin! You've gained some weight! Martin, your face looks like the full moon coming up over the bay!" He was trimmer now, but he did not have a look of authority or importance, even though, in his real life, these were qualities he possessed in some small way. This failure of his to match up to himself had always disappointed him. He was tall enough, but because of his thick torso and rather short legs, he looked stocky and bearlike—sometimes an endearing trait, he knew. His features, though, were so innocent and exactly arranged that his sweet, pale face set atop his wrestler's body was as surprising as the black dot in an exclamation point. His looks belied a mildly severe nature, and on airplanes he would have been pleased to look severe. He would have liked to look like a man who needed a drink to unwind. He didn't know that he had aged, and that his round, choirboy's face had elongated a bit with the pull of gravity. He had finally developed a faint air of irritation not so uncommon in people who otherwise have a look of boundless good nature. The stewardess accorded him due respect, though he didn't perceive it, and no one else was paying attention, anyway.

Vic met him at the airport, and he had not brought Ellen along just so he and Martin could discuss the *Review*. And they did discuss it all the way home. Aside from the two seminars he would teach at the college, most of Martin's summer would be given over to discussions just of this sort, and he was weary in the car as they passed through the Berkshire Mountains to West Bradford. He was relieved to be quiet at last and back in his house when Vic dropped him off. But he was perplexed, too, when he was left there alone. He opened the shades, even the ones over the windows that looked down on the town's single commercial street, and, most particularly, at a college bar and Laundromat adjacent to it. He had never found these buildings offensive; they weren't so very near, just easily seen from the height of the house. The house was silent, but Dinah's energy seemed to emanate from every corner and cubby of those rooms, and he was unnerved. When Martin was in this house he liked it; he always had, but now the rambling shell of the building shrouded him in a peculiar eroticism. He was more aware of his wife's impact on these rooms now that she was *not* in them. His family's artifacts were every-where around him, and that was what buildings were to Martin: simply containers. He had no other vision of them, though he had tried at various times in his life to think of them apart, as art in themselves. But now, when he sat down in a chair, he never even considered the color of the woodwork or the very walls and the manner of their con-struction. He sat in a chair in his living room with the tall trees swaying in the yard outside and was aware only of the remnants his family had left behind them.

What puzzled him unaccountably was the unperturbed order settled into every cranny, up the stairs, into the bath-rooms, bristling at him from the closets and the cupboards. In the usual course of events this was a household state seldom attained, and even then attained only after the expenditure of great energy and fury, and always attained temporarily.

"We're terrible in this place together," Dinah often said when they were in the midst of battling back the disorder that occasionally enveloped their lives so that they had to stop and put things right just to get on with their work. "You only understand neatness, and I only care about basic sanitation. You'd think it would work out so that we com-plemented each other, but instead we never really get the place either neat or clean!"

When the house was put in a state of domestic efficiency—with every towel folded, beds made, sinks clean—the arrangement was tenuous. And it seemed ominous to Martin, just for a moment, that throughout the summer, with only its lone inhabitant, the household would function with a calm and gloomy regulation.

As he walked around in his house, he found numerous plastic bins filled with carefully sorted toys. Each year, before they made the trip to Enfield, Dinah rearranged and straightened and cleaned all the rooms, because she didn't want him to suffer from her habit of casual disarray. He discovered plastic building blocks in one bin, miniature cars in another, and so forth. In the kitchen there were two laundry baskets beside the clothes dryer. One was filled with clean clothes, through which he would sift this week, finding what he needed, and then he would deposit those same clothes, once he had worn them, into the companion basket —only to begin all over again after doing a wash. The drawer from which he took a paper napkin to set the table for his meals was full of wire closures for plastic bags, substitute tops for open soda bottles, checked-off grocery lists:

Milk
½ & ½
granola bars
chicken
tomatoes
Toby's sd. drsg.
chick-peas (4)

He was overwhelmed with the sweet triviality of these things left behind, in the same way he would have been affected if his family had all gone off to war. In their bedroom he was even more overcome. Dinah's books were shoved beneath the draped quilt which covered her round night table. A basket by her bed still enclosed a plethora of small articles she gathered throughout a day and deposited there at night when she emptied her pockets; she would sort them eventually. There was a book of matches, though she didn't smoke, a child's rubber eraser in the shape of a little car, spools of thread, a large cat's-eye marble, etc. He sat on the edge of the bed transfixed, heady with the presence of his wife. He remembered when he had fallen in love with her, or at least he remembered the feeling of being in love with her, when there had been a sultry kind of tension between them, and now he would certainly say he loved her— he did love her—but that struck him as too simple a description. It was more as though she and he anticipated the other's moods and longings so exactly that they forever wore the other's persona like a cloak. Martin played the radio or the television most of the time the first few days of every summer to dispel the uncanny silence.

Into the second week, though, he fell into the rituals of

isolated domesticity he had developed over the many summers of Dinah's absence. The world *beyond* the house became suddenly erotic to him as well, so that even at the grocery store as he was sorting through the onions he might look across the aisle at a stringy girl choosing among the bell peppers and be stunned by desire. Ordinary people all at once seemed extraordinary in their mundane surroundings; their images leaped out at him from a hazy background like those photographs from SX-70 cameras in which the colors are more than real.

He grew even trimmer, because there was no comfort in having his meals alone at the kitchen table without his family. He took up his summer life as usual, relying more and more on Vic and Ellen. He spent a great deal of time with them, often bringing food to their house to be cooked and shared with them for dinner. Ellen's sister, Claire, was there for the summer—or perhaps forever; Martin had long ago stopped asking Vic and Ellen for information about themselves when he had at last discovered that they would only look back at him with a smile—ironic and mysterious. It baffled him, but it stifled his curiosity.

When he and Dinah had first come to know the Hofstatters, the four of them had been inseparable. They had all, for a while, felt that they had found soulmates— two happy couples, intelligent, young—and then subtly Dinah's disaffection began to settle into a solid enough persuasion so that Martin became aware of it. At first he had suspected jealousy, because Ellen was many things that Dinah was not. She was petite and exact and careful in her housekeeping, just as Vic was so precise in all his habits. Ellen had a mind and temperament like glistening, cool metal. She could be sharp; she was slightly inflexible. Martin knew that Dinah did not think *he* particularly admired those traits or even thought much about the difference between the two women. He thought Dinah might be jealous solely on her own behalf, because Ellen possessed qualities of order and emotional discipline that Dinah had longed for all her life. But one day Dinah had walked quietly into Ellen's kitchen while Ellen shelled peas at the sink and found Martin, taken unawares, contemplating Ellen's brown legs, muscular and supple in her brief red shorts. Dinah had looked at those legs, too, with a cool eye —his conspirator—until Ellen turned from the sink and the moment was over. When he thought about Dinah's detached and aloof assessment, Martin decided her new and private disenchantment could not be due entirely to jealousy, after all.

During those long evening conversations, over glasses of beer, about what America really meant, or the particular sort of world view that must be brought to the writing of great literature, Dinah began to grow more silent. When Ellen leaned her elbows onto the table, with her hair swinging forward in its long, curly triangles against her forearms, and spoke in her soft, intense, persuasive voice, he had begun to notice more and more that Dinah retreated into the haven of her bentwood chair. And one day his suspicions of Dinah's inexplicable disdain had been absolutely confirmed. They had all been working in the Hofstatters' garden, and Martin looked in the direction of the two women to see if it was almost time to stop. Ellen had bounced on her haunches as she stooped to gather beans from their intricate vines, and she began to sing some song in a gentle voice, but Martin saw a look cross Dinah's face which pronounced it all artifice—the entire enterprise. There were the four of them working in this rural garden while the sun went down, and Dinah's expression proclaimed it all artifice. And so, gradually, their association with Vic and Ellen had waned.

But Martin didn't see artifice in the lives of his two friends; alone, he took pleasure in their company in the summers. And he knew Ellen had a special interest in him, just as Vic did. An unusual intimacy had come about over the years; he felt more than ordinarily included in their lives. He would arrive, for instance, just as Ellen had lost her bra in the pond while she and Vic swam, and she would sit in the rowboat glimmering and topless, her breasts drooping a bit and touchingly vulnerable to scrutiny, while Vic dove and searched through the muddy weeds. She and Martin would chat quite naturally, but always for some reason—the flash of her white, white teeth in a small smile, a raised eyebrow—he understood that he was meant to know this was not just common friendship. Vic would emerge nude, guileless, and dripping, with the sodden brassiere held aloft in triumph, and Ellen would turn her back while he fastened it for her. Martin enjoyed this special informality, and it fascinated him, because he knew that Dinah would view it with scorn, but he couldn't think why.

In his own house, however, he still longed for his family. He would dream of his wife and wake to find she wasn't there. Her clothes hanging in the closet made him sad with yearning. He thought and thought about her, and her incredible energy seemed to have remained behind her, like thwarted intentions. He found her bedraggled winter night-gown on a hook on the back of the bathroom door, over the hot-water bottles suspended from their plastic tops, and it made him intolerably melancholy. It was as personal to him as her skin.

Martin wasn't a man who noticed buildings or paintings or clothes, and he had not even been aware that, day after day, Dinah had washed her flannel gown and worn it again that night. He hadn't known until he woke up one morning to find the bed empty of Dinah, and the house, too, he had thought after looking. He finally came upon her enclosed in her bathroom. When he called her name, she didn't answer, and so he rattled the door and called her again.

"It's all right, Martin," she finally answered him, but her voice was full and tight in her throat, so he knew she was crying. He had only been able to stand at the door, sleepy and irritated and puzzled, not knowing how to proceed. But she opened the door and leaned against the doorjamb in that ragged flannel gown printed with little candlesticks, and held her hands over her face and wept as heartily as Martin had ever seen her.

"Oh, God, Martin," she said. "How can you love me? How

can you? I don't think you do. I don't think you could!"
She cried on and on, and he didn't touch her at all he was
so surprised. He didn't even know what she could mean. He
felt the beginnings of a vast exasperation that sometimes
becomes a chasm between men and women. He was tired;
he was angry, and he was helpless in this one instance
because of the disparity of their separate male and female
histories.

"Look at me! Just look at me! I woke up in the middle of
the night with the most awful feeling. Oh, Martin, I haven't
slept! I felt my whole face change; I felt my skin pulling
and sliding. Why didn't you *tell* me? I thought I was still so
pretty! Damn!" and she slapped her hand against the woodwork in teary fury. "I wouldn't have cared so much if I had
known! Why didn't you tell me? I have circles under
my eyes—bags under my eyes—and creases where I smile. I
can feel them from the *inside!* My hair doesn't shine anymore. Oh, God, oh, God, I used to be all shiny the way
young girls are. I used to *be* a young girl!"

David, then just eight, had come to the door of his room
and was watching them solemnly, but when his father
turned and saw him, he went back inside and closed the
door, embarrassed. Dinah was at last simply leaning against
the wall, her head back, and her hands hanging limply at
her sides. Her face was blotched and puffy, and her pale-
blue eyes looked rabbity, underlined as they were just then
with flaring red rims.

Martin was so taken aback that he only stood there and
thought how awful she did look at this moment. Maybe she
was right; why hadn't he told her? She wasn't pretty now;
she *was* getting older. But he was thoroughly struck through
with sympathy all at once, and he reached out and held
her against him, with one hand cupping the back of her
head to his shoulder. "I love you, though, Dinah. I just do
love you more than anything."

She cried and cried. "God! I'm sorry, I'm sorry, I'm
sorry," she said.

That evening she had looked as beautiful to him as

always when they went out to dinner. He looked for circles beneath her eyes and didn't see any; he noticed her soft, blond hair curling gently at the nape of her neck where it was tied with a blue scarf. She was, as usual, charming, enchanting, and unconsciously intimidating to the young couple they were entertaining. Martin had always seen that other men watched his wife, and they did tonight. He had no idea that there was beginning in his wife that subtle reliance on style rather than substance that gives to some women in their thirties and forties a particular grace.

When they were home she came to bed in a cream-colored, silky gown, very lacy, and he knew that she wanted him to hold her and admire her, and he *did* admire her, so that was exactly what he wanted to do. But it wasn't the way they always made love; she was rarely ever so vulnerable; she wasn't often a victim of vanity. That night she was the subject of her own censure; she kept herself under careful control. She lay beside him for a while, and he knew that she was still tense, but he wanted to sleep. He also had the idea that she didn't want him to realize her need; she wouldn't want to be approached again. Finally, she slipped away into the bathroom and came back in the tatty, tacky flannel gown. When she caught his glance she smiled at herself. "I sleep better in it," she said. "Well, it's so comfortable."

Martin didn't care about that at all. But he thought he might cry, in fact, lying there in the dark, when he remembered that all day he had been able to both pity and love his wife simultaneously. He thought that must augur well for the future.

But so early on in the summers these reminders of his family life were hard to take; they made him restless in his own house, and he roamed too much about the rooms, up and down the stairs. So he often fled. He set up a routine; he had his summer schedule. In the evenings Vic and Ellen arranged chairs for them all behind their old farmhouse, in the yard they had thrashed out of the tall weeds and black-berry bushes, and everyone would sit and have a drink and gaze down the hill at the pond and the slow horses meandering through the meadow in the afternoon. There were four adults regularly this summer, now that Ellen's sister had come. And Claire would sit among them placidly, not so intense as Ellen, but prettier in a traditional manner. Her little girl, Katy, would wander about, and the adults would talk peaceably until it was time for dinner.

They watched Claire's child, and she was lovely in the evening grass, beyond the enforced lawn, moving with care among the lanky weeds that dampened her thin arms as she made her way down the hill toward the pond. There was no doubting it, and the adults, sitting there on the lawn, were —each one of them—thunderstruck by her sudden, astonishing beauty. She was so ordinary up close that each person observing her in that instant had a clear idea of her future, and each person felt that shudder of awareness that accompanies so definite a promise of time that is bound to pass. So there under the slanting sun was a tableau that would seem to have been prearranged: Claire, sitting cross-legged on the grass, frozen in that quick glance she sent her daughter's way; Martin, so awestruck that his expression of perpetual preoccupation—a look that made him handsome —had flown from his face and left him as surprised as a little boy; Ellen and Vic, lovely both of them, all of themselves, sitting so that the sunlight struck down over their faces irradiating their assurance that this moment was only what they had always expected. Theirs was a look of proprietary smugness.

"Not to get too wet, Katy," Claire called out to her daughter in such a light voice that the message just barely undulated over the rippling grasses, but Katy did turn back to drift, waist deep in the weeds, in their direction.

The group resumed motion. Ellen snapped the tough ends off the asparagus and then began the painstaking process of peeling each slender stalk with her little paring knife. "I hate peeling this asparagus," she said, by the way. But no one heeded her or replied, because she peeled it for herself; she preferred it thus.

Martin sat quietly, at ease to be in company, and thought idly about Claire's long hair—such odd hair of a peculiar color between brown and gray. No color at all, really. For these few moments he was suspended in his summer, just himself, alone. For at least that small time this became the essence of his existence, with no comparisons to be made.

CHAPTER THREE

ONE DAY

In the mornings Dinah always felt hopeful; mornings seemed so promising, and now with the uncommon languor she retained from the flu, she lay in bed just a little longer than usual, dozing and waking, and turning over in her mind the carefully ordered events of her day. One day's schedule, firmly set, had become the schedule of all the summer days. Monotonously reassuring, just as she thought summer days should be, with their variety afforded only by some one person's unexpected irritation or pleasure, or just by some offhand remark that might turn one's thoughts in an interesting direction. All in all, she led a limited life here, and it was soothing.

She anticipated an easy day, imbued with a luxurious kind of boredom, because she needn't put any thought into this day's structure, although she did intend to write to Martin this morning. This mild order was a relief from her winter life, which had a frantic pace, and in which she had to allot her energies with such care.

Dinah awoke in the mornings to that picture at the end of the bed of the pretty girl running. It was oddly invigorating, and encouraged Dinah to rise, to exercise, to shape her day. To the left of that picture was a portrait of the girl's mother, Mrs. Horton, who looked out into the room with a sweet and shy expression on her rather long, oval face. Dinah liked confronting these two people every morning—the one getting right up and getting on with things, tough-minded, self-assured. The other woman was more wary than her daughter, and had more reasonable expectations, but was still prepared to find goodwill and cooperation through every hour; that was what her face said.

The curtains at the bedroom windows blowsed out in the light morning breeze, and Dinah could lie in bed and look out at the village of Enfield. It was her hometown, but only recently had it become a place that other people came to on purpose. The Hortons had been the first; they had come here to make this their winter home, while they spent their summers in Europe. Enfield was only eight miles from Fort Lyman, which was a town of no particular consequence, but which provided services and such mundane necessities as weekend people often need. It was only forty miles from the Columbus airport, and real estate was cheap. So the Hortons had been the pioneers of a movement, only gently afoot, to restore and rejuvenate the village, because soon after they bought and restored this large and even elegant house, other commuter families from nearby cities began to buy up the fine old houses in the town. Dinah could look from her second-story bedroom window all up and down Gilbert Street, which was the right-hand side of the "H" that was Enfield. She could look out through the tall maples at the several handsome houses now in various states of renovation.

When Dinah's parents had finally separated after years and years of stony accommodation, Dr. Briggs had bought the house directly across the street from the Hortons'. After her parents' silence had literally been shattered with a bang, after her father had been shot under such peculiar circumstances, and then after he had been so long recuperating, he had finally bought the house on the corner of Gilbert and Hoxsey Streets and come home to it alone. Dinah's mother had taken on the interior decoration of it; she met with him at his house or at her shop just as she would have met with any other client. That's what she said; Dinah knew it couldn't have been so simple. Eventually, her father had begun the direction of the exhaustive physical renovation; he had never found a contractor who suited him. The work was extensive and tedious and still in progress after many long summers. So on clear mornings when the hammering and the shouting of the workmen would begin across the street with the earliest light, before the heat built up, Dinah would wake up and look out at her father's house without really thinking about it. It only caught her eye there, before she moved off into her life and the pattern of her day. She could look out and see with what perfection these workmen were applying the copper flashing along the ridge of the roof. It shone brilliantly in the sun; by this time next year it would have weathered to a fine, muted, greenish gold.

The entire establishment intrigued her; it intrigued her that her father was overseeing all this activity with such painstaking care and apparent deliberation. She noticed that each detail was being executed with determined fidelity to the era of the house's original glory. Last year she had watched the slate roof replace the asphalt shingles and had been amazed at the beauty of the square gray tiles lapping over the scalloped ones, which were the color of dusky rose. The roof had turned out just like a wedding cake in a bakery window, symmetrically assembled, and now iced with shining copper.

She could not account for this aesthetic gentling of her father. He had scarcely seemed even to live within the walls of her childhood house—Polly's house—and he certainly hadn't ever shown any interest at all in its structure or appointments. Besides, Dinah invariably believed that a household was a manifestation of the woman who lived within it, no matter how undetermined or careless her influence seemed to be. No matter how little that woman herself might perceive or care about it. It did not seem to Dinah that men belonged to houses; she thought that in spite of themselves they could always only be tourists in their own rooms.

She knew, for instance, that Martin relied on her to interpret his environment for him if she happened to be there. Even as small a gesture as touching his arm at a party might settle for him the fact that the gathering was hospitable, not unfriendly. Dinah could discern the nature of the atmosphere immediately by taking into account even the rugs on the floor or the arrangement of the chairs. It was not the quality or stylishness to which she gave credence, but she was alert to any sympathetic alignment of the most ordinary objects. The place need not be handsome; it was just that about her surroundings Dinah was like a dog: some rooms raised the hackles on her back. If Martin saw her come into a room and relax and enjoy herself, then she knew he could enjoy himself as well. So it puzzled her that her father had come to such an involved domestic situation independently. She sometimes wondered if the girl jogging along in the picture had one day run right up her father's sidewalk and sat down with him there on the porch, where he had a drink each evening—Dinah watched him from her window sometimes. Perhaps that girl had engaged him in conversation and had managed to ask him all these questions —about his house, about how he liked it—because Dinah didn't visit her father anymore; they were so estranged.

This morning the hammering and carrying about of ladders and such had begun very early, and finally Dinah got up and went down to the kitchen, thinking to anticipate the children. She meant to make them some special morning treat, since the noise hadn't awakened them yet and she would have time. But now Martin was so much on her mind that she sat down at the round wooden table with a legal pad she had found in a drawer and a ballpoint pen, and began a letter to him.

But the truth was that Dinah was frightened of writing down words. She felt that as the word spread itself across the paper to the left of her pen point, then there she was, more and more committed to that paper, pinned there like a butterfly. She always thought that it was essential to get down precisely what she meant, and she never realized how relentlessly she relied on a gesture or a touch to convey a message. She was restless as she struggled with her letter, and she thought with envy of the skill with which Martin could dash off a note. He didn't even watch the letters forming as he wrote, or reconsider the intent compressed within the skeleton of words he established with authority in his thick, full handwriting. His written words rolled exuberantly forward, while hers lagged back toward the left-hand margin, as though they might flee the page altogether.

With all that Dinah meant to say to Martin, what could she write? Anything she might want to tell him, and all that she meant, could only look trite on paper. How could she be anything but mute about her caring? And sometimes this speechlessness reminded her alarmingly of her parents and the long, bewildering looks that had passed between them in lieu of ordinary communication. Whenever she wrote to Martin and folded the paper and sealed the envelope, she felt as though she held a potential explosion of misunder-standings and possible injury. Her letter already reeled with underlinings and parentheses, because she could not help but labor toward reproducing the exact emphasis with which the words proceeded in her mind. She sat poised over her letter in exasperation.

In any case, here were the children, who had been asleep only ten minutes ago, but who were now wandering around the kitchen, bumping against the table and jostling her pen so that it made unexpected leaps across the page. She had every reason to put away this letter; in fact, she had no choice. These were bright little children with minds as sharp as razors, and she could never remain absorbed in her own sensibilities for long with their energy directed her way. She knew, but hoped that they had not discovered, that in this landscape of her childhood, her parental authority was halfhearted at best. With relief, she arose to fix them food or do whatever they might require.

"Oh, Lord, you three," she said with irritation, "how do you always manage it? As soon as I sit down . . . I was just trying to write a letter. Now what do you want? Let's see. I thought I would have five minutes of peace."

Dinah listened with mild curiosity to her own voice, ineffectual at the moment, and blond as she was herself, fading into the bisque walls, just as imperative to her three dark children as the many buzzings, creakings, and abrupt settlings of this big house. It was only breakfast they wanted, of course.

"But not eggs, Mama," Toby said. "I just want plain cereal. I hate that wheat toast."

She took a frozen coffee cake out of the freezer and turned on the oven, then she did begin to break eggs into a bowl in order to beat and scramble them; someone would eat them. Toby climbed up the step stool to look into the cupboards to see if there was something to be had immediately, and Sarah tried to follow him.

"Get down, Toby," Dinah said. "I'll give you something in a minute."

David was still sleepy and still in his pajamas, although the other two already had on their bathing suits. He sat at the table watching them all with his serious brown glance and the suggestion of a scowl. Inwardly, Dinah quailed at so judgmental a look from this ten-year-old, even though she knew that he was probably doomed to love her unreservedly. She was titillated, somehow, by the presence of her own children in this town where she had grown up. All day, as they came and went in and out of the house while she carried out any number of homely tasks, she might look down at her hands as she cut out a dress pattern and observe the beginnings of the many tiny pleats and wrinkles around her knuckles, the creases along her wrists, and she would feel a sudden pause. It made it inevitable that she absorb the fact of her own adulthood. And so she quailed before them all, considering what lay ahead, considering their potential, considering that perhaps there would be an eventual reversal of dependency. Subtle, she hoped, but probably inevitable.

She settled the children at the table and served them the coffee cake and the eggs she had scrambled, and then she turned to wash up the bowls and pans at the sink while she took occasional sips of her coffee. When she turned around she saw that Toby had left his place and was not in the kitchen, and that he hadn't eaten at all or drunk any milk. She started up the back stairs to find him and bring him back. To tell him in a voice like God's own that if he didn't eat his eggs and drink his milk he wouldn't get strong, he wouldn't stay well. He had to take her at her word that she knew these things. But she found him at the top of the stairs at the landing, folded up on himself, and when he looked up at her she saw that tears were sliding down his face. And sorrow overtook her; he was such a wiry, pathetic bundle huddled there on the floor. She sat down on the step below him and held him in a hug.

"What's the matter, Toby?" she asked, but not without a certain wariness.

And, in fact, he said, "I *hate* eggs, Mama! You know I hate eggs. I didn't want any, but you gave them to me."

It was left to her to decide if this was an accusation—she had served him the eggs—or simply an explanation. "Well, for God's sake, Toby, don't eat them, then."

He put his head down on his knees and didn't move. She and Toby had these battles too often lately, and their warfare had left her vulnerable. She tried to coerce him. "There's your favorite coffee cake. The butter-crunch topping. I don't care if you eat your eggs or not, sweetie. I just put them on your plate without thinking. Come on down with me." She won this much by retreating down the stairs, her back turned to him, so that he would have to follow if he expected any further concessions. He did follow her and resume his place at the table.

She gave up the dishes and sat down on the kitchen stool to finish her coffee. She gazed at the children seated around the table, but she didn't really take them in. She was thinking about Martin, who could joke with Toby; she was thinking of the letter she hadn't finished, and she was thinking of the errands of the day. She took her purse off the counter and rummaged through it for her wallet to see if she needed to go to the bank. She glanced over an old shopping list, and she mostly just sat there with a blank mind, waiting for the children to finish so they could get on with things.

When she looked up, she saw that Toby had removed, with surgical precision, all the eggs from his plate and carefully deposited them on his napkin. He had done this, she supposed, so that they could in no way sully his coffee cake. But the steam from his eggs had condensed all around them so that the napkin was a soggy rag, and she knew that he had achieved a small victory. She cleared up the table in a silence they all knew, and the children very wisely dispersed and played together with remarkable and uncommon good nature. She was sure they knew how deeply she begrudged them these triumphs.

She packed the children into the car and picked up Pam Brooks and her little son, Mark, and they all went to spend the morning at the Fort Lyman Country Club, by the pool. The two women sat under an umbrella at one of the tables and played canasta with two decks of dampish cards. They kept watch over their children, who played in various sections of the pool according to their skills. Sarah spent a lot of time in the wading pool with Mark; otherwise, Dinah would stand in the waist-deep water at the shallow end with her while she paddled around fairly efficiently. It was at one of those moments, with Dinah leaning against the side of the pool where the water sloshed in the ceramic gutter, that she happened to catch sight of Toby standing in the unshaded cabana, drinking a Coke from the bottle, and stepping back and forth from one foot to another because the bricks were far too hot to stand still on. For one second Dinah could even taste the cold, sweet trickle of Coke as it made its way through the ice that would have frozen at the top of the bottle. That pungent trickle was tantalizing and more delicious than anything on earth; that's how it had been twenty years ago when she had stood in that spot herself.

On the way home from the club, they stopped at one of the hamburger places that had sprouted up, along with cavernous discount stores, on the road between Fort Lyman and Enfield. Dinah's mother complained of them; she thought they were tacky, but Dinah was always happy to find food that contented her children in any corner of the country. It made life easier. Today she and Pam had seated the children in a booth and taken their hamburgers for them to the self-service counter and prepared them to order, as per each child's wishes. Just as the two women sat down to their own lunch in the adjacent booth, Dinah looked beyond Pam's shoulder and saw that once again Toby was quietly crying, leaning back into the upholstered booth and staring out the window into the parking lot.

But this time she was filled with irritation. It was irritation that crept over her whenever one of her children was difficult for any prolonged period of time—any spell of several weeks—and it arose from the fear that perhaps that child had settled, this time, into his permanent personality, that he or she would be forever unhappy, or difficult, or unkind, or vulnerable. Her anger and irritation were really just her fury that the fates would play so cruel a trick on her own child. A child she must somehow protect.

She rose from her table and went swiftly over to the children's booth, leaning over David to grasp Toby by the shoulders and turn him toward her in a sort of shake. "What *is* it, Toby? What's the matter now?" She glared down at him with terrific urgency, and so his answer was more timid than it might have been. "You put mustard on my hamburger, Mama. I only like ketchup."

Dinah straightened up, and out of pure vexation tears came into her own eyes. "You're being a brat, Toby. A real brat!" She didn't lower her voice; she meant to embarrass him just as he had embarrassed her. "I'll go get you another hamburger, but this is the very last time I'm taking you out for a treat like this. There are people all over the world who would give *anything* for a hamburger like that!"

Pam had gotten up, too, and was right at Dinah's elbow,

and she caught Dinah's arm and smiled at her. "It's all right. Here you go, Toby. I forgot to put mustard on mine, and I only have ketchup, so this will be a trade that's good for both sides." She deftly switched hamburgers, and Toby deigned to turn his gaze away from the parking lot and look down at his fresh hamburger.

"Oh, Toby," Dinah said, "what do you *say* to Mrs. Brooks?" But Toby just ducked his head, and Pam waved her hand in deprecation at the idea of being thanked.

Dinah discovered every day how great were the variety of things that she and Pam did *not* have in common, and yet she had come to like Pam and to count on her. Pam was one of those few, rare people who have such a strong sense of goodness that no motivation or expectation lies beneath it. She possessed effortless virtue and self-assurance. Pam seemed really to believe in grownups, and she even believed that she herself was one.

Dinah had scarcely ever been as impressed with anyone as she had been with Pam the day she and Pam and the four children had made a foray into one of those immense discount department stores which spread in every direction like an airplane hangar in the middle of what had once been a pasture. Row upon row of fluorescent lighting stretched across the ceiling, because there were no interior windows except those at the front of the store, plastered with signs. Cameras were strategically placed to record the influx and outgo of customers. The white light everywhere was so unforgiving that even the glossy skin of those four pretty children took on a mealy look. Dinah's spirit shrank. As they made their way into the store, past the gum-ball machines and electric ponies that the children—all but David—begged to ride, they were stopped by a straggly-looking girl with muddy skin who insisted they check their beach bags with her at her little raised cubicle of an office. Immediately, Dinah had been filled with unreasonable guilt, and she had handed hers over with alacrity and an air of apology. But Pam just moved forward into the store, her beach bag slung over her arm, ushering Mark before her like a little sheep, until the girl stepped down out of her box and called after her. "You have to check bags and large purses here, or you can't go in," she said without any inflection.

Pam stopped and turned full around to her with a surprised and dazzling smile. There was a long moment's pause as Pam made herself understand. Then she shook her head with slight bewilderment and said, "Well, if you think that the manager of this store wouldn't trust me enough to let me in with my purse . . . Well then, of course, I'll be glad to go somewhere else." Her voice was very pleasant; she was a kind woman. "You know, I have some things in this bag that I value very much. I couldn't replace them, you see." She continued to hesitate in that one spot, facing the girl, just smiling self-confidently and absently running her hand through Mark's hair as he leaned disconsolately against her knees.

"Oh . . . Well, then . . ." And the girl waved them on.

Dinah had found the incident staggering, and she had been so struck with admiration for Pam that she had related the whole thing to her mother that afternoon, but her mother had just nodded absentmindedly. Her mother had never been in a store like that.

Now Dinah sat in a booth across from Pam and felt grateful to her, because she was sure Pam was not judging her, was not even thinking of it. Pam never generalized; she would not assume that one mistake, one loss of temper, would inevitably lead to another. She would not, in fact, assume that one mistake indicated anything, really, one way or another. Dinah hoped that Pam would never be deceived in any way by virtue of her good nature, that she would know when it *was* necessary to draw conclusions. But at the moment Dinah was relieved because she believed that Pam's tremendous competence had not led her to feel either smug or superior. She and Pam did not have to be rivals; they could just be uncomplicated summer friends.

In Enfield the days were long, and most evenings Dinah's three children, with Mark Brooks toddling along behind, roamed around their grandmother's house long after supper while Pam and Lawrence and Dinah and Polly sat out on the patio with their drinks. Once in a while Buddy would join them when he came over from Fort Lyman. After a while Dinah would gather up her children and they would walk back through the village to their own summer beds, where they would sleep easily after their long day. But in the late afternoon Dinah sat on her mother's patio suffused with lethargy, yet always aware of an unsettling presumption that something was going to be made clear to her momentarily, in the fuzzy light.

Pam was talking about Mark, about how absurd she and Lawrence were about him, monitoring his slightest progress. Her voice filled the space between the four adults sweetly, and Dinah heard the adamancy behind her self-deprecation. Mark *was* the finest and most fascinating child in the world, she was saying, beneath her words. Dinah remembered knowing the same thing about her own children. She looked across the patio at Lawrence, and she had known him for such a long time that it was unfathomable to her that he should be a father, that he should feel it deeply.

"But, you know," Polly said, "it's hard to know about children. Well, they never *tell* you anything, do they? They're mysteries to me, still."

Polly had arrived at one of her disconcerting moments of animation. Suddenly she would reveal herself to be, after all, tangibly connected to the world. Those moments always took Dinah unawares. And, at Polly's words, Dinah's mind went dizzy with the naïveté of her mother's conclusion. To hear this from a woman who had floated through her own children's childhood in a private, efflorescent silence! But she looked at her mother and found that she could, at the moment, only reaffirm her in her opinion that one's children told one nothing, because Dinah could think of nothing to say to her mother on the subject. But Polly turned to her, "You know, though, Dinah, it does seem to me that you ought to do something about Toby. He walks oddly now and then, he's developing a limp, and he's gotten into a bad habit of stuttering. Have you done anything about his speech?"

It always amazed Dinah that her mother would sit down and calmly impart information to her about David and Toby and Sarah as if she, Dinah, had only a passing acquaintance with them. "Well . . ." Polly moved her hand around their little circle, motioning them all into her affection and amusement. "Now there's a child who will tell you *everything!* I imagine that's why he stutters so," she said fondly, "he just has so much to say! If he could only make himself clear. I've told him to slow down and *think* before he talks. Oh, I dote on him, really." She meant it; Dinah thought that Toby was her mother's favorite grandchild. "But he won't listen to a thing I say to him, of course. He's a child who wants to be seen *and* heard!"

Pam looked down into her lap and turned her glass in her hands. Dinah said quietly, "Oh, he'll be fine, Mother. All children get growing pains of one kind or another. Not to worry." She didn't know how to talk to Polly and explain to her that she was worried about Toby. That he was lonely this year, and not playing with the local children as he used to. Toby made a desperate issue out of the smallest incident; he wanted constant attention, and he was sometimes so sad. She didn't know how to explain to her mother because she herself had heard Polly say to Toby, "Now just *calm* yourself, Toby, before you try to talk. Just take your time." So Toby didn't follow hopefully in his grandmother's wake as he once had.

Dinah had finally understood after a very long time that her mother's ease at passing judgment was in direct proportion to her absolute lack of spontaneous or natural compassion. Her mother meant to be compassionate and could be very sorry for the masses in the abstract, but she was never touched with immediate empathy for the mundane miseries of humankind. Her innocent mercilessness in its mildest form amounted to no more than simple tactlessness. Polly was an honest woman who believed in her own good intentions. That was all Dinah had been able to determine about her, and she often sat there in the afternoons expecting her mother to reveal herself in some new way, so that Dinah could catch hold of it.

When Buddy and Dinah were children they had often played with the Brooks children, Alan, Lawrence, and Isobel, who had for a while been Buddy's wife. They had played in this same twilight among the trees and flowering bushes while Polly sat in a chair on the lawn with her drink, just waiting for their father to come home from work. For Polly's two children, as they bobbed around her chair, these moments were as close to true conversation with their mother as they ever came.

Sometimes Polly would reminisce and offer out little pieces of her past. One evening when Dinah was almost ten, Polly had begun to talk about her own days away from home, when she was at college.

"Well, I was down at a dance at Princeton," she had said, "I don't remember who I was with, but I had on a beautiful dress—it was a black dress with a halter neck and one of those wide skirts, cut on the bias. I had bought it in New York just for that party. And I was very pretty, you know, but not at all glamorous or especially chic. While I was dancing with some boy there was a great stir. The band stopped playing in the middle of a song, and all the couples sort of fanned out around the stage to see what was happening. I thought there was going to be an announcement of some kind. But the most amazing thing! A girl was up there—she had just hopped up on the stage, I guess—and she started playing the drums! So the band played with her, too. I was awfully impressed. She had on a dark-blue dress, and she had that terrible color of red hair that's mostly orange, really. Her face was a little like a pug dog . . . around the nose, somehow. But I thought she was the most attractive girl I'd ever seen! I would have given my soul to have been able to climb up on that bandstand and play the drums! She had such fun that she was a great hit, of course."

Her mother had spoken all of a sudden that evening, prompted by who knew what impulse. But Dinah remembered what she said—all those bits and pieces of her mother's recollections—she remembered them verbatim. The words her mother had used to frame her own memories had gone spinning out into the air like winged maple seeds, and they had taken root in Dinah's mind. So, with the growth of the host, the memory itself became enlarged beyond any action that ever engendered it. Now those memories belonged no more to Polly, their originator, but were the property of Dinah, for whom they were the only definition of her mother.

Every now and then, Dinah would approach Buddy with these images, these ideas she had about her mother. "Don't you remember, though, when Mother talked about the time she made herself a strapless dress out of a satin bedspread? Very daring at the time, I guess. Can you imagine her doing that?"

Buddy would look up from his book or away from the television. "Oh, really?" he would say, raising his eyebrows in good humor. "I don't remember that, but you're right. It's hard to imagine." Then he would go back to whatever he was doing, not having tried to imagine it at all.

But it had been Buddy who had phoned her at college when her father had been shot.

"What do you mean, he was 'shot'?" Dinah had said, after she understood that he was all right but in the hospital.

"Oh, Lord, Dinah! It was just some seedy thing in a motel. There was some other couple, too," Buddy had answered, sounding more put-out than anything else about the whole business.

"Do you mean Mother was with him?" Dinah had been absolutely at a loss.

"Lord, Dinah! You know Dad!" Buddy was angry at *her*,

which made her feel unreasonably apologetic as she tried to piece the whole thing together. "Good Lord, grow up! Of *course* she wasn't."

When she had insisted on flying out, he had discouraged her. "You can see Dad when he gets out of the hospital. I don't think Polly wants any company, really. Not right now, at least." So Buddy had understood something about their mother that Dinah had not, because she had come home, anyway, and she had been useless and in the way. On the plane going home, however, she had imagined all the circumstances that might have been possible. The exotic ménage à trois. She was not altogether surprised, because her father's nature was so extreme that, once she thought about it, she realized something just this dramatic had always been likely to happen.

While her father was in the hospital recuperating, Dinah stayed with her mother, but she could not help her mother deal with what was quite plainly just relief. Polly's habitual expression of mildly penitent suffering had fallen away and been supplanted by a look of almost triumphant resignation which settled over her features and her tense body. She had loosened and gone lax at every joint. In the post office and at the grocery store the whole thing was discussed and puzzled over, because her father had been shot in the hip and leg at a little motel on the outskirts of Fort Lyman. Both the man who shot him and the woman with the man were said to have been drunk. By the time Dinah saw her father, she had been made too embarrassed to ask, and he was no less fierce; he didn't seem to feel he owed her any explanation. He wasn't feeling guilty or apologetic at all; in fact, he even seemed amused, which fueled Dinah's imagination like kindling.

The story, as it circulated around town, was confusing, and everyone wanted to get at the core of it, though no one, of course, asked any member of the family about it. They simply offered their condolences when Dinah went down for the paper, as though her father had had a stroke. But Polly had begun at once, as though something had been confirmed, to sort and pack up her father's belongings.

"Oh, of course he won't be coming back *here!*" she said to Dinah with impatience and irritation, obviously wishing Dinah would not ask questions of her. And any questions Dinah did ask, Polly met with a look of exasperation. "Oh, Dinah, for heaven's sake . . ." and she would trail off to one room or another or go take a long bath.

Her father's recuperation had taken a long time, and, indeed, he had not ever come back to Polly's house. He had lived in an apartment in Fort Lyman for about five years. It was near the hospital, where he underwent physical therapy for a while, and close to his office. Eventually, he bought the house in Enfield, and came home to it. When he did that, he officially discontinued his psychiatric practice, so that he wouldn't have to commute even the short distance back to town.

Dinah could look from her bedroom window, across the street, directly into his study with its long french doors, and she often saw him looking through his papers or reading a book late into the night. She could watch his progress as he stacked the papers on his desk and made his way into the central hall and up the stairs, turning the lights out as he went. He moved slowly, dragging the leg that had been left damaged by that shot. But with his tall, spare figure and arrogant hawk's head silhouetted in the windows as he passed them, he never aroused her pity. She only watched him, bemused. At last the light in his bedroom would go off, and Dinah would go to sleep.

Dinah had watched one day three summers ago from her window while two of her father's gardeners erected a sign on his meticulously kept lawn. It was a cleverly designed sign, hung in the fashion, Dinah supposed, of the period of the house. Three narrow white boards were suspended one from the other by little chains. Three separate messages. All three were then suspended from a black iron bar and post by two sturdier chains. She could not read the messages on the slender boards, though, not at such a distance. When she took the children out for a walk and to get the mail, she stopped by her father's wrought-iron fence for a long look. The three signs said:

PSYCHIATRY

ELECTROENCEPHALOGRAMS

FORTUNES TOLD

It was after the sign went up that people talked to her about her father as though he and she were not related. They were absolving her from responsibility. The people in Enfield were no less sophisticated about human behavior than people anywhere else, and some of them had always understood her father's brooding cynicism. Almost everyone understood that the signs were intentionally amusing, but in the end they had come to think that beneath the surface of that slippery humor lay insanity of a sort. Dinah was not sure herself. She had sometimes considered the possibility of her father directing the force of his intellect, and his gloomy wisdom, to the outermost limits of sociability. Beyond the reach of sociability at all, perhaps, so that his keen intelligence would be cut asunder to range around among the most grotesque facets of his mind. Out of civilized bounds. She felt an obscure pride in the fact that it would be a profound madness, not any pitiful eccentricity. Sometimes she wondered what her father thought if he looked out his window and saw her with her three children ambling by his doorway on their daily walks. Did he have any compunction about his loss of her—her loss of him? But after eight summers she had become more and more accustomed to this peculiar arrangement.

Even so, when she was at her mother's house in the evening fixing dinner or tending the children, she was roused to a great, repressed rage if she had to hear those nightly telephone conversations between her parents, to whose silences she had devoted the whole passion of her youth in her efforts toward mediation. This evening, as she sat with Lawrence and Pam among the flowering spirea, she did not move a muscle when the phone rang; she let Polly get up and go to it. But her body went tense, because she was so disturbed by this ritual. Her parents kept up a running chess game, too, in this manner, telling each other their moves over the phone and then rearranging the pieces on their separate boards. Whenever Dinah came across her mother's board, laid out on the table in the study with its little ivory pieces all set up in the current positions, she found it inexplicably maddening. So she sat quite still while Polly went to answer the phone.

Dinah and Lawrence and Pam were sitting on the patio just at that moment before the onset of evening. As the day breaks away, the light settles on the edge of the horizon, seemingly sullen, not giving an inch, just a long horizontal bar of whiteness stretching on and on beneath the graying sky. Then it dissolves into a gentleness so unexpected that the dense and hazy quality of the air seems to be the embodiment of relief. The relief of the burden of that one day.

CHAPTER FOUR

A PARTY

Dinah did her grocery shopping at the little village store, even though the prices were higher than if she drove into Fort Lyman. She liked the sociability, and she would take the children along to the post office on the opposite side of Hoxsey Street, collect the mail, and then cross over to do each day's shopping while the children dawdled behind her. In the summers she didn't shop in great quantities. She didn't need to, for one thing; she didn't have the Artists' Guild shop in West Bradford to attend to—a burden she shouldered almost exclusively September through May—and also she had to carry these groceries home in her arms. Besides, it was her summer luxury, with no other pressing duties at hand, not to think ahead, not to plan in advance.

She was having a dinner party of sorts this evening, so for once she had come to the store with a careful little list written out on a spare deposit slip she had torn out of her checkbook. Pam had taken all the children swimming that morning, so Dinah lingered among the limited selection of produce. She had tended the Hortons' vegetable garden with sticky and ill-tempered determination in the afternoon sun, but now as a result she had lettuce and beautiful tomatoes, some splitting with ripeness on the vine. She began to sort through the potatoes in their metal bin; most of them yielded too readily to the pressure of her fingers.

She found five that would do and put the paper bag of them into her cart.

She turned the corner of the aisle, which brought her to the meat counter, and there she came upon her father, who was just being handed whatever he had selected in a brown paper bundle tied with string. He looked predatory there with his neck projecting lengthily from his collar. He peered down at the meat in such sincere deliberation that with his height he was like a great, melancholy buzzard. He turned and saw her and smiled with that rather supercilious amusement he always assumed when they met in town.

"Hello, Dad. How are you?"

"Oh, I'm well. I'm well." And he leaned down to give her a kiss on the cheek. Then he took his package and went off to the checkout. Just as he was walking away from her he turned back obliquely, hindered by his stiff leg from turning easily around. "Say, Dinah," he said, having to turn his head somewhat over his shoulder to catch her eye, "I really like that little boy of yours," he said and then continued on his way.

Dinah moved along to the dairy section, because she saw that the butcher, Jim, who owned the store and had known her all her life and knew all her history, had been embarrassed at having to witness this confrontation. She looked over all the little cartons of cream—real cream, not the chemical-tasting, ultra-pasteurized variety—until she came upon the most recently dated ones, and she put two of those into her cart. She bought some unsalted butter in one big block, not in sticks, because it was so convenient for cooking. Dinah and her father met often in the village; it was unavoidable. They were civil; they weren't sorry to see each other. But neither of them attempted a conversation of any length. When she saw that her father had left the store, she moved back to the meat counter to study the choices in the display cases. She wanted to grill shish kebabs tonight, and she was hoping to find a sirloin tip roast.

Jim was washing and drying his hands on the other side

of the counter. "He almost never shops for himself, you know," he said.

"Oh, no?" she asked.

"No . . . no. He had a girl helping him out for a while. A secretary, I guess. She used to come in sometimes. Now he usually sends one of those boys down. One of those people who works for him. I think that girl must have quit."

"Oh, yes," Dinah said pleasantly, drawing out the vowels a little to show her interest and also so as not to seem affronted. She wouldn't have hurt Jim's feelings.

"Well, he's come in pretty often, lately. He just buys a few things at a time. I don't think those boys ever get just what he wants."

Dinah explained what she needed, and Jim went back into the meat locker to get a side of beef from which to cut it. When he returned and was standing at his porcelain table sideways to her, he continued his part of the conversation. "It's a funny thing, though, about Dr. Briggs, you know. Sometimes I think he's kind of gone to pieces. Do you remember my son, Pete? He's up at OSU now?"

Dinah nodded.

"Well, last year he had to have an operation." He looked up at Dinah with a reassuring shrug. "He's fine, now. It turned out not to be anything serious. But, anyway, he was pretty scared beforehand. He was working here in the store with me, and he was real worried about the idea of being cut open." Jim paused to pull out a long sheet of paper, in which he would wrap Dinah's roast, from the serrated-edge holder over his table. "Do you want me to cut this into cubes for you, or do you want to do it yourself? It's no extra charge."

"Oh, no. I can do that," she said. "I don't know exactly what size I want them."

Jim nodded in agreement, and went on, "Well, I really got to be afraid he wouldn't go through with it, and I finally called up Dr. Briggs, you know, and just asked him if he would talk to Pete about it. I knew your dad was still seeing some patients, and he's known Pete all his life. Anyway, he said he'd be glad to. He asked me if Pete could bring along some meat and groceries when he came, just to save him the walk that day. I guess your father has some pain still, getting around."

By this time Jim had wrapped and tied the meat and put it on the counter in front of Dinah, but he was standing with both hands resting on the glass and leaning toward her, so Dinah didn't take up the package yet. She saw he had more to say.

"Well, Pete took all the groceries over to him. He carried them through to the kitchen for Dr. Briggs and waited while your father checked over them all and put them away. But your dad had ordered a thick T-bone"—and Jim held his fingers up to approximate the thickness—"and he didn't put that away. He just put it there on the table, and began to ask Pete all about his operation and when it was going to be and all, while he was unwrapping that steak. And then when he got it all untied, and the paper off of it . . . well, then your father took one of those long carving knives out of a drawer. The kind of knife you use to carve a turkey or a ham, Pete said. And he kind of flung it point down into the beef, so that it stood straight up there on the table. Then he looked up at Pete and said, 'You see, your surgery won't be any different than that. No different than that at all.' " Jim looked earnestly over the counter at her, declining to judge the incident, but anxious to impart it, nevertheless.

Dinah just stood there a moment, struck dumb by so much information. But finally she responded, "Well! That's terrible! Poor Pete. What did he do?"

"Oh, Pete went on and had the operation. It turned out fine."

Dinah had all the things she needed, and she paid the cashier and walked out of the store into the sunshine dappling down onto the shaded sidewalk and went slowly home carrying her groceries. A smile slipped down over her face; she was intrigued by her father's splendid misbehavior —well, cruelty. The smile stayed there; it took over her entire face, but she could not excuse her peculiar pleasure. After all, a little kindness among the civilians was what she had longed for and valued above all else in her life. Nevertheless, her father's performance had a certain gruesome elegance that she admired. But as she walked on down the street, careful along the sidewalk, which rose and fell precariously over the ancient tree roots, her smile dried on her face as though it were set in clay. Her smile lay over her lips, and her eyebrows remained lifted in amusement, as if her expression had just been extracted from a plasticine mold. It was one of those times when her mind raced ahead with new thoughts and neglected to signal her body of the altered direction. She stepped carefully along, embracing a brown paper bag with each arm, thinking about what her father had said to *her*. What boy did he mean? What child of hers could her father have access to?

When she passed by her father's house in order to get to the corner where she would cross, she slowed slightly and turned her head, still with its rigid, powdery smile, to that house being so elaborately turned out. She was suddenly so uneasy that a tingling spread down her back and arms. She was beyond judging this situation; she didn't even attempt to reach an objective state. She only knew that she did not want her children to encounter that evanescent, chill cynicism her father possessed. She did not want that cloud to envelop David or Toby or Sarah.

But all she saw of interest as she approached her father's house with an eye out for something sinister was the large gray cat hunched on his doorstep, and he only stared at her audaciously, assured of his domain. Her father doted on this cat; Dinah saw him in the evenings allowing the cat to climb over him and sit on his newspaper as he was trying to read it. She had watched from her window as her father cut up bits of cheese from the tray of hors d'oeuvres at his elbow and fed the little pieces to the cat. Sometimes the cat would eat a bite, condescendingly, and sometimes he would flick his tail and walk away around the corner of the house. Dinah had come to a standstill at her father's gate, and all at once she put her groceries down on the sidewalk and stooped so that she could reach her hand through the wrought-iron bars and wriggle her fingers enticingly at the cat. "Here, kitty, kitty, kitty." But the cat just looked back at her solemnly, unmoving, and Dinah found herself stooping there, feeling the kind of fool that only a cat can make you feel. She picked up the two sacks and went home.

D inah was a good cook. She often suspected that the pleasure she found in preparing a meal, step by step, with careful calculation and order all around her, was a substitute for the pleasure she would have felt if she could have applied such sensible organization to the other aspects of her life. It wasn't everyday cooking she enjoyed, and in fact, that had fallen by the wayside, a victim of her summer listlessness. Sometimes in the mornings, though, she would decide to make a stew for the children's evening meal. She would begin meticulously, peeling carrots and slicing them on the diagonal so that she could carve them into little ovals, and then she would carve the potatoes the same way. It gave her great pleasure to serve a stew with coordinated vegetables. All the little olive-shaped carrots and potatoes would lie in segregated heaps on waxed paper next to the sink, and then she would cube the meat, carefully cutting away all the fat. But when she took out the wide skillet in which she would have to brown each separate cube of beef, she would envision herself standing there by the stove, closely monitoring the heat and turning each little cube from side to side—six sides for each, in all—so that when she finished, the sizzling oil would have risen from the pan in a transparent mist that would coat the stove and her hands and the teakettle on the rear burner. With that picture in the back of her mind, she would carefully rewrap the cut-up meat and put it in the freezer, and she would drift out of the kitchen indecisively to begin some other project. In the evening she would open some tuna and canned peaches and make do one way or another, and the children preferred this laxity. Meanwhile, as the children slammed in and out of the back door during the day, they would pass the sink and take up a few of the delicately carved carrots and eat them out of hand. When Dinah cleared away the dishes and cleaned up after dinner, she had only the little pile of graying potatoes to dispose of.

Now, with a party to cook for, Dinah took stock of all the little cans and bottles of spices lined up so carefully by Mrs. Horton, who had left a note encouraging Dinah to use them up. Dinah had cubed the sirloin for the shish kebab, and with rubber gloves over her hands she rubbed each separate piece with a cut clove of garlic and then with powdered ginger, being sure that the deep golden powder adhered to every surface. She stirred the cubes into a marinade of sour cream, rosemary, and bay, and left the bowl in a shady place on the counter.

Pam kept the children for most of the day, and Dinah was lying on her bed, idly watching television and resting when she saw Pam's car pull up in front of the house about four o'clock to drop them off. When she looked out to see that the children had been delivered home, she was surprised to find that she had become inordinately interested in the show she was watching. She didn't want to get up and leave it, but she did, because she needed to feed the children their dinner early. Her guests would arrive about six o'clock; since they would eat outside tonight, she must cook while the light held.

She gave the children a dinner of hot dogs and potato chips and then suggested that they ride their bikes down to the school playground, where there were swings and a jungle gym. She knew they were tired, and she had noticed that Toby was limping again slightly when he had come up the sidewalk from Pam's car, although he seemed to be fine now. Dinah wanted them out of the house, because she knew she was too preoccupied to be kind to them if they were hanging about to hinder her dressing or final preparations for dinner.

It was Sarah who objected. "I only have a Big Wheels, Mama! I can't go as fast."

Suddenly Dinah was feeling very tense about the evening ahead, the dinner she would serve, the dress she would wear. She felt uncomfortable at the idea of giving a party without Martin to back her up in the face of any emergency, irrationally uncomfortable, since Pam and Lawrence and Buddy and her mother—her only guests—knew her at her most casual. But she bent down to Sarah and encircled her with one arm.

"Sweetie, David will watch you. He'll just walk his bike down, and you won't have to cross a street, you know. It isn't very far." She looked at David, but he didn't make any sign of disagreement, and she recognized that this was one of those rare moments when she had stepped into the scope of the children's empathy. They had caught on to her nervousness, and it crossed her mind fleetingly how foolish it was to require these three children, whom she cared about so desperately, to accommodate her in order that she might impress other people, whom she could only regard with mixed affection and wariness. But the children went along, Toby and David with their bikes, and Sarah clattering horribly over the pavement with her wide-wheeled plastic tricycle.

Her guests arrived all at once; they had walked down together through the village from the direction of her mother's house. Dinah saw them coming leisurely along the sidewalk. Lawrence had dropped back to walk alongside her mother, and Pam and Buddy were walking more briskly, several paces ahead of them. She sat in the living room with a glass of wine and glanced out at them through her windows. All the preparations were made, and she had no reason at all to be uneasy, but the wine was comforting even so.

She went outside to meet them so that she could lead the way around the house to the narrow space of yard between the vegetable and flower gardens. They all sat under the oak tree and around the table, over which Dinah had simply spread an unhemmed length of brilliant green dotted swiss. Down the center of the table she had aligned six little clay pots of begonias interspersed with short, fat candles set out in miniature versions of the same clay pots. It was all very pretty, and she knew at once that it had been a mistake. Even this simple decoration said plainly that this was a party, and the inherent demand in that idea made everyone stiffen a bit. But when she brought out a huge jug of California wine and passed around plastic cups, an ease fell over the group.

"This is nice, Dinah," Buddy said. "It all looks so pretty." He poured wine for everybody from the heavy bottle.

"Well, I was just in the mood to do something special," she said. "Thank you."

They began to enjoy themselves, all of them together, because it was so usual to be this way. This gathering seemed perpetual; sometimes Dinah thought it might be a way of capturing a bit of immortality at its most elusive— the imprint on time made by this particular selection of people.

When she began to arrange the charcoal in the grill, Lawrence came over to help, and he put his arm around her waist in a companionable hug, so she leaned against him as one does with a friend. These hugs and casual touches of hands between herself and Lawrence were new since any previous summer, and she was glad they had overcome their long uneasiness with each other and could relax again. When they were sitting under the tree once more, Dinah found herself looking at Lawrence and Pam as they sat there across from her. Lawrence was still attractive, but they were of an age, and he had altered in the same ways she had: his cheekbones more prominent, small creases at his mouth and eyes. When she looked at Pam sitting beside him, so much younger than the rest of them, she felt aged all at once. She evaluated her thoughts to see if it was jealousy she was feeling, because for years she had been slightly possessive of Lawrence.

For a long time it had been Lawrence, not Isobel Brooks, his younger sister, who had been Dinah's closest childhood friend, even though she and Isobel were the same age and Lawrence two years older. But so much of their childhood Dinah and Lawrence had spent together in exclusion of Isobel and Alan Brooks, the oldest of the four of them. One afternoon she and Lawrence had been sitting in her bedroom playing checkers while she held her cat on her lap as she pondered the game. Lawrence knew all the strategies and often tricked her into a position where she could be triple-jumped. He almost always won.

"I wish I were Thompkins," Lawrence said, all of a sudden.

Dinah had looked down at Thompkins's notched ears and battered head in surprise, until suddenly she was paralyzed with a shock of understanding as she observed how comfortably Thompkins was nestled in the space made by the triangle of her legs as she sat cross-legged on the floor over the checkerboard. That was all he had said then, but they had played together less and less after that, and for a while she had resented and been intrigued at the same time, that he had brought such a thing out into the open between them. She had lain awake long nights thinking about it.

All at once, about age thirteen, Dinah had become pretty after being ordinary for such a long time, and she began to gravitate to the company of Isobel, who had always been, and continued to be, lovely to look at. From that point on, and even now, Isobel was her closest friend, but since Isobel and Buddy had been divorced she had moved away from Enfield and was busy living her life all on her own.

But not so many years—maybe three years—after that checker game, Dinah remembered quite distinctly lying awkwardly with Lawrence one summer evening, hidden by those same flowering bushes still thriving between their two houses. She had been only half undressed and very embarrassed at their mutual lack of grace. They kissed each other as best they could—she knew now that neither of them had understood a kiss—and she had just held on to him around the shoulders. But when he had moved his hands down her hips and along her thighs, and then brought them up to spread her legs a little and slip his finger gently inside her, she had forgotten all about herself and how she might be observed by him. The inside of her began to relax and tense all at once, and a shaky, liquid warmth spread over her as he pressed his hand up against her and inside her. Her arms had gone lax in their hold on his shoulders and fallen limply onto the leaves around them. But when he had withdrawn his hand to unzip his jeans and had suddenly come pounding into her it had hurt, and she came back to self-awareness with a shock. She only lay there stiffly with Lawrence between her legs, which were pressed flat against the grass—she had no notion of embracing his long back—and felt dismayed for them both. She had no idea what her response should be, and nothing occurred to her spontaneously. He had suddenly collapsed full length on top of her, and before she had revealed her own discomfiture, she realized that he was happy and pleased with himself. She lay absolutely quiet, because she didn't know the etiquette that encompassed this, and then he started moving in and out of her again, with short, swift strokes—she lay still, but she longed to have his gentle hand play over her once more. Finally, he had rolled over next to her, with his arms and legs splayed out, exhausted. He had been smug, she thought, in a dreamy, heavy way. "You didn't think I could do it twice, did you? I bet you didn't think I could do it twice."

Dinah had been baffled, because she didn't know what had been accomplished from his point of view. But she had smiled and risen on one elbow to lean over and hug him; she had been delighted to find out that she possessed a body he would care to fondle so urgently. For a few years her relationship with Lawrence had been like looking at herself in a mirror—he was the mirror—she adjusted herself to find the most flattering reflection.

Now she wondered if she had been equally illuminating to him, but she thought not. She thought that while she was trying to find out what best pleased him—therefore what would best please *all* men—he was trying to find out what best pleased himself. In other ways, in ways of conversation, and wit, and how to have his hair cut, she may have been a mirror for him of sorts, but as soon as they were making love once more, he became entirely self-absorbed. They had been very young, and, too, it had never occurred to Dinah to find out what best pleased her. All of her adolescence had happened at a time when mothers said to daughters, or one girl said to another, with a condescending scorn at the very edges of their voices, "Oh, well, *men!* It doesn't matter what you wear or what you say. They all have one thing on their minds, of course. Any one of them will undress you with their eyes even while you're just walking down the street!" And Dinah had tried her best, but she had never been able to undress them with her eyes.

But even with all this behind them, Dinah and Lawrence had each remained a person of the other's childhood. They had been very young conspirators. Dinah thought that that was so as she looked across the table at Lawrence and noted that he was still a nice-looking man but that he could never have been as attractive as she had once thought he was. Nevertheless, as Dinah talked softly to Pam sitting so near her beneath the tree, she couldn't help but think that Pam's face had no more piquancy than a pale, smooth honeydew melon. She had those soft, muted features—a look of dense skin—that were often described as sensuous. But Dinah didn't think so. She thought that to be sensuous one must have all the senses available right at the surface, and it seemed only logical that the very quality of creamy waxiness that Pam's smooth skin possessed would naturally preclude that.

Dinah brought the shish kebabs out to the grill, but the fire was not yet ready, and they all had more wine. Polly excused herself from the gathering and went inside for a long time, so that Dinah knew she had gone to phone her father, who was just across the street. The children had returned and came darting around the corner of the house, past the little porch, like fierce, dark arrows in their intense game. They were good children, and polite children, and they did not interfere with the grownups, who sat quietly talking on the lawn and sipping wine.

Dinah was still amazed that she had these three children of her own, and still congratulated herself on her unexpected affinity—not talent, especially—for motherhood. She watched them running across the yard, and just briefly she thought with pity of Polly, who had somehow never grasped hold of the idea that she was anybody's mother. Dinah turned to Buddy and reached out to touch his arm and catch his private attention.

"Do you remember, Buddy, when Mama broke her violin? Backing up like that in the doorway? Oh, I think about it every now and then . . ."

Buddy stretched his legs out in front of him and leaned his neck back a bit as though he had become slightly stiff sitting in the cooling air in one position. He looked over at Dinah with what seemed to her to be a little irritation. "Oh, well . . ." He looked away and then back at her again, and she was surprised to realize that he didn't want to talk about it with her. But then he said, "You know, I always thought that was one of the biggest burdens off her mind. Getting rid of that thing!"

Dinah drew her hand back to her lap. She went blank for a moment with something that approached a kind of defensive anger, but which never quite materialized. She did understand that he was warning her against sentimentality. "That's really an amazing thing to say! I don't understand why you did say it." Dinah was agitated and searching for a better response. All that she could come to at this moment, though, was the image of the episode itself. It stuck in the forefront of her mind with the persistence of an engraving, leaving her a trifle spellbound and mute with her ideas.

When she was very young—almost four—and Buddy was approaching eleven, he and she had come racing into the house just as her mother had finished practicing her music and was coming toward them through the doorway at the other end of the hall. They had raced to her, demanding that she mediate some dispute, and as they came nearer, reaching up to her, she raised the violin away from them, above her head, and backed up out of their way. The violin had hit squarely across the door frame through which she had just come, and splintered at its tapering neck.

Now, sitting near her brother over thirty years later, she could only look at him and wonder if he had seen the same thing. Finally, she said to him, "But, Buddy, she never played again after that." She said it very mildly, with the slightest hint of a question in the phrasing of her statement.

"But that's got to have been a real relief to her," he said, and got up to pour himself some more wine. "She started so late. How good do you think she ever could have been? She could always have bought herself another violin, you know. There was nothing especially valuable about that one." He imparted all this with a peculiar and rather tender coerciveness, and when he sat down, a silence fell for a few minutes which Dinah felt no compulsion to fill. The limbs above their heads creaked as the large oak was forced to flex with the breeze.

Polly came back out to them, looking serene, and she settled into her chair while Lawrence got up to get her some more wine and pass the olives and nuts Dinah had set out at the last minute. Dinah gave instructions to Buddy, so that he could grill the meat, and this time it was she who left their little group to go to the kitchen and prepare the rest of the meal.

She busied herself with the mechanical preparations. In the early afternoon she had picked five beautiful, small, even-sized tomatoes, and now she lined them up on her cutting board and sliced them each in half across the middle, not intersecting their stem ends. She put the large skillet on the stove and began to melt four tablespoons of the unsalted butter slowly, so it wouldn't burn without warning while her back was turned.

All the while she moved around the kitchen she still had that vision of her mother, with her hands upraised while the violin snapped above her head. It was an idea she had had of her mother for a very long time; she had latched on to it as one more clue to Polly's nature.

When the butter began to bubble slightly, Dinah placed the tomatoes in the pan, cut side up, pushing them gently around until all ten halves would fit. She stood over them as they sautéed, looking for just the right translucency to set in at the cut edges before she turned them.

It was only beginning to become clear to her that while she and Buddy were growing up, the two of them had often been witnesses to the same domestic event. An event itself subject to various interpretations, she supposed. She thought that the very selection of an interpretation by either one of them was as close as they ever were to come to mastering their own fate. Those crucial interpretations—in some instances destined to be chosen as they were—were as near as any human could come, probably, to forming his own personality. This entire thought oppressed her, and she turned her tomatoes rather dejectedly and pierced the skin of each with her bacon fork so the steam would not wilt them altogether. She elaborated on this new idea a little; it meant that no one could ever be entirely independent or free of the past. The thought that one *could* eventually be disburdened was an illusion she had cherished.

Dinah added heavy cream to the bubbling tomatoes and shook the pan until the cream and the butter and the tomato juices mixed into a pale golden sauce and thickened; then she carefully tilted the skillet and transferred the contents to a large platter she had found in Mrs. Horton's pantry. She placed the dish in the oven with a casserole of potatoes and switched off the heat, leaving the door slightly ajar so they would only stay warm and not continue to cook.

Then she called out the back door to her guests to come and lend a hand, and all together they laid dinner out on the table and began to serve themselves. The meal was a success; everything had turned out well.

"What are these tomatoes called?" Pam asked. "They're wonderful!"

"Tomatoes in cream," Dinah told her.

"No, really, Dinah," she said a little crossly, "what are they called? I'd like to try them; we have so many tomatoes from the garden, now."

"Well, they're called *tomates à la crème*," she answered, and everyone laughed, as she had known they would. But it was true; that was what she had found them under in an old *Gourmet* magazine of Mrs. Horton's. Pam just glanced at her suspiciously, not sure if the joke was on her, and Dinah was sorry. It was the first sour note between them.

She had not made any dessert; she had just bought a large, iced watermelon, and as she cleared the plates from the picnic table onto a tray, she called the children to come join them. She couldn't see them in the front yard anymore now that the light was fading.

She carried the tray to the kitchen and began a careful sectioning of the melon so that everyone would get a part of the heart. The children came around the side of the house, beneath the kitchen window, in an argument, or it sounded to her like an argument from the tones of their voices. She was about to put her knife aside and go stop them when she began to hear what they were talking about. Then she stood very still to listen.

"Well, you shouldn't have left me all by myself with Sarah," David was saying. "I just had to push her on the swing the whole time or she kept starting to cry. I didn't get to ride my bike at all."

Toby didn't say anything to that.

"Where did you go?" David was a little persuasive now.

"Oh . . . I just rode around some."

"By yourself? How come? Where's your bike?"

"I guess I left it somewhere. I'll get it in the morning," Toby answered, seemingly unconcerned.

They passed by the window, not angry anymore, anticipating the melon, and Dinah could hear Sarah's Big Wheels clattering relentlessly along the front sidewalk. But still,

Dinah remained where she was, with the knife poised in her hand above the melon. Then suddenly she put it down and quickly climbed the back stairs and went along the hall to her own room, where she stood at the window, peering out into the dusk. She could just make out the shiny fenders of Toby's bike as it lay on the grass in her father's side yard across the street. Nothing at all came to her mind; she just stood there for a moment staring out, and then she went back down to the kitchen to finish cutting and distributing the melon.

As everyone ate and talked to the children, Dinah sat sipping more wine and staying very quiet. Her mind remained blank, not searching for conclusions, and the progress of her thoughts veered off just short of clarity. She was tired, and she was thinking just now that this particular dusk was weighing with loathsome heaviness on the trembling leaves of the pin oak; each leaf was so tenuously attached by its fragile stem.

When everyone had gone, and the children were in bed upstairs, Dinah poured herself even more wine and set about the business of clearing up the kitchen. She rinsed the plates and put them in the dishwasher and put the casserole in the sink to soak. But when she came to the platter with the last of the shish kebabs she hesitated. Finally, she slid two of the large cubes off the long skewers and carefully cut them into smaller bits, and then with the blade of her knife she scraped all those little pieces off the cutting board into her hand. She started toward the back door, but she had to stop and remove her shoes, because in these high heels she was beginning to wobble.

She went to the edge of the front yard, directly facing her father's now darkened house, and stood there in her stockinged feet. She stood there for a few minutes until she could make out the eyes of her father's cat sitting just behind his fence, staring back at her.

"Here, kitty, kitty," she said. "Here, kitty, here, kitty." And she stepped along backward, dribbling the little pieces of meat from her palm in a sort of trail as she called all the while to the cat. Finally, she reached her own back door, and she went in and washed her hands and went up to bed, carrying her cast-off shoes with her.

In the morning, when she looked out on the back steps, she saw that all the little pieces of meat leading up to her door were gone, but of course who could tell what animal had eaten them?

CHAPTER FIVE

HOUSEKEEPING

Martin had no idea that he had accumulated over the years—say all his years past age ten—so many alternatives to an apology. It would have been especially unusual for him to turn to anyone, particularly a woman, and simply say, "I'm sorry." It was not because there was anything of his pride at stake; it was because men have other ways than women do of making amends. Not many men have ever understood how disarming, how unarguable, an admission of guilt and culpability can be. Martin could only stand at the window tap-tapping his fingers on the sill and look out while Claire sat on the floor of his living room, cutting and wrapping and tying ribbons on the presents she had selected for her daughter, Katy. In this instance, anyway, sorrow, or even guilt, might not have been the precise sentiment he would have had to accommodate. Nevertheless, he remained preoccupied. At other times in his life he had rubbed two fingers over his lower lip, abstracted; he had put his hand over the late-evening stubble of his beard and gazed out of some other window to avoid an issue. In none of this behavior was there intentional deceit; there was really only an element of reticence and tradition and simple clumsiness. Martin couldn't have thought of any way to say to Claire that when they had entered his house, and he had watched her spread out the wrapping paper and ribbons and go to work with the tape, his immediate impulse had been finally to put his hands at her waist, with his thumbs pressed against that vulnerable cleft just below her winglike rib cage. It was all he had thought about as he watched her, because over the summer weeks his house had become a neutral territory, empty of his wife and not under the influence of Ellen. Summer after summer, he had experienced the same melancholy during the absence of his family, but his dejection always took him unawares. It had never become a habit. He hadn't caught the knack of nestling gloomily into it so that it might even have been of some use to him. Vic and Ellen had always been his mainstay during the two and a half months his wife and children were away, but never before had he been offered any other distraction than simply that of their calm company. But now, since Claire and Katy had come to live with them, and even the Hofstatters' lives were becoming complicated, he was drawn more and more into a new and separate domesticity.

The souvenirs of Dinah and his children, dispersed throughout his house, had lost their significance, and the usual communal state of the household had gradually elapsed into an entirely personal order controlled only by himself, and he was seldom there. He had taken to sleeping on the couch many nights at the Hofstatters' house in the country and staying in town only on the two days he had to teach. There was so little gas, and the cost of going back and forth was too great. He had forgotten, in some respects, that he was responsible for any house at all. And night after night he had thought about Claire, and he had convinced himself that she expected and desired just what he expected: that at last, like children growing up and leaving home, they could do just as they liked, now that they were alone together. Thus the lingering feeling that he should explain something to her, since they weren't doing anything at all but wrapping packages. But she worked with incurious concentration, and not only could Martin not have said anything to the point or even formulated what was to be said, but his mind adapted with singular beauty to the situation and leaped over his original intentions. He was only looking out the window wondering where they could get all those balloons filled with helium.

He and Claire had waited an hour in line at the gas station to fill Martin's car, and he had expected to be able to have the balloons inflated at the same station, but he had found that they didn't offer that service, and, in any case, this was a poor time to make the request. In answer, he had been given only a vacant stare. But Martin had latched on to the idea of helium balloons for Katy's party, and he was not to be persuaded that they weren't necessary. He had become privately morose, standing against his car waiting for gas and listening to people insult each other. The poor, gangly attendant burst into apprehensive perspiration under the accumulated fury of his customers. In the unusual heat the cars glistened ominously, and Martin even became fearful. All summer he had protected himself from the sudden desperation of a previously complacent society by steeping himself in what he considered to be the remarkable serenity of Ellen's house. It was a balm for his spirit. One could remain convinced, in that carefully contrived environment, of one's relevance in the world. But in that gas line the only things that seemed important, all at once, were fuel and food and sex. And—also—the helium balloons.

He turned to Claire, who was still working with ribbons there on the carpet. "I think we might be able to get them filled at Newberry's," he said.

Claire didn't care about the balloons so much, but she looked at him with an expression of resignation. "Look, why don't I phone first? It's so hot to drive around, and we'll only waste gas. Where's the phone?" Martin showed her through the house into the kitchen and rinsed their beer glasses while she telephoned discount stores and any dime stores she could find listed in the book, but she had no luck. Finally, they gave up and carried all the presents Claire had bought and wrapped out to the car, leaving behind them a litter of tiny slivers of paper and odds and ends of ribbon strewn across the rug where she had been sitting. It hadn't occurred to either of them to sweep them away; the house didn't seem to be anyone's property. Their plan was to take the party, completely assembled, out to the farm, because it had become apparent over the week that Ellen had no intention of making an exception to her habit of non-celebration, even for Claire's daughter, Katy, of whom she was very fond, and who would be five years old on Saturday. In fact, Ellen had seemed cross and edgy all week, and Martin had boxed himself into the position of being Claire's conspirator.

One evening Martin had been sitting down on the grass with Katy and Claire so that they formed a triangle. Katy was talking about her birthday. "Well, Katy," Martin said then, "you're probably feeling very sad. In a few days you'll have the very last evening of ever being four years old. Think of that! It will be the last time you'll look over and see those horses with four-year-old eyes, the last time you'll go swimming in your four-year-old skin. And you'll never wake up four years old again!"

His own children usually took this up wildly: "And the last time I have to go to bed at an eight-year-old hour! The last time I'll get an eight-year-old allowance!" But sitting there in the grass at age thirty-eight, and looking around him at Claire, who was frowning, and Katy, who watched him with alarm, Martin realized what he was saying, and he was ashamed of himself.

"So," he went on, "your mother and I will go into town Saturday morning and buy everything that's simply too old for a four-year-old but just right for someone as old as five. When you still had so long to go before you would be five, I didn't want to tell you how much better it is than being four. You'll be much smarter, and you'll be able to swim faster, of course. And you'll be surprised at how soon you'll even be much taller!" But all the while he talked to Katy with her tiny wedge of a face and wispy, colorless hair like her mother's, he was plagued with sorrow that year after year he had remorselessly inflicted on his own children the desolate message of their mortality. Why had he done that?

And as though it were a joke? Perhaps he had thought that they could avoid it if they knew about it, because that was what he wished; they were the repository for all his life's care.

Claire looked up at him, relieved. "If you really would drive me to town on Saturday, it would be a big help. I haven't wanted to ask Ellen or Vic. I'm not so sure they're too enthusiastic about this party."

As a rule, the Hofstatters did not give parties, but their summers went like this: People arrived in the morning or after lunch on some days and didn't leave until late evening. If Vic was at work on his own writing, or if he was going over material for the *Review*, the company might not see him at all. He would have settled himself into the big upstairs bedroom for the day, only appearing now and then to make a sandwich or get some coffee. If this was the case, the visitors would register their arrivals and departures with Ellen, who moved around the downstairs rooms to attend to many and various small tasks. Sometimes she would sit at her desk in one corner of the dining room and work at her poetry, and then people came and went without disturbing her. The wide front door, mortised in a traditional double-cross pattern, stood open. The central hall was illuminated on sunny days, or if the sky flew with clouds, it was as though the shining wood floor was darkening and lightening of its own accord. The guests arrived dressed to swim, or they changed unabashedly in the long grass at the edge of the pond. Some simply took off what they had on and waded in. It was established that no visitor judged any other as to their apparel.

Some of the company were friends who just came out to enjoy the pond, and others were carpenters or plumbers or rural neighbors who stopped by on farmers' errands. People brought gifts. They brought cakes, tomatoes, cut flowers, books.

Martin had a niche in that house into which he settled customarily, and of which he was the sole occupant. He and

Vic could consult each other if need be, but otherwise they could weed in peace through the unsolicited manuscripts sent in to the *Review*. They could work well in the tranquillity of a busy house that nevertheless functions methodically. The two of them could work with the assurance that other things were being taken care of.

Ellen was their protection. She had almost made Martin believe in the feasibility of living a life that was only immediate. One night, as they sat watching the news in the Hofstatters' small sitting room off the kitchen, they had suddenly been confronted with the plight of the Vietnamese boat people set afloat precariously on dozens of swaying, tottering ships. The people were packed so tightly aboard that they could only stand, and they looked out at the camera with apparent apathy. In that instant Martin was overawed by sorrow. His instinct was to cover his ears and close his eyes, although he only sat there looking, filled with hopelessness, and then also affected with fear for his own children, who would be, who must be, eventually, threatened by the world's condition. But Ellen rose from the floor where she had been sitting and turned off the set. She sat back down to the crocheting she was doing, and her features were so bleakly determined in her anger that Vic was surprised into alarm. "Ellen . . ." he began, and Martin, too, thought that she was so saddened that she couldn't bear it.

But, in fact, he hadn't understood. "It's an obscenity," she said, "to have that on the air. What can we *do* about it? Why do we need even to know about it? For God's sake, why do they tell us?"

Anyone could have answered her, and might have if she had not been so angry—and her anger was at the people themselves, all those people crowded on board those bathtublike boats. Martin was shocked; he saw that her empathy was so far away, so isolated from any external influence that she would not be touched. From that moment he would regard her more warily, and yet she had given him a peculiar comfort. She managed to sanction a life lived within the bounds one delineates for it. In some way Martin was absolved of responsibility by her attitude, and yet his affection for her was subtly diminished.

But it was Ellen's determination to live her life within her own house that made Martin's summer a respite from normal cares, and made it a time in which he could do work that was important, for the most part, only to himself. He set himself up in the large living room and spread his material on the coffee table, while he stretched out comfortably over one or the other of the huge, matching butterscotch leather couches. When he and Dinah had first visited this house and sat in this room, Ellen had been very charming and precise in explaining it.

"Well," she said, "when we decided it was time to buy some furniture we were in Boston, and we simply walked into a store that seemed to be completely filled with very swank, leather furniture. You know the sort of store. Chrome lamps and glass tables. There was brown leather, black leather, white leather, beige leather . . . well . . ." She shrugged helplessly. "I became very taken with it all. I just walked around and around that store loving the smell of all that leather, and we bought these two couches and those three armchairs and quilted leather pillows! I was carried away." She tilted her head down with a deprecating smile. "And then, as we were leaving the store—after we had arranged for delivery and so forth—a man was coming in, and I just stopped dead still and put my hand out to make him stay there at the door. I was astonished, you see. I just couldn't grasp it. He had on one of those sports-car hats—suede—and I said, 'But, Vic, we've forgotten the hats! We haven't got any leather hats!' "

Martin and Dinah had been delighted, and a little mesmerized, to discover such furtive and superior humor let loose in their midst, and they were all four complacent in their mutual grasp of each other's wit.

The vast leather sofas continued to be exotic and mis-placed there in the living room of the old house, where the floor was still covered with black-and-white linoleum. Sometime during the summer Vic and Martin would pull up those tiles, however, because they had removed a small section and found grand, wide, primitive walnut boards beneath. They would pull up the tiles and strip off the glue and varnish. They would sand the floor and perhaps they would stain it, and then they would cover it over with a final coat of polyurethane. Meanwhile, Martin didn't mind the black-and-white linoleum at all, he was so used to it. And when the heat and humidity grew intense and hung for a long time in the little valley where the Hofstatters lived, Martin pitched in and helped remove the film of greenish mold that blossomed overnight on the exposed surfaces of honey-colored leather.

Each summer Martin accomplished the greatest portion of what he considered to be his work. Not his job, because his job was teaching, and he enjoyed it, but the *Review* was his work. The four of them, Vic and Ellen and Dinah and Martin, had conceived the idea; they had planned it as a collective editorial effort, but both women had drifted away from the project and from each other. Martin had never taken time to ponder this; it hadn't seemed unusual as it had happened. Dinah was increasingly involved with the Artists' Guild shop, and Ellen became more and more wrapped up in her own writing, which she regarded as strictly her own affair. She did not intend it for publication, in any case, so the *Review* could not be a useful instrument for her, and Vic and Martin never even saw her work. She did mail it off to a few friends across the country, and to favored ex-professors. The *Review* became a thing of Vic and Martin's making, and it gave them great satisfaction, but the work was often tedious. So Martin thought of his summer as a time in which he truly labored.

This summer, though, a new intensity of purpose suffused the air like pollen. Ellen moved about these days taut-limbed and with severe and controlled intentions—setting up for herself more and more arduous tasks and insisting on completing them by her own arbitrary schedule. Her tension was picked up by everyone in the household, even the visitors and carpenters and plumbers, who did their work in half the time and departed. Her tension was picked up by all but Claire and Katy. Therefore, Martin gradually realized that there was an eccentric insistence in Ellen's behavior that had as its focus Claire's blithe disregard for the gravity of everyday life. Claire proceeded through each day as need be. Of course, she cooked and ate and cleaned and cared for her daughter. She did all the irritating or pleasant chores of any day, but she went along with comparative frivolity; she never acknowledged or even seemed to think of any long-term goal.

Martin had always watched Ellen with wonder as she ran her household. She laid out her days like playing cards, he thought, so that one felt she must be bound to complete the deck. Each task was carefully thought out in relation to something else. "You know, I can't bear it—it almost makes me ill—to have anything in my house that isn't beautiful of its own accord," she had said to Dinah one night years ago. So she persuaded herself of the beauty of things which had always seemed quite ordinary to Martin. She even insisted that Vic mow the lawn with an old-fashioned push mower she had found in a junk shop, because she said it pleased her by its simplicity. "I don't see why all the objects we're forced to live with, just because of a sort of imposed civilization, shouldn't have aesthetic value. Well, the thing is, I think I'm diminished in some way if I allow myself to use inferior tools—or inferior methods." Martin had known at the time of that discussion that Dinah would be intimidated and irritated at once by even such a notion. As it turned out, the reverse was true, also. Ellen had been ill at ease in Dinah's house with its almost systematic chaos. In those early days, when the two women had been friends, Ellen visited Dinah at the shop, where tranquillity reigned. But this summer Martin observed Claire and Ellen and began to think that Ellen's passion for perfection amounted to an obsession. As this came home to him, he realized that Ellen herself perceived his slight disenchantment, and it seemed to drive her into a frenzy of worthwhile activity.

She kept at her writing, but she also applied herself relentlessly to harvesting blueberries and strawberries and all the garden vegetables, and laboriously canning and pickling and making jam. She baked loaves and loaves of bread—oatmeal, whole wheat, pumpernickel.

One afternoon, while Martin sat in the cool living room halfheartedly making notes on a manuscript, she called to him from the kitchen with such urgency that he thought there must have been an accident. He went to help and found Ellen standing in the center of the room looking forlorn—as he had never before seen her.

"What's wrong? Are you all right?"

She was standing, slowly shaking her head, and in her shorts and halter top she was too thin, too muscular. She looked like a drawn bow.

"Well, just look!" she said. "Oh, just look at that!" And she gestured at the window, where there were at least a half-dozen loaves of bread sitting on waxed paper on the sill.

Martin was at a loss. He stared and stared at them and then back at her, only to see her face turned to him with that widened look of expectation, so that the tension had left her features, and her expression had gone blank in anticipation of his sympathetic reaction. But he was so baffled and so naïve that his face, too, went blankly quizzical, and it infuriated her.

She seemed to Martin to leap in one bound like a cat over to that window, and she slapped her hand lightly across each little bread loaf as she spoke. "Well, just *look* at them! I like them all lined up and glistening like a little train. They sometimes look like a little train in the sun, and with the copper pots hanging over them they're just right. But *look!* They've all sunk in the middle! I took them out too soon, or the damned oven's off again. And they're too brown on top, too. They're ruined! They're just ruined!" And it ended up that Martin moved over and embraced her, and she just leaned into him in limp despair. Claire came in, too, from the garden, where she had been working, and sat down at the table to rest, while Martin stood at the window with Ellen.

"The bread's gone wrong, I think," he tried to explain, although Claire hadn't seemed the slightest bit curious. She got up and inspected the little loaves, and then turned to her sister with concern.

"But they'll be delicious, Ellen. They smell wonderful. They're only a little scorched on top." She finally understood that Martin was holding on to Ellen because she had gone absolutely still in despondency. "Oh, but, Ellen," she said plaintively, putting a hand on her sister's back as it was turned to her, "it doesn't make any difference. It just doesn't matter." But Ellen gave no response at all. She disengaged herself from Martin and left the room.

In the evening, when Martin was sitting by the pond with Katy and Claire, who both lay nude in the fading sunlight—their bodies not so dissimilar—on towels they had trampled down over the high grass, he finally asked her about it. "Is Ellen all right? Is that bread all right?" Claire didn't answer for a little while, and Martin thought she wouldn't. He just let his question drift out over the pond, but then she turned her head to the other side to look at him.

"Maybe she's just surprised that she's getting older," she answered finally. "She likes to be in charge. Well, I'm not sure. I'm not sure what it is. The bread's fine. I don't know what that was all about."

Martin was looking down at Claire's young skin and her narrow, childlike body as she lay there on her stomach next to her daughter, with her head buried in her arms and her wet hair splayed out over the towel, and so he wasn't listening, or caring, really, what she answered. But when he glanced up the hill and saw Ellen in her lawn chair snapping beans, he understood with perfect clarity that things had not gone as she had expected them to this summer. He knew now to expect a greater, a more dogged ferocity in the weeks to come. He remembered that at the first of summer, shortly after Claire and Katy's arrival, Vic had spoken out into their small company one evening almost in the manner of a warning. "All the people in the house," he had said, "anyone who comes by, they are all, for the time being, property of Ellen's."

Ellen had looked around at him severely and said, "Oh, yes? And you, too?"

"I come with the furniture," he said lightly, and after a moment she had smiled at him, pleased.

But when Martin saw Ellen looking down at the three of them there by the pond, then he himself suddenly saw Claire as an intruder and himself as her ally. She was a purveyor of propaganda simply by the resolute meaningless-ness of her everyday existence. The reality she made for herself was both alluring and threatening, and Martin, looking up the hill, saw that he might suddenly find himself an alien in that house.

But the morning he drove out to the Hofstatters' in his old, blue Chevrolet to pick up Claire for their birthday shopping spree, he was optimistic; he was almost joyful. He liked giving presents. When Claire came out of the house, however, to meet the car, he was a little disappointed that she had on her usual khaki shorts, so that her thin legs projected from them like parentheses, and that she wore her old T-shirt with the subway system of Paris stenciled on its front. He was dressed as usual, too, in old jeans and a faded shirt, but he had been thinking of this as an occasion.

"You've never seen Dinah's shop, have you?" he said to Claire, because he often spoke of Dinah; he had told Claire a lot about her. "She has wonderful children's toys. Why don't we drive into West Bradford?"

"The Artists' Guild, you mean?" Claire asked in a dubious tone, and was thoughtful for a moment. "Okay. That'll probably be fine."

When they arrived, it was disconcerting to see Claire make her way around the shop. She looked more than ever like a waif, especially since Martin was accustomed, in this build-ing, to the influence of Dinah's disheveled elegance and her authority. Claire handled a beautifully carved wooden train as though it were not, in fact, amazingly sturdy; she behaved as though she could damage it. She did linger for a while over the hand-sewn stuffed animals made in Vermont by three women who took care to embroider with great thoroughness all the eyes and noses on their creations. But she walked away from the toys while Martin still inspected them, and she drifted around the shop and stood on its small balcony, which was cleverly cantilevered out over the Green River. Wind chimes rang faintly under the eaves, and inside, every object was beautifully displayed on blond-oak platforms with raised edges so that the pottery and hand-blown glass could be set down on a bed of white crushed stone.

Martin joined her out on the balcony. She was leaning against the railing. "You know," she said, "the whole shop is really more beautiful than anything in it. Your wife is the best of the lot. As an artist, I mean." She paused and looked out at the river and the little park on its other side. Her voice was oddly toneless. "Well, I'm not much of a judge, probably, but it's a beautiful place. But, you know, all Katy really seems to want is a toy plastic shopping cart she's seen advertised on TV." She looked at him to see if he knew what she meant, but he didn't. "You must know the thing I mean. It's junk, but it has all those little pretend cans and bottles in it. It's the only thing she's asked for." She smiled at him but took up her large leather purse, ready to leave, and Martin felt as if he had betrayed his wife, even though he was somewhat mollified by his notion that Claire's smile was one of apology.

They went to a shopping center five miles away in Bradford and hastened through the oppressively dark mall lined with benches, where a great many old people sat waiting for someone or simply keeping their places in that air-conditioned tunnel and nursing some private and unspoken fury. Martin had to be especially invigorated whenever he put himself up to shopping here for the special bargains they advertised.

Claire had made her selections with what seemed to be slight consideration but great satisfaction, and Martin had bought all sorts of things. He had been carried away with the whole thing. They found the little cart Katy had requested and then brought all those toys back to Martin's house to wrap in birthday paper.

When they finally finished that chore and left his house, they stopped at the bakery to pick up a cake Claire had ordered, and then they drove slowly out of West Bradford in the summer tourist traffic back toward Vic and Ellen's. They progressed hesitantly along the main road and then through Bradford once again, stoplight by stoplight. While they sat still in the sun waiting for one light to change, Martin gazed ahead at a broad, grassless churchyard on the corner, in which some large activity was taking place. It looked like a children's fair, and he realized with a rising, gleeful ebullience that everywhere there were grubby, dust-covered children running around with helium balloons attached to their belt loops or wrists by a taut string.

"Let's stop, Claire," he said. "We might be able to fill the balloons here." He was terribly enthusiastic, thinking how excited Katy would be to run all around the meadow with a mass of party balloons bobbing high above her in the air.

"God, Martin. It's so hot. It isn't that important, really, do you think?" But his delight was so intense that he turned at the corner and parked the car in the church lot. He and Claire wandered through the crowd looking for the source of helium. It was a frantic group in that depressed section of town; the children moved about with a cocky authority that his own children did not possess. These children knew how to fend for themselves. The only advantage Martin and Claire had was their height; their status as adults brought them no special consideration. The other adults were mostly sad and pasty-looking women, hot and disheveled and defeated, who clearly had relinquished control long ago of whichever children were their own. But Martin spotted the helium dispenser and took hold of Claire's arm to propel her in the right direction. The man filling the balloons was enjoying a letup in their popularity, and he stood leaning against the outsized plastic clown which encased the cylinder of gas. He gave them a glum look as they approached with their two cellophane bags of birthday balloons.

"I can't fill all those balloons. This thing is for charity. I just hire out for a fee." He looked at them sullenly like an ill-treated dog.

"Well, what if I gave you ten dollars to fill them? Would that seem fair to you?" Martin asked, and Claire just lagged back, seemingly offended by the whole event going madly on around her.

"I told you, this is a charity thing. The kids get the balloons free. The church pays me."

"But we can't find anywhere else to get these filled. They're for a birthday party."

The man didn't seem to have any particular greed and no sympathy on which to play, but when he realized that Martin was going to continue to stand there arguing, he straightened himself and held out his hand resignedly for the balloons, which he fitted over a spigot protruding from the clown's grotesque smile. He turned the knob that released the pressurized gas. Martin took on the job of tying off each balloon and attaching it to a string, handing them to Claire as they accumulated. When the balloons had all been blown up, Martin turned to her to see that she was holding at least twenty balloons in each hand, and that she was absolutely radiant with the unanticipated pleasure of their buoyancy. He looked at her carefully; he had never seen her face so devoid of reserve, and when he turned to pay the man his ten dollars, he felt as if he might cry. But at the same moment, he realized that what he was feeling was an unexpected and nearly mournful lust.

It took them some time to arrange themselves in the car. Ten or twelve balloons fitted in the back seat, pressing against the ceiling. The others were left to Claire to hold on to tightly by their strings as they were suspended outside her front window. People honked at them and waved as they resumed their slow progress, with the balloons perilously in tow.

Martin drove along slowly, thinking of Claire when he had seen her nude, swimming and floating and diving in the deepest part of the Hofstatters' pond. Her coloring was so odd that as she had become tanned, her skin, and even her hair, had taken on the same muddy opaqueness as the water. All those times he had not really desired her. She was a friend; she seemed very much like a tall child. But he was suddenly feeling that he was in the process of experiencing a pervasive loss that could not be appeased. It had been made clear to him, when he had turned to Claire and seen that his enthusiasm for those balloons—for the celebration inherent just in the having of them—had been communicated to her, that all those summer days without his wife he had been thoroughly bereft. Now he would have stopped the car and made love to Claire in any field, but instead, of course, they continued sedately on, with the balloons buffeting about and squeaking against each other above their heads and out the window.

When they arrived at the Hofstatters', Martin drove up the long driveway in sudden embarrassment. It had only just occurred to him what an imposition they might be making on Vic and Ellen's careful schedule. But Ellen had seen them approaching, and she met them in the driveway full of goodwill. She immediately appropriated the party and made of it her own invention. She abandoned herself to its organization, although she insisted that it be held outside, so that any amount of running around would not matter. She brought out onto the grass an old wooden coat-rack and went about the business of attaching the balloons closely to its several arms. In the end she had created a glorious, multicolored, and bulbous tree, so the rest of the group sat down beneath it and left the arrangements to her. She dashed in and out of the house, and at some point she changed from her shorts into a long, flowered chintz skirt with a wide flounce at the hem, so she weaved and bobbed over the lawn as intriguingly as the beautiful balloon Katy had appropriated from the original bunch.

After they had all had a piece of cake and Katy had opened her gifts, Vic and Ellen and another couple who had dropped by to swim sat with Martin and Claire in the yard drinking champagne that Martin had bought for the festivity.

The balloons had been untied from their tree trunk and given over to Katy, who, just as Martin had expected, did drift through the meadow with all of them tied by their strings to her wrists. But it was somewhat disappointing, because the balloons were apparently too porous to be inflated with helium, and they floated limply now, not so far above her head. An obscure memory flickered through Martin's mind just then. One year when he had been in New Orleans during Mardi Gras, he had been edging through the crowds on Canal Street with friends when they realized that they were being bombarded with water-filled balloons dropped from many stories up by some drunken revelers. He had thought they were balloons, but when he noticed one broken on the sidewalk he realized that they were, in fact, condoms. Now he had driven twenty long miles from Bradford to the Hofstatters' with balloons that had had a remarkably prophylactic effect on his own rather doleful desire.

When he looked at Claire and poured more wine, he discovered that his desire had dissipated, that he felt instead overwhelmingly depressed, with a longing for his own home, his own wife, his own children. He had a heartsick need for that quiet and continual celebration of the spirit when it is bound fast by the expectations and wants and demands of other people whom one desires above all else to please and cherish and be nurtured by in turn.

CHAPTER SIX

THE FOLLY OF MOTHERS AND FATHERS

Now that the full heat of summer had slipped up the Mississippi Valley and dropped down over Enfield, Ohio, Dinah's perspective became as limited as the visible horizons. Her boundaries were as definite in the heavy atmosphere as if she existed inside an immense overturned teacup. At night, when the heat did not abate, she lay early in the dark, still as stone, with the sheets thrown off and the windows and shades up so that, with an elaborate system of fans and closed-off rooms, she could feel a faint movement of the air. But her mind could not move off into thoughts of its own accord; she had to motivate and steer her thinking with a will. She found that her imagination was as encompassed by the heat and humidity as if she were asleep and possessed by a dream.

As the summer evolved, she began to think that her actions *did* have the insubstantiality of the actions of dreams. She awoke early each morning as soon as the light came through the unshaded windows, and because of the moisture that had settled into the room overnight and made the sheets cool to the touch, she would look out at the glistening leaves—each one glittering deceptively in minute movements on the distant branches—and be persuaded of coolness. She counted the clarity of the atmosphere as a seductive trick. She expected to be able to see the heat as one can in the East, where it hovers honestly like a fog, or in the South, where it shimmers up warningly from the ground. Enfield sparkled in the transparent mornings, and each summer she finally remembered that she had to school herself daily against the hope of relief, because, once she began to move about, the debilitating temperature would hinder her again.

She lay in bed until she saw Lawrence make his morning circuit of the village; he jogged resolutely through the quiet streets; she could even see his bare back and shoulders shining with sweat. Then Dinah would get up and perfunctorily pull her hair back from her damp temples and wrap it in a twist at her neck. She had no need to dress up for Lawrence; he had always, since childhood, been privy to her company at its best and worst. When they were very young friends of eight or nine years old, Lawrence had often sat chatting with her in the kitchen, where she stood wrapped only in a towel, drooping her head over the sink, while Polly washed and then combed out her long hair. It never occurred to her now to adopt an artful modesty. So she would only slip a light robe over her nightgown and go down barefoot to the kitchen while the children slept. She tried to believe she was surprised every day when Lawrence showed up on the steps after running his five miles, but each time she would have to consider the fact that she had taken two cups and saucers from the cupboard before he appeared. He would put an arm around her shoulders in a friendly hug, and she would scald the cream and pour it into the cups simultaneously with the coffee. They would sit together on the back steps and sip the steaming mixture, even though it made them much hotter.

They had been several days into the heat the first time he had appeared at her back door. She had been sitting at the kitchen table in that coolest moment of the day, so that her coffee wouldn't make her feel as sick and sticky as it had the day before, when she persisted in drinking it quietly after the children had had their breakfast. She didn't mind getting up so early if it would ensure her a private moment in which she could sit with her mind blank, until the coffee jolted her into the sense of the day. The door was open to let in the cooler air from outside, and she had looked up to see Lawrence standing at the latched screen. She motioned him to stay there quietly; then she took down another cup and saucer and brought him some coffee, too. They sat outside in the lightening morning, so as not to wake the children. "I saw the light on down here," he said. "I thought you must be up."

The next morning he had stopped again; this time he had wanted to tell her that his sister, Isobel, had called late the night before and was coming for a visit. Dinah had been delighted at the news and glad to see him. The morning after that, he had arrived without a message, just his company, and they sat together on the wooden steps shoulder to shoulder as if it were a long-practiced habit. It was in such a simple way that they began a trifling and unacknowledged conspiracy. No one knew that Lawrence stopped by, but surely no one would have cared; the two of them were such old friends. They discussed their families: their mothers and fathers and siblings, and especially Isobel, whose arrival had become a stable point on which to pin all the suddenly tenuous impressions of the summer.

"I haven't seen her in over eight years," Dinah said, "but even so, I suppose I still think of her as one of my only women friends."

"She comes back at Christmas, usually," Lawrence said. "She seems happy."

"Well, how is that for Buddy? Isn't that awkward for them both?"

The custom of having Isobel home from school for the holidays was so familiar from childhood—the excitement of it—that it evoked an undeniable pang in Dinah. She looked at Lawrence and saw that his face had closed to the discussion of his sister and Dinah's brother. She realized that it might be an issue on which one was expected to take sides, but she hardly believed that was appropriate. She hadn't made any judgment of Buddy and Isobel's divorce; it had caused her a good deal less confusion and anguish, in fact, than their marriage. "Well," she went on, a little apologetically, "they were married for pretty long. Almost six years. And, really, they've always been together since they were young."

"Oh, Lord! When was that?" Lawrence said. "No, we're amazingly sophisticated in Enfield, Dinah. All kinds of people are getting divorced nowadays." Dinah looked at him closely to see if this uncharacteristic cynicism was just a manifestation of the old jealousy he had had toward Buddy. They had all coveted Isobel's exclusive attention in those days. "Well, in fact," he went on, in a softer tone, "I think they're glad to see each other. We went together for a long time ourselves, you know."

Dinah didn't give that any real consideration, because the two of them had never made any pretense that there had been anything between them except curiosity and desire and simple affection. They had been protected against terrible vulnerability to each other by the fact that they had shared their childhoods from the earliest moments on, so they were safe from the other's most severe censure.

But Buddy had been so much older than the rest of them, and he had never been lightly connected with Isobel. On his part, there had always been a fearful intensity. Even in retrospect, who could tell how Isobel had ever felt, or why? She had been sought after by adult and child alike, and Dinah remembered how her own mother had so often spoken of Isobel with what Dinah could only think of as a sort of wistful admiration. "Oh, she was *born* forty years old," Polly would say. "That girl doesn't have a thing to learn!" Why had Polly repeated that so often and with such mysterious and unusual fervency?

When Isobel and Dinah had gone off to the movies together, as girls, Polly had ostentatiously given Dinah's spending money to Isobel for safekeeping. Dinah recounted this with infuriated pity both for her hapless mother, burdened with her own tactlessness, and for herself as her mother's daughter. Polly had never been able to understand that she didn't have to insult one person in order to compliment another. But, in fact, thinking about it now, Dinah understood just how wide Isobel's knowledge of life had been, and how mature her diplomacy. When the two girls were dropped off in downtown Fort Lyman to wander through the stores before the show began, Isobel had dipped her head down over her purse so that her hair swung forward, concealing her face, and then she had looked up to return Dinah's money to her with an expression that clearly indicated her wry amusement at the folly of mothers and of fathers. She had always had the sense not to disparage Polly in particular; her amused scorn had blanketed all the world around them. Isobel had, indeed, known all the things she needed to know. Dinah wondered if she still did, and if it would still be an attractive trait. Dinah wondered if it would be bearable.

She had never become settled in any one way of thinking about Isobel. Dinah was protective and possessive of their friendship and at the same time wary of Isobel's elusive affections. She had spoken with Isobel often over the years, long distance, and Dinah would be sitting in her own house and suddenly realize that she was in a room Isobel had never seen, although Dinah would have with her in that space Isobel's light, persuasive voice. Sometimes Isobel would talk at great length about her life and her friends— all unknown to Dinah—and Dinah would feel a terrible sense of loss. Isobel would occasionally describe trips she had taken with a lover or a friend, so that Dinah, at her end, would hang up the phone when they finished the conversation and find that her usual generosity of spirit in regard to Isobel had narrowed into a slender knife of jealousy. On the other hand, Dinah could scarcely give credence to the fact that her friend lived a life and moved through surroundings with which she, Dinah, was not wholly familiar. For the most part, she didn't believe in Isobel's separate existence, and because of that simpleminded conviction, she did not care that Isobel was not always accessible. But she would be delighted to have her back again for a little while.

So Lawrence and Dinah sat together every morning, not worrying particularly about conversation, just as they had sat together many years ago. One morning Lawrence had leaned over and kissed her lightly on the temple. He had said, "You know, we're just getting older, Dinah." They had both laughed, because that was a reasonable argument for the case that no damage could be done to either of them by further exposure to the other. They already knew all there was to know. Dinah wasn't even surprised, because, of course, she had already thought about his body; she had thought about his long legs, which she admired now for their strength. But they had not retained the gleaming elasticity of adolescence, just as hers had not. Each hair sprouted from the skin of his lean thighs from separate, dark pinpoints against the pale color of his legs, giving the flesh a very slight, powdery look of indentation. She had considered his body with affection and sympathy, but she didn't really take her musings any further.

None of this, though, was any reflection of her feelings about Martin; those feelings were secure, and carefully compartmentalized. In fact, it seemed to her that Martin and Lawrence were of entirely separate times, and it might be that she was slipping alarmingly out of the immediate moment. She had been seduced into this bond with Lawrence by the peculiar state of mind into which she had been thrown, and by the compelling surroundings of her own youth. The secrecy of these few minutes alone each day with a man she found attractive was as pleasurable to her as the luxurious, heavy taste of the scalded cream in her café au lait.

However, nothing about these quiet and private morning meetings had anything to do with the rest of her life, and Dinah never thought how Pam would view it, either. In any case, over the summer, Dinah's initial admiration for

Pam's matter-of-fact approach to whatever problems presented themselves day by day had turned into a gentle disdain of a practicality that, in Dinah's estimation, severely limited Pam's imagination. Dinah couldn't believe that her own friendship with Lawrence would have anything to do with Pam's feelings about the world. Dinah and Lawrence were innocent enough, and besides, Lawrence was her childhood friend; Dinah supposed that such an old association would always be sacrosanct.

Pam was Dinah's friend by virtue of their shared circumstances. It was becoming apparent that that friendship had reached what could be thought of as its saturation point. It had gone as far it could go. Neither one of them cared much any longer about gaining the other's approval, and so their acquaintance remained just that; it had lost the momentum that might have propelled it into a true camaraderie. Those long, card-playing afternoons at the club had grown wearisome, and the two of them had fallen into the practice of showing just their small disapprovals of one another in lieu of open hostility. It came down to the simple fact that there wasn't a redeeming affection between them that made their differences tolerable to each other. Every little thing was beginning to make them edgy.

During their days at the pool, for instance, Dinah would find herself disproportionately aggrieved that Pam packed careful, healthy snacks for her son, Mark. Then, when David and Toby and Sarah made their assault on the various vending machines, just a shadow of a frown would crease Pam's forehead. Dinah observed with some satisfaction that Mark never ate much of his peanuts or raisins, and she explained righteously to Pam that peanuts are a deadly treat for a young child. Much too easily inhaled and choked on. The celery sticks that Pam had so cleverly stuffed with peanut butter were intact and limply greasy by the end of the hot afternoon. The thermos of milk was foul. Dinah didn't like herself for her own petty delight at Mark's refusal to accept celery as a substitute for a Milky Way, or at his certainty that milk wasn't comparable to a Coke. She didn't like herself for being glad of these things, but there was no stopping it. She accepted the justice of Pam's unspoken but obvious disapprobation of her casual attitude toward the eating habits of her own three children, but over the issue of Toby's more and more obvious limp, Pam and Dinah had approached a real argument, and that would have made the rest of the summer awkward and embarrassing.

After several days of progressively less delicate comments and questions, Pam had finally turned to Dinah at the pool and been very blunt. "For God's sake, Dinah," she had said with real heat this time, not tactful coercion, "I'll make an appointment for you with Dr. Van Helder. He ought to look at Toby. He's Mark's doctor. He's very good, I think. I really want you to have Toby looked at! He's just not using that right leg, and he won't even swim today!"

Dinah sat there quietly in a complete rage, but she continued to study the cards laid out before her on the metal table in a game of solitaire. The last few afternoons Pam had been so solicitous of Toby; she had bent and catered to his every whim. She had chatted and talked with him; she had, in effect, certified this imaginary illness of Toby's. And the symptoms were becoming more severe because of it. "Look, Pam, if you would only stop *pandering* to his own idea that he's sick, he would get better. I've tried to explain it to you. *Please* just ignore it. He wants attention, and he needs attention, and I'm doing my best to give him lots of attention *apart* from his being sick! Do you see what I mean? I don't want this to become a pattern in his life!"

Pam was terribly agitated and quite angry. "Well . . . Oh, well, Dinah, I simply don't understand how you run your household!" And she had gotten up and begun to stuff towels and suntan lotion into her beach bag, making preparations to leave. The two of them were on the verge of an irreparable breach.

Finally, Dinah reached out and detained Pam by laying a hand on her arm. She said, in the most soothing and gentle voice she could summon, "Look, Pam, he's with my father every morning. Toby adores him, and he's just copying him. Don't you see? But, of course, Dad's a doctor, you know. Well, in spite of everything else, he's a very brilliant doctor." Dinah knew that Pam didn't like her father. "You don't really believe that if he thought there was anything physically wrong with Toby he wouldn't tell me, do you?"

Pam went on collecting her things and Mark's, and Dinah could see by Pam's face that, in fact, that explanation hadn't been especially convincing to her. But nothing more was said about it, and they gathered the children and left together, amiably enough. After that afternoon, they had taken to switching off lifeguarding duties on alternate days. The children were familiar enough with the rules and their own capabilities by now that it took only one woman to watch them, in any case.

But Dinah couldn't put Pam's comment entirely out of her mind, because she had given up all pretense of in any way running her own household. She would sit each morning on the top step of the back porch with Lawrence, and above her in the upstairs bedrooms each child slept separately in his or her own heat-shrouded privacy. The conversation between Dinah and her three children had become spare; their coexistence in this house had lost its chaotic, summer quality and drawn out thin like a straight line, plain and determined. Their four lives scarcely seemed even to merge at the edges, as they should be bound to. This turn of events swept over the household beyond her control, and she would ponder it, but she had no idea if she should or could effect any change. She was slipping in and out of roles that she thought she had carefully mapped out for herself. She was alarmed by and angry at her children— when she thought of it—for their surprising and inexplicable refusal to behave as if they *were* her children. After Lawrence left each morning, Dinah would shudder in anticipation of her day-long and aloof involvement with them. All at once, it seemed to her that those children were regarding her with an intellectual rather than an emotional judgment. It had come as an alarming revelation that she was even to be so considered, and she bristled at the injustice of it.

David had his secrets, but that wasn't unexpected; he always had. Lately, even Sarah had been muted in her irrepressibility, as though she had developed a dual judgment, at age four, and recognized in herself a reservoir of ideas that she could explore independently. It was Toby, however, who could in one moment reduce Dinah to despairing inertia. She thought he flaunted the possession of his own milky-sweet summer secrets.

Every day he, too, had a morning assignation. After Lawrence's visit, Dinah made it her habit to rinse out the cups and quietly return to her own room to rest until the children woke up toward the middle of the morning. She had watched each day for a week now and seen Toby slip cautiously over the lawn, cross the street, and sit down to wait at her father's door. Presently her father would join him, towering gauntly over Toby and greeting him with a restrained nod. Dinah couldn't tell if they spoke. The two of them would make their way around the flower beds, where her father bent to inspect a plant here or there. She had first witnessed this with astonishment; it paralleled so precisely the ritual of her own childhood when she would linger with her father through the garden and tag along throughout the much more serious business of checking on the corn and tomatoes in the plots that had once been so carefully laid out behind Polly's house. She had particularly remembered the immense pleasure her father had taken in the startling panorama of the blossoming gladioli, which speared the air with their scentless and waxy height and color. He had cut masses of them for the house, but Polly disdained them. She claimed that they had no delicacy, and Dinah thought, now, that that had been a telling point. Her father could not or would not see how gauche such blatant flowers would be to Polly's aesthetic tastes.

The very first morning Dinah had happened to look out and see her son with her father, she had felt the weight of nostalgic tears pressing at her eyes, until she had taken in the scene a little longer. Her father progressed slowly through his garden, his lame leg dragging behind him, and Toby, too, matched him step for step, limping alongside. Dinah had gone rigid in immediate panic. She saw a quick flash of an image of herself standing among her children as they silently slipped away from her. As she reached out to them to plead her dominion, her hands splayed in entreaty, it was as though her control were a tangible substance sliding through her open fingers, and she was stupefied with helplessness.

It wasn't until a day or so later that Dinah finally realized that Toby was limping all the time now, as well as in her father's company. He lay on a chaise longue at the pool, scarcely moving, or he was quiet and languid on the couch at home, and when he did move, he leaned down heavily on his left leg and brought his right leg forward with great and maddening hesitation. Dinah was so angry and appalled that she couldn't bring herself to say anything at all to him, though she had heard David ask about it. Toby had scarcely answered him; he had shrugged it off, and David had lost interest. Dinah felt betrayed on all fronts.

Even her mother, who might not know that Toby was with his grandfather each morning, pressed her on this point. Polly's usually inert curiosity was piqued, and she was a woman whose curiosity assumed a gently aggressive character.

"Do you think you're putting too much pressure on Toby about something or other, Dinah?" her mother had asked her one afternoon as the two of them sat reading the evening paper on Polly's porch while the children played in the yard. Dinah sat there a moment, hopelessly depressed by her mother's uncanny ability to phrase this question so disingenuously that there was no satisfactory answer to it. She didn't answer at all and just looked out at the children instead. David was lying on the ground reading a comic, and Sarah was digging a system of canals with one of Polly's silver teaspoons. Toby was wandering around in his own world, oblivious of the rest of them. Dinah repressed her fury as she watched Toby move around the yard with such apparent and truculent difficulty.

"Well," Polly persisted, "he's under some sort of strain, Dinah. His stutter is even worse, and that limp . . . I remember when Buddy did that. Isn't that odd?" she said, suddenly led away from the mainstream of her thought and sounding a bit vague, like a very old woman all at once. Dinah was caught by this note unexpectedly, in the middle of her resentment. She glanced over at her mother with involuntary compassion to see the narrow, aristocratic regularities of her mother's profile held dead still and starkly outlined against the gentle, muted movement of the tree-filled landscape. "It was just after you turned two, I think, and your father was away in the army. He was stationed at Fort Dix, you know. Buddy was just nine." She seemed to think she had explained something, but Dinah drew no conclusions; she just let her mind go blank. Her senses registered the trace of moisture that lay over her skin like a coating of oil, irritating and emotionally defeating. "You were everywhere," Polly added. "I've never known a child who made her presence more felt. That's when I first hired Jeannie. She used to come every day." Jeannie was a local woman who had always been in and out of the house doing various jobs of cleaning and baby-sitting. She came regularly now only once a week. "That's when Buddy stopped using his left hand and arm. He's right-handed, of course, so I didn't pay much attention, at first. But, you know, I don't think children do those things *intentionally*. I helped him exercise it for hours a day. He was so jealous of you, and he was feeling absolutely deserted. He needed all that attention, and it finally worked."

The implications of all this information—so unexpectedly offered—were inescapable. This must mean that in some way Dinah had to be responsible for the past as well as the present, she thought.

She got up and went to stand at the porch rail. She stood there for a while, just gazing into the yard, until she was sure she wouldn't cry in pure frustration. She felt suffocated at the idea that she would be forever imprisoned in her mother's mind as her two-year-old self. How could she ever rectify what wrongs she may have done? The injustices she may have perpetrated? She thought she might cry at the impossibility of ever, ever making herself clear—of ever justifying herself—to her own mother, who should know her so well. Her own mother should know her at least as well as Dinah herself knew her own children!

"Oh, Mother! Why do you always end up saying things like that?" Her voice was very quiet, but not ominous, just truly sad and quizzical. "Toby gets lots of attention! He knows we love him! How could he not know?" Real sorrow enveloped her as she spoke, not an apprehensive sorrow, just an overwhelming sadness for all human beings. She also felt awfully sorry for herself and all the people she cared about. Dinah had no idea if Toby did understand how much he was loved; every now and then she became very worried about that. When she thought of Toby, she sometimes imagined that she and he were like television lovers, running toward each other across a great, grassy distance, their arms open wide in expectation. Dinah wondered if the two of them were charted just enough off-course so that they were destined to hurtle past each other, heavy with love and good intentions, but inevitably missing their target. Her mother didn't comment further, and Dinah hoped she had lost interest, for the moment, in Toby and his happiness. A little later she gathered up the children, and the four of them wandered back to their own house.

They never arrived home that the cat was not waiting for them. Dinah had stopped feeding him, and he was uninterested in the restrained attentions of David and Toby, and he openly shunned Sarah's gregarious affection. Dinah could not understand their attraction for him, but over the last few weeks her father's cat had become a more and more dubious conquest. At any hour of the day he might be found lounging on the steps or under the shrubbery if he sought the shade. She didn't even allow the children to feed him the scraps of their dinner; he was a sleek creature, and she had immediately despised herself in the first place for her initial, petty enticement of him.

Dinah kept going—she got by, day to day—on a belief in her own decency. In general, she had very little *hope* of anything; she was not an optimist, and hope would have been foreign to her nature. In fact, hope would have indicated a certain sort of faith in something—even simply in the nature of the universe—that she had given up even considering. She was not as nice, certainly, as she meant to be; she didn't believe that anyone was. But she was determined to believe in people's intentions of decency and kindness. She was also aware that because of that belief she was probably circumstantially naïve. But at least she didn't extend to herself the easy charity she extended to everyone else, and she was particularly contemptuous of that small remnant of childishness that often led her into pursuing revenge. She was ashamed of herself every time she contemplated the company of that handsome cat, and she was obliged to think of him often. In spite of her discouragement, he seemed to find the activity of their household especially interesting. And, oddly enough, he had taken to courting her.

Those early mornings when she went down at dawn to open the house, she would often find on her porch a freshly dead but unmarked little corpse—a mouse or a mole. The first few mornings the cat, whose name, Toby had told her, was Jimmy, would be sitting apart from his gift, looking into the yard with satisfaction and apparent disregard. He sat there, suspiciously immobile, and she knew that he was attuned to every nuance of her discovery of this tribute to her. However, subtlety had eluded her in this instance, and upon first coming across a small, dead, furry animal, she had naturally recoiled and shut the door to think how best to dispose of it. She returned with a trowel and squeamishly used it to transfer the little body to the garbage, while all the time the cat appraised her from the porch rail. This continued, to Dinah's dismay, for several days, but Jimmy had become dissatisfied with her response, and now she would often find just a severely gnawed head or an undigestible, bony leg. It angered her, each time; she wondered at that cat's lust for murder.

It was bound to have been Toby who would be the one to come in full of delight one afternoon, in search of her. When he found her in the living room, he coyly held both hands behind his back. "Guess which hand!" he said, for the first time in weeks, shy with immense pleasure.

"That one," she replied, and he brought forth a handful of silvery-gray feathers that caught the light from the bay windows so that the web could be seen as a composite of its separate, delicate filaments against the rigid quill. Without waiting, too full of excitement to carry on the game, he also held out his other hand, palm flat, on which were displayed two knobby, brownish bird feet.

Her face immediately and involuntarily was cast over with distaste; subtlety deserted her here, too. "But, Toby, those are from a dead *bird!*" she said at once, idiotically meaning to impose on him the initial brutality that had yielded such trophies. She had looked up from the feathers and feet to see the pleasure leave his face, and his mouth and eyes become still and guarded.

"I found them on the back porch. I didn't *kill* it," he said.

"Well, no," she said, striving for kindness now; who was she to judge mercy? "The feathers are beautiful, Toby." She picked one up and held it to the sun, so he could see it as she had. He stood politely with her and then silently took his leave, disappointed in her, it was clear. He ponderously made his way toward the stairs and his own room.

Dinah was so distressed that the air of the room and every object in it took on an ominous substance. Once in a very great while, and always unexpectedly, all the freewheeling elements of her senses came to a dead stop, so that the impression of that instant would be printed on her mind for all her life. Such occasions were rare, and she sat in thrall, watching Toby progress away from her for the many hours it seemed to take him, while she sat so apart, her assessment of time gone murky with the intelligence—suddenly communicated to her—of all the terrifying havoc and harm she might cause in the world. Then the moment passed; time picked up as though it were her pulse revived, and she sat still on the couch as Toby began carefully to climb the stairs. With both hands encumbered, he couldn't make use of the banister, and his ascent was clumsy and precarious because of his refusal to use his right leg as he should.

In the next instant, Dinah was caught up in a terrible rage, and she leaped up from her seat in the quiet living room and raced up the stairs past him, turning at the top to face him as he approached, slowing in alarm.

"Toby, I just can't stand this anymore! I don't even know what to say about it. If you're sick, you've got to tell me *why!* If I'm doing something that makes you miserable, for God's sake, tell me what it is. Are you mad at me about something? My God, Toby, it's like being tortured! I can't stand to see you so unhappy. Don't you *know* how much I love you. And your father loves you!" Her anger had lost its force almost at once, dispelling itself in her voice, which became a breathy, plaintive rasp as she lowered herself to sit down on the landing and receive Toby as he made his way steadfastly upward, his hands still full. "I just don't understand what's wrong. Would you like to talk to someone, Toby?" She was pleading with him by now, staring at his lowered face as he stood next to her on the top step. What she wanted was for him to tell her how to give over the responsibility for his ease and comfort in the world. "You know, maybe we could talk to your grandfather." They looked directly at each other in their first acknowledgment of that association. Here, at least, was a truce. "He's good at helping people who are unhappy, and he's told me how fond he is of you. Or, Toby . . . if you want to talk to him when I'm not around, that would be fine. If *I'm* making you unhappy, sweetie, you might want to see if he could tell you what we could do about it. Toby, I don't mind anything you tell him. Don't try to protect *me!* I want you to be happy and to feel good again!"

She was holding Toby around the waist as she talked to him, although he wasn't bending into her embrace; he was standing rigidly beside her. He looked at her quite honestly. "I don't think I'm very unhappy about anything," he said at last, and resumed his slow progress to his room.

Dinah put her head down on her knees in sorrow and exasperation. It was clear she had no leverage with which to pry him away from his sullen, sulky, obsessional illness, and since she loved him with greater determination than she could have directed even at herself, her expectations of him and for him were enormous. She was having difficulty forgiving him for his recalcitrance.

Dinah began to try to foist off her own apathy, which she thought might be causing the widening breach between herself and her children. In fact, she began to infuse a really dreadful cheer into their days. She made clever little meals, designed to appeal to children, and they all sat at the table together as her resentment grew when the children ate the food suspiciously and without any particular gratitude. She thought of activities they could all do together. They went to the Amish museum; she took the children to the zoo in Columbus, where they were all made miserable by the heat. She discovered that Toby's malaise had caught on. She couldn't shake it, and she furiously resented the force of her own empathy. In this state of extended sensitivity, she imagined that she had practically *become* Toby; she suffered so for him in spite of herself, and all to no avail. It served no purpose, this anguish, except to communicate itself to David and Sarah as well, so that a pall hung over the household. She had no choice but to try to improve the situation, in however trite a manner. She didn't really believe for a moment that she could put things right, but she was bound to try.

She had decided to go ahead and give Toby an early birthday party. This was always a celebration of summer, so it wasn't quite so out of the ordinary, and Dinah had some notion of distracting Toby, if only for a few hours, from his preoccupying melancholy.

One afternoon, when Pam had taken all the children with her to the pool, Dinah settled herself in the living room with a notebook and pencil and began to make plans for the party. She sat making lists of guests, lists of party favors, clever ones for the adults—grim as she always thought it was when everyone must openly appreciate the stale humor—and some little things that would entertain the children. She had never enjoyed giving children's parties, just as she didn't think she had ever had fun at one as a child, and she made out her lists with no great hope of a successful celebration.

She paused for a moment and was looking up, vacantly staring through the front window, when she saw her father leave his house and come down his front walk. She just watched him without thinking of anything much, until she realized he was crossing the street to her house. She was thrown into that juvenile and abject state of alarm in which one craves approval and worries about appearances above all else. She jumped up to go to the mirror and see how she looked. She wished she were nicely dressed. She wished she had put on lipstick. She felt a terrible apprehension, but she had known that he would eventually come to talk to her about Toby.

The past few nights she had lain awake wondering if her father was waiting for her to approach him first, because she knew he must be concerned. He had always had great respect for children. She thought that the years when her father had liked her best had been when she was still a young child. He had always been earnestly interested in her opinions and adventures. It had pleased him to be able to show her *how* to think about things. It was only later that she received the full force of his scorn or simple lack of interest. Their gradual parting had begun in her adolescence, during those long, futile years when she had tried, with as much disinterest as possible, to discover and solve her parents' differences. She hadn't known what a presumption that was. She hadn't known until she was married herself. But she had been sure that her father would be bound by his fierce conscience, and probably some affection, to take action on Toby's behalf. She had reached a state of such desperation that she wouldn't mind if it turned out that she must shoulder the entire burden of responsibility for Toby's mysterious and persistent sorrow. She wouldn't mind anything her father might tell her if only he could offer her a solution.

She opened the door as her father was mounting the steps, and she walked out to the edge of the porch to lean down and greet him with a light kiss. He smiled at her with what seemed to be a weary effort and followed her into the house.

"Come into the living room, Dad," she said. "I can get you some iced tea if you like." It should have seemed peculiar to be ushering her father into this house for the first time, and yet, oddly enough, the occasion seemed perfectly ordinary. But, then, her father was a close friend of the Hortons'; he was probably entirely familiar with these rooms.

"No, I can't come in, Dinah. I have to go to the post office." He held up a handful of letters in illustration. "I have to walk a mile every day," he said, "to exercise my leg. I just stopped by for a minute. I wanted to tell you that my cat, Jimmy, is dead. I thought that I ought to tell you so that you could tell the children. I saw them go off with Pam, and it seemed to me that this would be a good time to let you know first. I know how fond Toby was of him, and Jimmy was always coming over here lately. I kept telling Toby that he shouldn't encourage Jimmy to leave my yard . . . but Toby just didn't understand, I guess. Well, in fact, Jimmy was hit by a car this morning. He must have been crossing the street to your house."

Dinah responded immediately, as was appropriate, without having time to think of the gray cat or her father, so obviously saddened. "Oh, Dad, I'm sorry. He was a beautiful cat!"

Her father looked particularly pained, and he shook his

head in a manner that indicated a resigned futility. "Why in God's name do people always say something asinine like that about a cat? What difference does it make what he *looked* like?" He was making himself very angry, but he was also tired. She watched him with alarm and fascination. Dinah had expected such a different conversation that her mind had not really started to work on what he was saying.

"Well, Dad," she said, "that cat was pretty hard on the wildlife." Was she trying to justify this cat's death to protect Toby? To protect himself? She had never considered her father a sentimental man; she had always known, at least, that neither she nor her mother could ever touch any kernel of his sentiment. That's what she thought, at any rate, but now he leaned back against the doorjamb, and his face filled with a familiar look of gleeful irony.

"Yes, Jimmy was a great hunter." He arched his eyebrows with pleasure. "It was the only career I could get him to take up. He wasn't the least interested in the law, or accounting." Then he grew solemn again and was intent upon getting Jimmy's description clear. "He was a very smart cat," he said. "No, he was an *intelligent* cat. Not at all sweet-natured, but canny." She would have to think later about whatever it was he meant by this; she couldn't understand it now, but her father had always been a man who chose his words with stingy care. She knew she must give them some thought. "But, you know," he went on, "until he got so interested in Toby, he had always been a cat who was content to live in his own yard. I have that fence, you see. Dogs didn't bother him. Oh, well . . . well, will you let the children know?"

Dinah nodded. How could she ever explain to her father that it was she, and not Toby, who had seduced that sleek gray cat?

CHAPTER SEVEN

EASY LIVING

D inah stood in the doorway and watched her father retrace his path down the steps and along the curving front walk that wound around the corner of the house to the street. Usually, people in Enfield came to the side door and entered through the kitchen; that door was easily accessible, but her father was a man who always observed the formalities. Especially after so long a time, he had come to the front door, not chancing to presume he would be casually welcomed just like any other neighbor. His elaborate propriety suddenly brought to mind the long-ago Sunday luncheons at expensive restaurants, slightly grim occasions as were any gatherings that included the four of them, but nevertheless the event she had always anticipated most during the week.

The whole country had been naïve then. It had been rather an innocent age all around. The restaurants they had gone to had served very good but ordinary food. Baked Alaska was considered exotic. And the rooms were only rooms with painted walls, some mirrors, and pictures. No fantasy was involved; no room pretended to be Polynesian or Victorian, and those restaurants had names like The Capitol House or Pinetta's. One of her and Martin's favorite places to eat in Fort Lyman now was called The Spotted Zebra. She thought that it had been easier to define things then. She and Buddy and Polly and her father had sat together in a restaurant that smelled sharply of starched linen, luxurious carpeting, and secret edibles enclosed in silver dishes and wheeled on trolleys to nearby tables. The atmosphere had been sincerely respectable and reassuring as they unfolded their napkins into their laps.

Now, she watched her father walking away down the sidewalk, and a sensation of familiarity swept over her so entirely that she believed she knew the next move he would make, how the branches of the shaggy pines would flex as he brushed against them, the angle he would hold his head. She was at once enclosed in the same claustrophobic apperception that was becoming unbearably frequent these hot days. The simple tableau of which she was now a part seemed thoroughly of the past—as though her mind, having long ago expanded into a certain territory, must occupy it again if given the slightest prod. But her hand resting there on the intricately carved woodwork registered the sensation of being in the present, so even as she stood transfixed by her conflicting sensibilities, she could isolate that instant as a clear bubble of experience. She knew what had happened, and she thought that this particular manifestation of déjà vu was simply her mind's absolute refusal to admit the random nature of human events and of human connections. It was far too risky, she knew, to confront the fact of one's initial lack of choice. There was a degree of anxiety involved in understanding that it was not *reasonable* that she was who she was, tied to and caring about her inevitable relations. Her circumstances had come about only by chance, and her intelligence couldn't approve of that.

She stood there watching her father stoop to avoid the branches that protruded, untrimmed, into his pathway; he was too tall to walk beneath them. Before she considered it, she took up her purse and keys from the hall bench under the mirror and left the house to catch up with him. "I'll go along with you and get my mail," she said, and he nodded at her absently and smiled. They recrossed the street and walked along slowly next to the handsome iron fence in front of his house. Some new construction had been started. Dinah had observed it with mild curiosity for days. Raw-looking two-by-fours were erected in the rough skeleton of a box that straddled the peak of the roof. She regarded the house from its long side; she couldn't see the gable. "What are they doing there on the roof, Dad?" Her father came to a stop and looked up at it, and so she did, too.

"Well," he said after a moment, "that's going to be a cupola. I've always wanted one. I've always wanted a cupola and a gazebo. As soon as I have those, I'll be finished with this house. I even like the names. They have a nice sound, don't you think? You wouldn't think of one without the other."

Dinah didn't say anything at once. Her father had only asked her a rhetorical question, and they walked on. "Won't that be something of an anachronism on that house?" she said. "I guess a gazebo would be fine in the garden. But the lines of the house are so elegant." The thought of a cupola perched on top of that pristine slate- and copper-clad roof worried her unaccountably. She cared about the integrity of houses. But she knew even as she made this mild objection that her argument was futile. She had tried, off and on during her life, to abandon her own tendency to insist on getting things just right. Her father looked disdainful, as much as to say she had missed the point. But she already knew, anyway, that he liked what he liked, and that a mere architectural incongruity would be of no consequence to him.

"I always thought we should have had a gazebo out back in the far yard," he said, as though she hadn't spoken. "Up at Polly's, you know. But that didn't interest your mother at all." A faint nasal twang whined out into the middle of a sentence now and then as her father spoke, and it was an inflection that connoted absolute self-assurance. It was curiously attractive, but also entirely patronizing. Perhaps it was perversely tempting to an audience to be patronized; perhaps that accounted, in part, for her father's magnetism. Otherwise, his speech drew one's attention because underneath the distinctly enunciated syllables there was a faint tension of the chest and vocal cords. He gave the impression of speaking with a very tenuous restraint, and that, too, was compelling.

Dinah didn't care if her parents had ever talked about building a gazebo; certainly they never had within her hearing or memory. But she winced at her father's petulance about it now, which had crept into his manner right away when he mentioned it. That petulance was too reminiscent of childhood, when she had finally perceived that whatever one parent desired, the other was bound to despise. The two of them—her mother and father—had never understood that. They would approach each other time and again with various plans and schemes, only to be met with bland opposition once more. A plaintive resentment grew up between them and came to rest like a constant shadow over Dinah and Buddy. As a result, of course, Dinah was adamantly incurious about the unconstructed gazebo in Polly's back yard.

"Toby's birthday is coming up, Dad," she said. "I wonder if you'd come? I'm going to wait and have it when Isobel is here, because she's his godmother. They've never met, though." This still made her sorry, that her life and her friend's life could have progressed so far so separately.

He turned his mind to this question now, to Dinah's relief. "Oh, well, Dinah. I don't think so. I don't much like those sorts of things."

Dinah had never set out, had never intended, to invite him at all, and her first impulse when he refused the invitation was to tell him so. She was furious at his obtuseness. Now she couldn't manage not to feel his rejection, his lack of generosity; she couldn't be unaware that Toby, too, was rejected, even though, on her father's part, it was all unconscious. It was only an example of his own consuming self-involvement. But it laid Dinah and Toby open, in Dinah's view, to their own humiliating desires and dependencies. She walked on beside him in apparent calm, but she was laden with a disproportionate anger.

They paused in front of the post office, and her father readied himself to mount the steps. He shifted his weight and transferred his envelopes to the hand that would not clasp the banister. He assumed a look of concentration, and Dinah watched him with sympathy in spite of herself. "Look," he said, "why don't you bring the children over someday and I'll fix a birthday lunch for Toby? Something like that. I'll arrange it all, and you get Isobel to come, too. I don't think you've seen the house, have you?" He turned once again to gather himself up and take the steps, but he added in an abstracted and bemused tone, "It will be good to see Isobel again, too. She used to come over just to listen to music. Dave Brubeck. She never liked any of my Ahmad Jamal." He thought that over. "Well, I think she was probably right about that. They were just a shade too commercial. Now *she's* an attractive girl!" It seemed that he meant she was attractive in opposition to someone else, but Dinah didn't want to explore that possibility. "She must be almost thirty-five or thirty-six by now. She still seems so young! She came over at Thanksgiving just to say hello. I like to have her visit."

By now, in spite of herself, Dinah could not help but think of Isobel. All of their lives, the two of them had played at competition. She had a vivid impression of Isobel, all at once, as she had been the weekend she had been home from her boarding school when Dinah was in the Homecoming pageant at Fort Lyman High School. Dinah had been pleased when she had found out that Isobel would be home to see her celebrated. Isobel had been so glamorous! But Dinah did not want to hear her father name any more of Isobel's virtues, as much as she might agree with him. Now she was intimidated by her own memories.

Dinah put all this out of her thoughts for the moment, but she did accept her father's invitation to lunch, for Toby's sake, and for the benefit of her own curiosity. Dinah had forgotten, over the years, that she needed an armored sensibility and a sturdy ego to risk exposure to her own father. Isobel had always had both, and besides, she and Dinah's father had approached being the other's favorite person. This notion flickered alarmingly over the surface of Dinah's mind, laserlike, a beam of pure resentment that permeated her studious unconcern.

"Dad, I've been wanting to talk to you about Toby. You've noticed his limp?" She had caught his arm at the elbow this time, before he started up the steps, and he turned back to her with slight impatience. "Should I take him to a pediatrician or an orthopedist? Could it be something that ought to be looked at?"

"Oh, Dinah, for God's sake!" He looked at her with his head slightly cocked. Dinah had spent many years of her life learning all the subtleties of her father's expression, just as children must. When he raised an eyebrow and drew one corner of his mouth down ever so slightly, she understood entirely the implied derision. She understood entirely, once more, the horror of being anyone's child, subject to such terrors as the denial of approval. "I'll tell you," he went on. "It almost amuses me that, of all the possible traits he could have taken up, he chose my least attractive!" She was momentarily embarrassed, because just as they had walked along together this afternoon and she had watched her father's cautious handling of his body, she had remembered his huge and unabashed vanity, and she had become aware that his faltering gait was especially distasteful to him. But he went on, unconcerned apparently, and she remembered that people always suffered more for him than he ever did for himself. That was his best trick. "Martin's not here," he explained with exacting condescension. "Well, Toby's just at that age, I suppose. About seven? It's just a kind of hero worship. Toby's fine."

Dinah didn't mean to, but generally she believed what men told her. In this case, though, she knew that in some way Toby was not fine. "He isn't," she said.

Her father had gone ahead, laboriously, up two steps, and this time he turned to look at her in amusement. "Well, Dinah? What do you expect?" She just looked back at him; her mind wasn't moving with the conversation. She was thinking of Toby with a small but penetrating grief; she wondered if he was beyond her help. "Why isn't Martin here? Why *do* you come back here without him year after year? Of *course* that's on Toby's mind. You shouldn't imagine that children don't feel the weight of a situation like that."

She stood there astonished as he made his way up the steps and into the post office, struggling with his balance as he levered open the heavy door. She was not shocked by his audacity. She had long ago, and during the most bitter of their confrontations, given up expecting him to coordinate his advice with his own actions. It was only his own children who were expected to be immune to the effects of family trauma. But she continued to stand there after he disappeared into the dark interior, before she could register anger, before she formed a reply. She had nothing to say; she didn't even have anything to think. Her situation, her desperation, went unnamed and unaccounted for. All the loose ends of her life flew around her like unfettered ribbons around a maypole. The only thing she knew for sure, and what astounded her most, was that he misunderstood it altogether; he had it all wrong. In fact, when challenged in such a way, she felt the absolute solid certainty of Martin's reassuring existence in the world. As with every other summer, she had reached that stage of separation at which point the idea of Martin had become as slight as the rustle and final settled whisper of her letters to him when she dropped them down the "Out of Town" slot in the air-conditioned lobby of the post office. She often lingered there, because it was cool, and because she wanted to extend the moment. When she talked to him on the phone, they were both fairly matter-of-fact; they were well practiced, by now, at being in different places. But she had never thought for a moment that they were not closely bound. Now every facet of her mind suddenly reflected all the myriad aspects of their marriage into her consciousness, and for one moment all the day's persistent despair was alleviated. Then the moment was gone.

For the next few days, Dinah was in a rather exquisite

state of mind. She was wrapped up in a tender and fragile malaise, compounded of despondency, nostalgia, and wistful anticipation. Without thinking, she took care not to disturb that balance. She didn't indulge in introspection; she didn't allow herself anger; she was content to stay adrift. In the evenings she sat with her children, who were unusually and sweetly subdued because of the continuing heat. They sprawled over the furniture or on the rug in front of the fan to read or draw or watch television, being careful not to move too much. Dinah sat there, too, while the black-and-white television glimmered fluorescent light and shadow into the room, and she stared and stared out the window at the little village of Enfield.

The Hortons' study was a close and comfortable room, tightly pocketed between the kitchen and the living room on one side of the house. From its windows Dinah could see all the way down Gilbert to Hoxsey Street and count the maple trees planted symmetrically in corresponding pairs on either side of it. In the late afternoon the fading light came down in such a way that evening seemed to begin in the heavy dark heads of those maples and slip down slowly over their gray trunks. There was not one building in the village taller than the towering trees; the village had formed itself to suit the topography of the land, and that reinforced more than ever the pull of natural time on the shape of a day. It always had. When dusk came, the day was over. This was a great comfort; one was relieved of choice in these matters, and Dinah came back each year hoping that the rhythm of village life would once again—as in childhood—give a direction to her time. Most of her life she had moved through this particular village lulled by its unelaborate charm and civilized—even elegant—rusticity. This place was so much a part of her nature by now that it was no longer a place she could choose to leave. She could trace out her earliest years on a transparency, unroll it maplike over Enfield, and therefore interpret it. That was what seemed likely to her. And now, wherever she might go, she would have to impose any other manner of living upon those early learned habits of gentle expectation.

Sometimes in the quiet evenings Toby mentioned to her that he wasn't feeling good, and she knew what a healthy sign that was. She would have liked for him to tell her more, but that was all he would say. She held him on her lap, although he had grown much too lanky for either one of them to be comfortable that way. She told him about his upcoming party, and she listened to his suggestions, pinning great hope on his enthusiasm. She told him about the luncheon her father was giving solely in his honor, and she talked to him about his godmother's arrival.

She was aware when she spoke out into their quiet company that her voice had the disembodied intonation it had in her own dreams, but the children listened and didn't seem to notice anything out of the ordinary. They were interested in the arrival of Isobel, although David and Sarah were jealous because it became clear that she was to be more Toby's than their own. That was galling; they had heard so much about Isobel, and they had no particular charity for their brother simply because he wasn't well. But they were not terribly envious, and in Dinah's case this was an easy way to live. The four of them, that small family, sat together in the study with an unexpected and soothing measure of contentment. Whatever had settled over their mother—her sudden nonchalance about the bothersome details of their lives—was beneficial. They preferred their mother's peaceful listlessness to her frantic efforts to energize herself on their behalf. They were all quite satisfied in their cool, shady twilights together, while the heavy air hung over the dark trees outside their window.

Dinah and Lawrence talked about his sister in the mornings when they sat together drinking coffee. The prospect of Isobel's company, in fact, had practically mitigated Dinah's need for Lawrence's; he paled by comparison. But she found a mellow pleasure in his physical presence. She would lean her leg in its nylon gown just companionably against his long, bare thigh as they sat outside together. When he got up and went away, the fabric would be damp from his perspiration. She would go in and rinse their cups in the kitchen with the moist, sheer nylon clinging to her leg, and she enjoyed that warm, pleasurable sensation so fondly felt that it amounted to the reminder of her own sexuality and little more. She saw him every morning, and he always gave her a hug in greeting and sat close beside her, but in some singular way neither of them sought to carry their familiarity beyond that. This event, Isobel's arrival, loomed ahead of them as it had intermittently all their lives. She was more important to each of them than either was to the other, so they couldn't explore what might happen between them until this other anticipation could be overcome.

Even Polly was restless, apparently, in her accustomed rounds. She set her own hours for her work, and lately she had taken to showing up at Dinah's now and then during her usual office hours. She had become oddly loquacious and curious, and disconcertingly less distant. Now and then, during Dinah's childhood, Polly had been alarmingly lifted out of her habitual repose, and then she had become vigorously active in her pursuit of some problem that whetted her curiosity. She hadn't ever had much appetite for involvement, but once that appetite was roused, it was not easily satisfied. There had always been a few things Polly must find out, and there had even been a few things that had brought her to anger. But they were arbitrary events, never predictable, and she seized upon them as a terrier digs for groundhogs. So no one in Enfield, really, could be sure of being left in peace until Polly settled whatever it was that was on her mind.

She dropped by one afternoon when the children were off with Pam, and Dinah was sitting lazily in the living room with a book she was reading but not absorbing. She was watching for her father, idly, although she had not admitted it to herself. She had taken to walking with him often if she happened to see him when he took his daily exercise, but she only walked as far as the post office and then went on to do her shopping and other errands in the village. Those few occasions when she had caught up with him and kept him company hadn't been at all remarkable. It was as if they had been visiting with each other regularly for years. Her father was never surprised to see her.

When Polly joined her in the living room, and Dinah brought in tall glasses of iced tea for them both, she was ill at ease and realized that she wanted Polly to leave so that she would not miss her father. Polly was sitting in a chair with her back to the long windows that looked out at Dr. Briggs's front door. Dinah sat down opposite her, and they talked about Isobel a little, about her mother's bridge club, about her decorating business, about David and Toby and Sarah. Dinah could not make out exactly what her mother's purpose was, if she had come with any.

"I think Toby's improving," Polly said.

"He says not," Dinah replied, startling herself by the brusqueness of her own voice. "He complains about his leg now," she added more softly. "I talked to Dad about it. He says it's just one of those stages, so I've tried to ignore it." She understood what had given such an abrupt edge to her voice; it was nothing more than the somnolence of the room itself. Each piece of furniture was upholstered in a slightly deeper shade of plum than the piece next to it, although the impression was of a happy accident of harmony, not a conscious design. Dinah knew that this was Polly's doing; she had done the whole house for the Hortons. A flat-blue, pierced screen stood in one corner, cutting diagonally across the edge of the broad Oriental rug. The air was drowsy with the heavy colors. Not pastels, but deep, plain, chalky colors that seemed to exude something of their own essence into that confined space. Any voice—any but Polly's pale tone—would have been unsettling and inappropriate.

Polly made a gesture of dismissal with her hand. "If Toby's *talking* about it, that's the best thing yet, isn't it?

Once he brings it up, you can find out what's at the bottom of it. Have you talked to Martin about it?"

"Only a little," Dinah said, without attention. Just as Polly had reached up and pushed her hair behind her ears in a characteristic gesture of settling in, Dinah had caught sight of her father leaving his house. Polly twisted in her chair to follow Dinah's gaze. "What is it?" she said.

"Oh, I was going to walk along with Dad to the post office. He might be able to tell me the best way to talk to Toby, you know. Toby visits with him every morning. Well, that's where he picked up that limp, of course."

"Oh, yes," Polly said. But Dinah wasn't sure if that signified any previous knowledge or not. "Well, we can catch up with him if you like. I have to talk to him today, anyway."

This idea unnerved Dinah, but the two women rose. Polly picked up her purse and Dinah her mailbox keys. They didn't hurry, because her father's slow pace made it unnecessary, but they left behind them their two glasses of iced tea sitting in puddles of condensation on the delicately carved ivory coasters.

Her father saw them from across the street and stopped to wait. He turned to study the construction on his house, and when they joined him, Dinah fell in between her two parents and felt peculiar about it. They walked together for a moment before any one of them spoke, and then her father began to speak as if they were all simply continuing a conversation.

"You know," he said, "I've just been sorting through my records. You ought to come over and listen to some of these!" It wasn't clear who he meant. "They're marvelous, some of them. It seems to me that Isobel likes Charlie Parker better than she likes Dave Brubeck. She always did. Now, I wonder why? I can't understand it, but I know she likes Miles Davis and Charlie Parker. I remember that. I guess that was the thing to do." This last was a question, but Dinah didn't answer, and her mother smiled at him with surprising indulgence. The disharmony over this very subject in the household in which Dinah had grown up was still vivid to her. Her mother, of course, hadn't liked any of it, and had said with her unimpeachable scorn that it was not, as her father insisted, the classical music of the age. She discouraged the idea entirely, refusing to entertain it at all. It was beneath her consideration.

"I need to find out when you want us to come over for lunch, Dad," Dinah said. "Isobel will be in late tonight."

As they walked along three abreast, they were suddenly accompanied by a great, happy golden retriever that circled and trailed them, dragging a long chain behind him. He wove cheerfully among them, smiling and stopping to raise one foot in pleased and foolish attention. They had to move along fitfully to avoid the silly dog as he interrupted their progress down the sidewalk.

Polly shooed him away ineffectually with her hands. "Go on! Go on!" she said, but he paid no heed, and they made their way slowly.

"Why don't you all come over about one o'clock tomorrow?" he said, and he sidestepped the dog. "You come too, Polly. It's a Saturday. And see if Buddy will come. We'll have everyone! A celebration!"

At first Dinah thought to object that the children would be far too hungry to wait for lunch at one o'clock, but that would have been petty; her children could observe this occasion with some small amount of grace. She would give them a snack beforehand. Besides, Dinah had lost her tongue. She had been thrown into a bewildering insecurity, as of a child between two adults, and yet she had never been persuaded of her parents' authority, or even of their majority; they had always been split in two in disagreement.

"Whose dog is that?" she finally asked into what was masquerading, she thought, as a companionable silence.

"Oh, I don't know," her father said irritably, because the dog was causing him a good deal of trouble, since he lacked their agility. "He's broken his chain. I don't know where he belongs, but I don't think he ever came around the house to bother Jimmy. I don't think I've ever seen him before."

They crossed the street, and the dog bounded behind them. Polly was talking to Dinah's father about an insurance policy that had just surfaced, which they mutually owned, although he didn't seem much interested. They had only reached the corner of Hoxsey Street, but Dinah wanted very much to be away from her parents just then. The remaining two-block walk to the post office looked to her to be too long a time to endure this disruption of her calm assumptions. In her mind she had resigned herself happily, and with relief, to each one of her parents being separate from the other, so she was thoroughly annoyed with them both, standing as they were, circled by the dog, her mother almost transparently blond and fragile in relation to her father's lean height. They stood, still talking, and her mother angled her face toward her father, who had turned around to her. Now she presented to him a tilted profile, glancing at him sideways, slightly and charmingly distracted. Dinah thought that there was, for an instant, that same intangible promise about them—which had fooled her time and again—of the certainty of their alignment. The idea made her unusually cross. They *must*, by now, be either one thing or the other. She could not bear it if they ever became again what they had been for so long: both together and apart. They owed it to her to give it up. It left her on too precarious a footing; all the meticulously constructed links to her past hung in the balance.

"You ought to *do* something about that dog!" she said to both of them suddenly, interrupting them before she took herself off to do some shopping, and they looked at her in surprise. "Well, *look* at him, Dad! He's dragging his chain. He could get caught up on something somewhere. Out in the woods! Well, you can tell he's lost. It seems to me that you would at least find out who he belongs to and let them know!"

Her parents watched her with attention all at once, as though they hadn't known she was standing with them at all. And she felt what they saw: a tall, grown woman with slightly graying hair, speaking out with the peevishness of a child. "Dinah," her father said, "I can't possibly take the time to find out who that dog belongs to. I'm sure he knows exactly where he lives, anyway. He just doesn't choose to go there right now. Frankly, that dog strikes me as a fool!" They all looked at the dog, who was dragging his chain through the bushes bordering the sidewalk, stopping now and then in absurd ferocity—when he thought he'd tracked a scent—to stare menacingly at the ground. Then he would abandon that hope and move cheerfully on to the next bush to raise his leg and sniff around. He seemed to Dinah to be an especially amiable and good-hearted dog.

"So few people have your special knack for making such absolute judgments!" Dinah said. "Even if he's a *terrible* dog, he's still lost!" Dinah was depressed by her own lack of control. Irony was lost on her father, and he would not brook disagreement, or even pay attention to it; she and he would only reach another impasse.

Her father was seldom angry, and now he was only hugely irritated; she was a bother to him just now. "For God's sake, Dinah, why don't *you* find out where he lives?"

"Well!" she said. "I don't even live here!" That was all she thought to say, and she left them as they resumed their walk to the post office; she crossed the street to the little grocery store. As she entered the market, other answers crossed her mind. "*I* can't do that, Dad," she should have said, her voice mild and quite reasonable. "I'm with you." She might have said that to him and to her mother. When she looked out over the tomatoes piled in a pyramid in the market's window, she saw her parents still discussing something, and still being wooed by the hopeful dog.

That evening she thought with charity even toward herself about that trifling incident and her overreaction to it; she saw that these little matters were always the trials of summer. The long sunny days and the soft nights were never enough to counterbalance her self-righteousness. It still seemed to her that she was the only member of the family who was bound to put an order to all their lives, to set them straight in their pattern. Then she wouldn't be needed any longer; she could relax, and they could all know how much each of them was loved by all the others. Everything would be much easier.

Buddy came by in the evenings sometimes, to eat dinner with her and his niece and nephews. He had come the past few nights, and he appeared that afternoon just as Dinah was starting to fix dinner. She was only making a chef's salad. He came into the kitchen with the evening newspaper and sat at the table reading the front page while Dinah ran cold water over the steaming hard-boiled eggs before she tried to peel them. She suspected that Buddy's company these past few days was due to his own restless anticipation of Isobel's homecoming.

Dinah began peeling the eggs under running water, but they wouldn't peel, and she was angry every time a sliver of hard-cooked white came away with the brittle shell. Buddy got up and hovered behind her. Finally, he took an egg from the colander and one of Mrs. Horton's teaspoons from the drawer and tapped the shell into minute fragments with the spoon's back. After this careful preparation, he slipped the shell and its underlying membrane off the egg as easily as if he'd unzipped its coat. Dinah noticed this with aggravation, but she left the rest of the eggs for him to do and began laying down layer upon layer of Boston lettuce in the salad bowl. She and Buddy had acquired from their father the infuriating habit of interfering in the most mundane busywork carried out by any other person. It was kindly meant. They could not believe—not one of the three of them—that they couldn't make life easier for some other person if only that other person would follow their example or advice. Oddly enough, in Dinah's view, since she thought they were so little alike, Martin and Polly dealt with this trait in the same manner. They listened docilely enough and agreed with any suggestion wholeheartedly; then they proceeded with whatever they were doing just as they liked.

In this case, Dinah's aggravation was momentary; she enjoyed having Buddy there in the kitchen with her. When he was in his teens and she had just become old enough to assess him, to wonder what he was like, he had had the lanky height of her father and something of the same edginess and restrained tension. There had been an uneasy promise about him like that of a tightly drawn wire under incessant strain. But he had thickened and become one of those tall, kind-faced, burly men—the sort Dinah would dare to stop on a city street to ask directions. He had become the kind of man who wore a beautiful suit and then didn't button the jacket, as though he wished he didn't have it on. He looked content; he looked successful; he had become an avuncular, well-pleased man, she thought. He finished the eggs and dried his hands and settled back at the table with the paper.

"Listen, Buddy," she said. "I hope you'll come to Toby's party tomorrow at Dad's. You could just come for lunch. Polly's coming, too. Would you mind? You're much easier around the two of them than I am." It was embarrassing to be making such a blatant appeal. "Isobel will be there. She's coming in tonight. Will that make any difference?"

"Oh, no. In fact, I'm meeting her at the airport. She's always coming and going. I'll be glad to see her." He leaned back in his chair and folded the paper. He had fallen into an awkward discomfiture, and Dinah was puzzled. She wasn't sure if he meant he was coming to the party or not.

"Will you come, then?"

He rearranged his big body in an apparent attempt to stall for time, in an attempt *not* to say something. She was so curious about this that she turned around from the sink and leaned back against its edge to wait for him to speak.

"You know," he said, "all this would be so much easier for you, Dinah, if you could just get it into your mind that some people are . . . just bad people."

She turned back around to her salad making and began to scrape garlic from the garlic press. She knew, of course, that he meant their father. Buddy had decided very early just how he felt about his father, but Dinah thought that might be due in some part to the natural rivalry between boys and their fathers. "Oh, well," she said, with not much inflection at all, "it's not that simple. I really don't think it's that simple."

"Damn, Dinah, it *is* that simple!"

"You can't really think that"—and she heard a mortifying quaver in her own voice. "No one sets out to be a *bad* person! Who would intend that?"

"Intentions don't have anything to do with it! Christ! No one sets out to be an *old* person either! Who would intend *that?* The point is . . . well, the point is that it's not worth it to try so hard to get things to work out. It's a waste of your time." He seemed almost to be pleading with her, but she was slightly baffled. "Well," he went on, "this really isn't worth talking about either, I guess. But your life could be easier. It could be a lot less complicated. And, by God, Dinah, having you worry about us all the time is hard as hell on the rest of us! I just wish you wouldn't expect so much. It's just going to make you tired in the end."

Dinah went on assembling the salad, with her back to him. She had made a little stack of ham slices on the cutting board and was carefully shaving them into slivers with Mrs. Horton's French knife. Her feelings were hurt.

"I'd like to come to Toby's party, though," he said, and she even resented it that he was offering her mollification. She thought that she, too, had learned a little about life. She wasn't grateful for his brotherly admonition.

Buddy turned a page of the paper and shook out the crease with a snap. "I've been worried about Toby, in fact," he said. "How's that limp? What did the doctor say about it?"

"*Dad's* a doctor!" She paused and measured oil into the cruet with care. "Toby's fine. This party will cheer him up, I hope." But by now she and Buddy were put out with each other. Dinah's voice was crisply matter-of-fact and polite, and every line of Buddy's frame, as it was arranged precariously over the small kitchen chair, suggested disapproval. He read the paper with aggressive interest and obviously refrained from comment only with inordinate restraint.

Dinah called the children in to dinner and carefully served their plates with all the ingredients of the salad meticulously segregated, and each one's favorite bottled dressing dribbled over everything. She tossed the remainder of the salad in the wooden bowl, with the garlic-laden oil-and-vinegar dressing she had mixed. When she did this, all the fragile, julienned cheeses and meats disintegrated, and the whites and the yolks of the carefully peeled and sliced eggs fell apart and were dispersed among the lettuce leaves. This was just how she liked it: a fine, pungent mélange. If Buddy preferred his salad beautifully arranged and sparingly sprinkled with dressing, he wouldn't say so, and she didn't care. She was irritated at him. Life was *too* easy for him. He didn't worry enough. He lacked the resonant contemplation of the married, the child-bound, the intimately connected. It struck her as a willful and selfish disassociation, and she resented him for it. So she heaped his plate full and gave him his dinner, and they sat for a while just eating while the children talked.

CHAPTER EIGHT

UNCLE BUDDY AND THE HOMECOMING QUEEN

Sometime during the night the heat had broken and Enfield was released from its heavy atmosphere by a steady penetrating rain, so that the town no longer lay upon the rolling countryside in its own comprehensive universe. Under a blanket of such heat, even the generation of normal human emotion had built up like static in the contained environment, but overnight it was dispersed. The release of tension was so sudden that it was not altogether a pleasurable sensation. Dinah woke up in that new, bland climate cold and surprised.

She ached from the chill that unexpectedly filled the room, and she huddled under the single, thin sheet until gradually the sound of the steady rain on the porch roof became distinct to her. The drops fell with such rapid but steady regularity that she knew it was not a shower but a drenching, persistent rain that would last the day. She retrieved the spread from the floor, where she had thrown it in the previous evening's heat, and tried to sleep again, but the heat was all gone, and her muscles were tight because she had curled into herself during the night in an attempt to stay warm. Finally, she gave up any effort to rest, and she got up in the near-dark and went quietly downstairs. She was jumpy, with a kind of ragged tension due to her need of more sleep, and the new, unsettling chill. She stood for a moment in the kitchen and looked out the window, watching the heavy drops that didn't even fly against the screens but only fell straight to the ground from the dead gray sky. The weather was a dreary promise; it was numbing to the spirit. She realized, too, that she was watching out into the gloom for Lawrence, who, of course, wouldn't be running this morning. Outside was only Gilbert Street, sheathed in rain, with the leaves of the trees bending darkly against the branches under the weight of the shiny moisture that clung to them. She finally felt the chill so much that she took her raincoat from the downstairs coat closet and put it on over her thin gown. She didn't want to risk going upstairs for her robe, because the children might awaken. She prowled the downstairs rooms uneasily.

It made her restless that Lawrence wouldn't sit with her that morning while she drank her coffee. Just as she had hated it, she longed now for the voluptuous heat that had held her in a trance, suspended in the summer. These first cold fronts billowing in from the west were always the earliest signal of the season's inevitable end, and as usual, that idea filled her with unwarranted nostalgia. It strengthened her belief in the everlasting myth of an idyllic summer. As she watched the rain, her ego was pained as well; she would miss the daily routine in which she and Lawrence balanced so cautiously on the edge of sensuality. Each morning it was curiously reassuring.

She ate some toast and had some coffee, and then she cleaned up, but she felt irritable and hungry still. Dinah was just standing at the front windows and looking out at her father's house when Buddy's car pulled up in front of her sidewalk. She didn't move at first when Isobel and Buddy got out of the car; she just stood there, in sudden panic, with her gown drifting out from under her knee-length raincoat and hanging around her ankles. She hadn't expected to see

Isobel so early, and she was not at all prepared. As edgy as she was, she hadn't entered a daytime sensibility; she was still in that hazy state that precludes the easy separation of dreams and reality. She didn't have her wits about her. She only watched from the window, and when Isobel stood there in the rain, Dinah looked on and admired and remembered that sheen she always had about her, as though she were undercoated with a pale gold wash. Through the falling rain, and in that lifeless white light, Isobel, as she stood there shaking the water off her hair, seemed to be the only animate thing in all the world. Buddy came around the side of the car, and Isobel gave up struggling with her umbrella. The two of them dashed for the house.

Dinah ran back up the stairs in her bare feet. She called to the children to wake them up and tell them to go down and greet the guests. She told them to tell Uncle Buddy to start the coffee. She was still coming out of a daze, and in spite of a natural nervous shyness, she was enjoying a sudden satisfaction that she felt only rarely, when everything seemed to fall into place at once. She continued to see her life in two parts: then and now. She didn't question that perception, but the idea of having Buddy and Isobel in the house with her this morning pleased her immensely, because she had always thought of Isobel, especially, as part of the elusive past. She had begun to ponder the question her father had asked her on the steps of the post office. She still felt the blunt impact of his austere, unfair judgment and conclusions. But she thought she knew now why she *did* come back here again and again. She had begun to believe that it was no more than an effort to homogenize her life, to resolve the schizophrenic images of herself that she had in her mind's eye, two ideas of herself that incessantly combated each other for dominance. She was baffled by the transition from child to adult—almost from victim to victor—and she wanted to understand and see a clear picture of how she had moved from her past to her present.

From the bathroom she could hear the children being loud and excited downstairs, but she couldn't hear the words they said, just the noise of it. There was nothing she could do about it right this minute; she felt she must pull herself together—gather her forces—before she went back down. The children adored their uncle; he could handle things for a while. She was so chilled that for the first time in days she ran steaming water in the shower and stood under it until she knew that in an instant the warmth would give out and she would be standing in a downpour the same temperature as the rain outside. She shut off the faucet but stayed within the curtain-enclosed tub in the remaining steam while she dried herself. It amazed her to find that her body adapted to the cold with as little grace as it had coped with the heat.

When she was dry, she put on a long, heavy robe that had been hanging untouched on the hook since the heat had begun weeks ago. She rubbed away the filmy condensation on the mirror with the flat of her hand and looked cursorily at herself just long enough to comb her wet hair straight back from her face and clip it tightly at the nape of her neck. Dinah imagined to herself that she strove only for neatness. Long ago she had intended to abandon competition with Isobel because of the futility of it. When she came to understand that at the very center of Isobel there was absolute self-assurance, Dinah had meant to give up the battle. There had been a time when she had thought this all out very carefully; she had calculated all the angles, but then Isobel would reappear and not be in the least arrogant, would seem possibly vincible, after all, and Dinah would be—time and again—lulled into the idea of achieving a victory. Dinah didn't think this all over now in great detail; after all, they were both grown women. Even so, Dinah's particular kind of beauty was never more impressive than when she turned her clean, bare face to the world without benefit of makeup or the softness of her hair wisping loose to modify the striking alignment of her bones, which eight years could not alter.

When she entered the kitchen, where everyone was gathered, she realized that despite her shower she was still in something of a fog; she wasn't properly alert to the present. She could only embrace Isobel mechanically in a show of greeting and retreat to the perimeter of the activity, because all her impressions were still insubstantial. She sat while the room shifted with movement and voices, and she had the sudden idea that the entire scene was a Crayola drawing in which only Isobel, so vivid against the pallid morning, had been outlined in black. In fact, as she sat there seeing Isobel for the first time in so many years, it occurred to her that Isobel's face *looked* exactly as if a talented child had drawn it. It was the imperfect arrangement of her friend's features that was so compelling, even against the precision of the room itself—all straight lines and perfect angles. Dinah thought that it must be the general expectation of balance in beauty that so enhanced the crooked perfection of Isobel's lovely face. That child who had sat down with a determination to get this portrait exactly right had concentrated so arduously on each separate feature that proportion had fallen by the wayside—but it had worked to the advantage of the finished product. It would be impossible, thought Dinah, not to contemplate Isobel's face repeatedly if one was given the opportunity. And, as always, Dinah felt a proprietary pleasure in the beauty of her friend. It was as satisfying to her as if she had said, "I told you so."

"It's wonderful to see you again," Dinah said across the heads of her children. "You haven't changed at all, I don't think. I don't think you've changed a bit."

Isobel could only smile across to her in the crowded kitchen. She had simply begun preparing the children's breakfast while she and Buddy waited for Dinah to dress and come down. These were children she had never met, however, and an entirely strange kitchen. Perhaps, Dinah thought, such necessary and compliant assurance and ease in the world is what really constitutes charm. She watched as Isobel made her way back and forth through the small, warm tide of animated children, and Dinah was unable to energize herself even to attempt to instigate order or calm them down.

David was too large for his own coordination in his sudden shyness, and he was brash and boisterous and clumsy. Sarah was in the way in her desire to help Isobel with everything. But Toby set Dinah's teeth on edge. It seemed that every sullen tension once embodied in the lost heat had resolved itself in Toby's dark presence. He was jealous, and he was whining and complaining about his leg and then about his stomach, and he was in a cringing, clinging mood so that he hung on Dinah. At the same time he was wired with an uncertain excitement, as if his body were circuited with auxiliary power; even his dark hair seemed to bristle out around his head in morosely intense and peculiar agitation. This morning his manifestation of some obscure but genuine despair only aroused in her a quiet fury, and it was an anger she didn't bother to explore. It wasn't a very sophisticated anger; Dinah wanted her life—even this moment as it was being played out in the boxlike kitchen— to be sincerely coveted by her good friend Isobel.

She sat at the edge of the room and looked at her children in the light of the immediate moment, without benefit of their complex history and with a blank mind. Just for an instant she erased the knowledge of her affection for them, and she saw that they were clearly burdensome; she was not to be envied just now. She felt uncharitable about the whole situation. Taking one look at their flushed faces, she allowed herself a rare luxury: she slid out of the present. Her mind took no account of her own past, and so she was absolved, temporarily, of any liability on behalf of these children.

Toby was in a constant state of motion around the room, studiously ignoring Isobel. "I can't *eat* anything, Mama. I just want some ginger ale. I don't feel good. My stomach hurts." He moved along the edges of the room, opening drawers, moving the appliances, punching the buttons on the blender. He moved jerkily, leaning against the counters and bracing himself while he pulled his leg along after him.

He and Dinah regarded each other for the first time that summer with mutual and unequivocal antagonism. Dinah needed Isobel's approval of her three children; if they would not seek it, then she would not cajole them; she would ignore them.

Buddy took up some of the slack. He was sitting at the kitchen table, and he put Sarah on his lap to get her out of the way; now he gathered Toby into one arm and held him so that Toby leaned against his side. "You feel hot, Toby. He feels pretty hot, Dinah."

Dinah just glanced at them. "It's your party today, Toby. You'd better eat some breakfast so you'll feel well enough to go."

Toby hadn't learned how to handle a celebration of himself with any grace yet, and Dinah remembered just briefly the torture of a birthday party in one's honor. When she was *aware* of being her children's mother, she loved and protected them above all else, and even against and in spite of themselves, but for the first time since their birth she found herself in conflict with her own instincts. Dinah needed to be unencumbered right now in order to deal with the subtle threat of Isobel and any success she might have had in her life. She needed that, or she needed to be the parent of three children who would render her life justifiable in Isobel's eyes. Dinah wanted her children to be the sanction of all her choices and alliances—her way of life, her marriage— in case Isobel had ever questioned their advisability. After all, Isobel had done what Dinah's father had wanted Dinah to do. She had chosen not to be married; she had chosen not to have children. So when David and Toby and Sarah persisted in being who they were, Dinah disregarded them as best she could. While Isobel and Buddy talked and saw to the children's needs, Dinah looked on distractedly, as though she was still not completely awake. She sat on quietly in the kitchen and appreciated, for the moment, the blessed anonymity of being eclipsed.

Isobel put out plates of toast for the children, and Buddy took up a piece and ate it over Sarah's head while she still sat on his lap. Toby stood where he was, leaning against Buddy, his face pale and his brown eyes fierce and quiet. Isobel lounged against the counter and ate some toast as well.

"I'm so glad you're here, Isobel," Dinah said in a voice that surprised her in its plaintiveness. She lurched into the morning and made an attempt to fortify herself against the summer's persistent reverie. "How *are* you? Well . . ." And she smiled in apology. "I really mean that. How is your job? Isobel, it's incredible how much you haven't changed! Really!" With one arm Dinah made a vague, pleased sweep to indicate the delightful magnitude of Isobel's sameness. But Isobel leaned back and nibbled her toast with a mystifying look of doubt and irritation. She didn't say anything at all right away; the children were talking to one another or to Buddy and not being listened to especially, and in the ill-lit kitchen Dinah immediately understood that there was something complicated in Isobel's life, but she didn't dare to ask yet what it might be.

"Well," Isobel said, with an oddly bitter note following so closely on the heels of her cheerful breakfast-making, "I've gotten eight years older, just like you have."

Dinah was angry that this hurt her feelings so much. Did Isobel mean that *Dinah* seemed eight years older? And if that was what she meant, did she also mean to hurt Dinah's feelings? Maybe she didn't even realize what she'd said and how it had sounded. Dinah began to remember uneasily that she always wondered these things about Isobel; Isobel's intentions were so slippery.

"Oh, everything is going pretty well," Isobel continued, no longer ironic, but reflective. "I guess everything is fine." She turned full around to Dinah to smile wholeheartedly, and Dinah believed her entirely, as she always did. "How do you suppose it happened," Isobel went on, still pensive, "that all the things we expected for ourselves actually came true?"

Dinah glanced at Buddy to see if he felt slighted by this last statement—Isobel was saying, apparently, that he had been unnecessary to her fulfilled expectations—but he was not even listening to them. He was contentedly reading a cereal box aloud to Sarah, and he sat there placidly with the children around him just as a cat sits with her kittens after they have eaten. Isobel was standing completely still, lost in some idea, and she shook her head slightly, so that her bronze hair swung like a polished bell.

"Well, you're still just lovely, Dinah. Of course! And all your pretty children . . . You have changed, though, I think." It made Dinah uncomfortable to be closely scrutinized. Some mornings she was lovely, some mornings not. That was the age she was. "Dinah, you look like a grownup!" Isobel was delighted to discover this, and then she became rueful again. "And I've come to be known as 'charming Isobel.' A friend said to me the other day that she didn't know anybody who didn't like me." She looked over at Dinah as if they were conspirators, but Dinah was blank.

"That's not altogether a compliment, you know," Isobel explained. But Dinah didn't see why not. Isobel intimidated her by the wily turns of her intellect. "But it's what I had planned on, and now I have it."

"Well, it's what we both planned on," Dinah said. "In fact, I was really surprised when I began to meet women who don't care if people like them or not."

Isobel passed over all this. "But you've become the grownup!" she said with that deceptive generosity with which she had many times bequeathed a fleeting victory to Dinah. This time Dinah knew it was absurd, and she was surprised, because she had never known it was a contest. Isobel had always been a grownup. That old instinct—like the one between two sisters—to protect Isobel from any criticism save Dinah's own flooded through her, and she got up and took her friend by the shoulders to shake her affectionately and then just embrace her lightly once more.

"My God, Isobel, of course no one dislikes you! How could anyone? Why would they?"

Isobel's expression remained reflective, even though she smiled to thank Dinah for her loyalty. She ate a few more bites of toast and still seemed to be mulling over some thought or other.

Dinah began to make herself busy around the kitchen in sudden nervous apprehension. She didn't want to know of any threat to Isobel's happiness or peace of mind. She didn't want to believe that either one of them had changed very much in relation to the other.

"Come on," she said, "we can go into the living room and have some coffee while the children watch television." Toby was right behind her, so that she stepped back into him and then leaped forward in irritation. "What, Toby? What's the matter?"

"Why is he limping?" Isobel asked quietly from across the room, and Dinah waved the question away but then turned her head in Isobel's direction just to say softly, "Well, possibly this morning it's all for your benefit." But before she turned back to her son, she saw Buddy's face cloud over with vexation aimed in her direction, so she stooped down to Toby with a concern only she and he knew was tense and partly counterfeit. "What's wrong, Toby? What do you need?"

"I don't feel good. You said I could call Daddy before my party. Can't we call him now?"

Dinah stayed as she was a moment, stooping there, looking at the determination and self-righteousness on Toby's face. It was so peculiar, this morning, to be slewing uncontrollably back and forth in time. She meant well by Toby; his well-being was as involved with her own as if they were the same person, but she was so oddly distracted by Isobel's presence, and by Isobel's unexpected vulnerability, that she could not consider Toby at all in any way right now. She could only make promises to him to buy herself time, because the evocation of her own youth had overcome Dinah this morning in the damp, chill air.

"We will call Daddy. Okay? You let us talk and have our coffee in the living room without bothering us, and then we'll get ready for your party, and we'll give Daddy a call." Toby looked at her with embarrassed scorn; she was underrating him; she was talking to him as if he were so much less wise than they both knew he was. She could only turn her expression into a mute plea, and so he subsided sullenly into a kitchen chair and turned a wan interest toward the miniature television on the counter.

Buddy slowly disengaged himself from Sarah, and the three adults made their way out of the kitchen and into the living room. Dinah carried a tray with cups and saucers, and she made a return trip to the kitchen to get the coffee and to heat the cream. While she stood over it watching carefully so that it wouldn't boil over, she experienced a pleasant nostalgia at the idea of Buddy and Isobel sitting together in the Hortons' living room. That seemed fitting, and it pleased her to be the connection between them; she was necessary now to their involvement. She had been ambivalent about their marriage and then about their divorce, but since she cared so much about each of them she had carefully not asked questions in either instance. She sometimes wondered how complicated their separation had been. They could have simply fallen out of love, and she assumed that if that was mutual, it might be an easy process. But she was glad to be the link between them once again, even briefly.

Dinah and Isobel had always been ambitious in one way or another, and they had their own plans and ideas, but growing up as they had in Enfield, they had always had to circumvent the town's high and paralyzing expectations for them. They were pretty girls, easy-limbed and pleased with themselves; anything could have been anticipated on their behalf. They showed such promise; people wished them well and were excited by the prospect of their having great, perhaps unqualified joy in their lives. There used to be girls about whom such things were conjectured, and it had been hard not to believe for a while that Dinah and Isobel might attain absolute happiness devoid of responsibility, as only a woman would be able to. No one expected anything of the sort from any boy. The handsome, brilliant boys who came on the scene would certainly be likely to have a good future, but that was a different expectation altogether—solid and earthbound—and only acquired with plodding difficulty. *Joy* was not presumed. Dinah and Isobel were, from the beginning of their adolescence, objects of almost frivolous speculation. Something on the order of a bolt out of the blue was expected for those two girls, and Dinah's father had always been thrown into a frenzy of disapproval if he began to suspect that either girl took this too seriously. And, in fact, his caution was justified, because those enormous expectations were debilitating in so many ways. It was not really expected that either girl would have control over her own fate. It might have been that, alone—that presumption of dependency—that had finally forced Isobel out on her own. Certainly, it would have been hard for her to bear; it would surely rankle. But when they were young, she and Isobel hadn't understood all the ramifications of their celebrity. They had come shimmering across Enfield's limited panorama in their disarming and flexible youth, and for a little while they had captured the town's attention with the poignant hopefulness of all the possibilities in their lives. And still, early that morning, even Dinah had felt a surge of delight and a sudden frisson of recognition when she had caught her first glimpse of Isobel in such a long time. There she was: a golden girl. In Dinah's mind there was not so much difference now, really, because Isobel still seemed to her to be a woman of endless promise and potential.

She came back into the living room and put the coffee and scalded cream down on the tray and was arranging the cups so that she could easily balance them when she passed them, when she had that alarming sensation, straight out of childhood, of being the odd man out. The impression was so extreme that she looked around sharply, thinking to catch a signal or a glance passing between Buddy and Isobel. She saw nothing at all, and she realized that they hadn't even been talking to any purpose during her absence. But that was just what it was! They were at ease, and they were smug and complacent, and in an instant she understood why Isobel had been able to be so self-effacing when they were chatting in the kitchen. Isobel had spent the night with Buddy! Dinah was so affronted by this new and absolute certainty that she had consciously to keep from registering dismay. She was desperately depressed by what she considered to be their sly hypocrisy. She didn't care anything about the fact that they had made love, but she did care that the whole night through, restless or at peace, they had shared a bed. They might have awakened together whenever the rain had begun; one of them may have gotten up to shut a window so that the other wouldn't be chilled. Even in sleep, one registers the comfort and discomfort of one's partner. But she herself, sleeping singly in the wide double bed, had curled up for warmth. Those two would have the familiarity of a whole night behind them. Having shifted to the other's weight and accommodated themselves, when necessary, to the other's repositioning, they would be bound, by morning, to be more lenient toward the other's flaws. But not to hers.

This notion so infuriated Dinah that she was rigid for a moment as she bent over her tray. All at once the exact reason she had come back here to this town time and again became clear to her! She grasped the sudden idea with her mind and held it as if it were a prism that would send out irradiations of light from all its sides. She had come back because she wanted an apology! She wanted an absolute, blanket apology from Buddy and from Isobel and from Polly and her father! She wanted from each one of these people an acknowledgment of all the injustices of her childhood, of all the misfortunes they might have prevented. She wanted to resuffer all her illnesses and be adequately consoled; she wanted an admission that at one time or another some one of them might have ignored her, hurt her, deceived her. And she had no doubt that this was her just due even though she, too, might have inflicted an injustice now and then. She had paid in plenty for it by now, and she was therefore exempt from any more responsibility. Isobel was right. Dinah saw clearly now that she was probably the only grownup in all the world, save

Martin, and because she was a grownup she had had to contend with a terrible fate—she had *mortal* children, and she had to recognize it and deal with it every moment of her days. Now she wanted everything else resolved so that she could get on with adjusting to her perilous situation. She was possessed by a need to find the right place for all the free-floating resentment that had traveled with her through the years like a cloud. She bent over the tray, icy with indignation, but she had no idea, really, of acting on it. All she did was pour out coffee for the three of them, and she took her own cup to the rocking chair in the bay window.

No one spoke while they took their first sips of coffee, and Dinah knew herself to be powerful with the knowledge that this was not a friendly silence. Isobel and Buddy sat at ease in their chairs, while Dinah's entire intellect had gathered itself into one spare judgmental beam, which she turned on them through a haze of hindsight. She twisted her coffee cup nervously in its saucer with the intention of imposing rationality on her runaway emotions. She considered the transparent and slight ring of coffee that always remained on a saucer under the china cup. Why was it always there? Was the china so porous that it couldn't entirely contain the liquid? But at last she looked up, and without any purpose clearly in mind she said out into the room, "You know, it's interesting to be here all together. Well . . . there's something I've always wondered about, and now that you're both here . . ." Isobel looked up restlessly; she had been absorbed in other concerns altogether. It was clear she hadn't been thinking of the people in this room at all. Dinah looked at Buddy, too. "I've always wondered about the time I was the Homecoming Queen. You remember? That weekend both of you were home from school?" She tried to give the title an ironic twist, to disparage the idea, but in fact her voice trembled. No matter with what disdain she meant to look back on that event, she had never forgotten being chosen. No one does. But as she finally faced these two with it, she was horrified to realize that she was going to have to fight tears.

"Oh, Dinah!" Isobel said. Dinah was surprised to see her so blatantly reveal irritation; usually she was harder to pin down.

"Well . . . I'm sorry . . . but I want to know. I mean, what really happened that weekend?" Dinah sat there dead tired of her own timorousness in any confrontation. Her fear of battle only served to make her grudges run deeper. She was very tempted now to let this issue pass, but she managed to sit quite still and let the question remain in the room.

Buddy leaned back comfortably in his chair, and his features assumed a look Dinah hadn't seen since childhood; they assumed an expression of delighted culpability. He couldn't seem to prevent himself from smiling sheepishly, and he put his cup down and rested both large hands on his knees in the manner of an artful storyteller. "Lord, Dinah! Do you still remember that, too?" He was apparently pleased at the whole thought, and she was so shocked that she didn't say anything. She got up to make a circuit of the room, offering more coffee. Isobel wasn't watching either of them; she was looking out the windows at the steady rain.

"You know, Dinah, why *didn't* you let Lawrence be your escort that night?" Buddy didn't ask this with heat but with the condescending amusement of a big brother, and at this Isobel glanced at Dinah—their eyes caught—but Isobel's glance was noncommittal. Buddy hadn't ever developed the knack of avoiding heavy sailing. Dinah thought briefly that it was odd that so many men lack that innate radar that would warn them of rough water. Sometimes the lack was endearing.

"God, Dinah, I had to come all the way back from Baltimore and drive you around the football field! Dad insisted. Nothing else would do!"

Dinah just let that glance off her mind; she couldn't believe her father had interceded on her behalf. In the beginning, her father had only made good-natured fun of her for caring about the pageant at all, but then over the space of a few weeks he had embraced the entire concept as a new cause. Eloquently and adamantly, he had refused to have anything to do with it, but even then, and even though she was mortified by his eccentric passion, she had known that these spates of furious intellectual partisanship were necessary to her father's very idea of himself. He would not be her escort, as was customary for Fort Lyman High School Homecoming Queens, because it was an absurd and sexist and perhaps tribal custom by its very nature. He had never understood that he was a grown man, an independent man, a doctor, an outlander who could afford his condescensions. Dinah must live as a native of her own hometown, an equal to her peers, and this ritual which he so abhorred was absurd perhaps, but it was also a custom of her country.

"Still, I think the only thing that really got me to come all the way back here," Buddy was saying, "was that you were going to be home, Isobel, and—damn!—I don't think you even went to the game. I don't think we went out at all the whole time I was here, did we?" For a moment a vague and woeful shadow moved over Buddy's face. "I think you spent that entire weekend in one of those goddamned interminable conversations with Dad! I remember that, by God!" And he shook his head in baffled recollection, but then seemed to come around again to his cheerful and puzzling complacency. "Oh, Lord, Dinah! You were really something that weekend!" He was so amused, and it turned Dinah's mind right around. She went full circle from her narrow focus of self-righteousness into the realm of rationality and real life in which the possible consequences of this conversation finally became clear to her.

"Oh, well, Buddy . . ." she said, really out into the air, just a vague wisp of a truce floating in the room. This wasn't worth the price. Suddenly she didn't care much about any sort of apology. She was afraid if Buddy remembered it all now, that in the end he would be embarrassed and dismayed, and she realized with a pang that he had never before recounted it to himself. She realized with a certain wonder how little time he must ever have spent in speculation, puzzling over what *she* was like. She had spent a great deal of time wondering what he was like, her own brother. But she didn't want this conversation to continue, because she was one of those rather cowardly people for whom it is less painful to suffer embarrassment themselves than to have to stand by cringing and witness a justified discomfiture in someone else.

Isobel had arrived home from boarding school two days before the whole festivity of the Fort Lyman Homecoming had begun. Right away and unwittingly, she had diminished Dinah's ingenuous pleasure and anticipation. Dinah remembered sitting in her bedroom watching Isobel's cunning, foxlike face with that curious gleaming expression it took on as she shared all sort of confidences and told Dinah amazing anecdotes about her decadent life away at school. Dinah had been disheartened even then, as she had had to reckon with the immense differences in their lives at that age. On the night of the Homecoming game, the night Dinah would be presented to everyone in the stadium as their queen, would be handed an armful of roses and kissed by the captain of the football team—before it all began—Isobel came over to chat with Dinah while she prepared for it.

Sitting now, curled in a rocking chair in the Hortons' living room and wrapped in her own soft, heavy robe, with her own mind, her own bones, her own blood encased in her showered thirty-six-year-old skin, Dinah was suddenly knocked almost breathless by the involuntary assumption of her sixteen-year-old self. At once she became the same girl in her bedroom, leaning into her mirror to rub a thin film of Vaseline over her teeth just as she had been instructed to do by the pageant coordinator, who was otherwise the third- and sixth-hour gym teacher. She had been told to do this to prevent her smile from sticking to her teeth in case of nervousness.

As she had looked into the mirror, she had seen Isobel behind her, lounging casually on the foot of the bed, dressed in flannel slacks and a creamy Shetland sweater. She had on very plain, gently fluted, circular earrings that she said all the girls wore. Isobel had bought her own, she said, and pretended they were a birthday present. Even though Dinah had been touched that Isobel had confided this small charade, she had still been filled with dismay, because it was all so far outside her experience; she couldn't hope to touch it; she couldn't hope to catch on. Isobel sat there serenely, and her hair was held cleanly in place by a plain black velvet band, so that her lovely narrow face pierced the picture reflected in the mirror like an arrow. Dinah had contemplated her own complicated, beauty-shop, tulip-shaped hairdo with sinking expectations. There was Isobel, relaxed and comfortable; she appeared to be accustomed to her clothes, which had only pointed up the fact that Dinah, incredibly adorned, was not.

Isobel had declined all their invitations to go to the game; she chose to sit with Dr. Briggs in the library and drink Scotch and listen to jazz. She had said she already knew how beautiful Dinah looked, and after all, she didn't know anything about football. Buddy and Dinah had been standing just inside the library door while Buddy tried one more time to persuade her to come along, when Polly descended the stairs, beautifully dressed and bespeaking anger with every movement and gesture she made. She stopped outside the library door to pull on her gloves. "You see," she said with that terrifying exactitude of enunciation that indicated her infrequent but wholehearted disapproval and disdain, "your father has always and *will* always just manage to miss the point! He never has learned to be the sort of person he imagines he is—an *aristocrat*, I think!" She said this with breathtaking scorn and the most passion Dinah had ever heard her muster. "Do you see what I mean? He hasn't really got the slightest drop of sophistication in his blood! Now, that's odd, isn't it, since it's the only ambition he's ever really had. To be sophisticated. Even just to be jaded." She turned around and looked in at him through the library door. "Well, it's not something you're ever going to pick up, and you weren't born with it, by God!" The whole company had been stunned; even in retrospect, it stunned Dinah. It was the most Polly had ever given away about herself. Her father had sat perfectly still, and finally Isobel had smiled at Dinah and wished her good luck. Just as Dinah and Buddy and Polly were leaving, her father slammed the library door with a furious bang. Buddy's face had gone immobile and frozen across the cheekbones.

And Dinah *was* the Homecoming Queen. She waved and smiled; she accepted the roses; she was kissed by the football captain; but the event progressed for her in unsynchronized motion. At one moment she felt speeded up, as though she were moving through a tunnel at a terrifying acceleration, and then the proceedings would take on the nightmare aspect of slow motion, hideously exaggerated, so that she had the alarming notion that her frozen smile hung luminously over the stadium long after she had taken her seat, just like the Cheshire cat's. By the end of the game she was sick and sad sitting there on the dais surrounded by the pretty princesses of her court. She might have been sick; she had felt terrible, and she had been unable to believe, anymore, that this event was special or fun. She was supposed to go on to the dance with Lawrence, but she asked him to pick her up later at home, and she would go back with him if she felt better. She was encircled by friends and teachers, and she had seen from their faces that she must look as peculiar as she felt. Her mother had already left the game in her own car, and so Dinah asked Buddy to drive her home in the borrowed convertible before he returned it, and he had sullenly agreed.

"Maybe I'm just hungry, Buddy. I was too nervous to eat. Would you mind stopping to get us something to eat?" She had been beyond caring that he hadn't answered her at all but had just pulled up in front of the only pizza place in all of Fort Lyman. It was nothing more than a little closet of a building sandwiched in among a string of sleazy bars and restaurants. Buddy had gone in, and Dinah had leaned her head against the seat to wait for him. In a little while he had come out and bent over the side of the car to hand her the pizza and the keys.

"You go on home, Dinah. I'm going over to Snow's. I'll get a ride home later, and I'll take the car back in the morning."

Now she looked across the living room at Buddy, but she felt more as though she were looking from the bottom of a well at someone peering down from the top. "Why did you leave me there with that pizza, Buddy? Why were you mad at *me*?"

"Good Lord, Dinah," he said, and grinned down that distance to her, about to laugh. It made her numb that he still viewed this as a prank. "That whole weekend you had just about driven us all crazy. You were so damned *pleased* with yourself!" He shook his head in renewed wonder. "You were wearing that horrible dress—really horrible. The kind girls wore then, like a net wedding cake." He laughed. "And when you left Lawrence behind at the stadium, he just about died. He wanted to drive that car, too. Oh, I don't know . . . I guess I just couldn't resist it."

When Buddy had left her sitting with the pizza and the keys outside the greasy little shop, she had struggled to slide across the seat and arrange her hoop skirt so that she could drive. Just as she managed to adjust the seat and start the car, a short, thickset man came bounding out the door and leaned into the window. "Hey, that guy said he'd be right back to pay me! I don't have any money for that pizza!" He had stared at her aggressively; he didn't even seem to notice that she was unusually dressed. She had been dumbfounded for a moment, trying to put it all together.

"Well, I don't have any money with me. I'll have to bring it to you tomorrow," she said. "I just came from the Homecoming game"—and she gestured down at her billowing white dress, but he hadn't paid any attention.

"Listen, you're not leaving here with that pizza! I don't like this a bit, I'll tell you! Don't you think you're going anywhere!" He had leaned farther into the car and she had felt that his swarthy, angry face represented real menace. She had apologized to him with as much guile and charm as possible.

"Well, here," she said, holding the pizza out to him, "take this back. I'm just so terribly sorry all this happened."

"Are you kidding me?" He was beside himself. He was incredulous. "That pizza will be dead stone cold by now. It's no good to me!"

So it ended up that she stood waiting in the little pizza parlor in her great mushroom of a skirt and her rhinestone tiara for a long, humiliating interval while Isobel drove into Fort Lyman with some money.

For all she knew, now that she thought of it, Buddy may never even have known the consequences of his own actions; she had never had the energy to tell him about them. He was still sitting on the couch vastly entertained by his own idea of that weekend.

"Dinah, do you *remember* what you said the day I picked you up at the shopping center after you'd had that dress fitted?" He laughed now with affectionate goodwill. "Lord, you came out of that store and got in the car and said, 'Buddy, not one of those people I passed—not a single one —knew that they were walking right past the Fort Lyman Homecoming Queen!' That knocked me out! It really did!"

Dinah thought that Buddy had this all wrong, all of it. She thought that he still did not know his motivations for the bind he had left her in that weekend, but she sat there listening to her brother relate this last incident and reflected that surely she had never, never been so innocent as that. Surely not! Suddenly she said, "I never forgave you for that, Buddy. I never really forgave any of you for that night!"

Buddy grew serious very slowly in the long silence that deadened the room, and Isobel got up and moved restlessly to the windows, pacing from one to the other like a housebound cat. Then he was thoroughly abashed. "No," he said, "well, I don't guess you have. Well, there's no reason you should, either. In fact, I felt pretty bad about it right away.

I think I did." And he looked especially sorry just now, and so Dinah had an apology of sorts, but it didn't fill any need. When she grasped on to it, it had no more substance than a balloon. "In fact, Dinah," he went on in a voice suddenly devoid of any reminiscent glee, "what I really think is that you *have* forgiven us. I think you don't really blame any of us enough!" So now, even Dinah's need for an apology was confirmed. She sat there motionless.

Isobel paced clear around the room, and finally she turned on Buddy. "Jesus Christ! What are you talking about? If ever there was a winner—if ever there was one—it's Dinah! Dinah's always known the key! She'll always be one step ahead of the rest of us. Good God, Buddy!"

Dinah had the feeling she was seeing an old argument rekindled, and she didn't do anything but sit there transfixed, and then Isobel turned to her, much calmer now. "You've always known, haven't you, Dinah . . . Well, and the thing is, you've always been able to *do* it, just sit back and do it! You've always known that it's much better to be more sinned against than sinning."

Dinah just sat on quietly, not quite realizing she had been asked a question. She sat there pondering that suggestion and wondering if she could believe that and still be happy, if she could believe that and still like herself at all.

CHAPTER NINE

SORROW AND RESPONSIBILITY

The three grownups stayed as they were in the living room for a few moments, and Isobel finally turned to Dinah with an elaborate shrug, lifting her hands in a pantomime of helplessness, so that the gesture might be taken for a diffuse apology. She moved to the tray to pour herself some more coffee. Buddy sat frowning down at his own empty cup. "I guess you always have been jealous of Dinah, then," he said, but there was no force in his words; they didn't require an answer from anybody, and if anything, he seemed to be bored with the situation.

Dinah heard what Buddy said, but his tone reflected her own mood. A kind of dolorous unease had settled in, a peculiar tedium, as it always did at the possibility of a confrontation. Dinah remained in a state of suspended judgment about Isobel. It wasn't the moment, just now, to wonder if there was any truth in Buddy's idea. But Isobel *did* know her so well, and Dinah sat rocking gently in her chair with the unwelcome knowledge that it was absolutely true that for a long time she had made a great virtue out of being wronged. Her assurance that she had often been reproached at moments when she was, in fact, beyond reproach had been one of her greatest strengths; it had seen her through her worst depressions. "But I was right," she had always been able to say. Dinah worked hard to like herself; this new notion jeopardized her well-being.

Toby and Sarah came into the room gradually, because they had mastered the art of making their presence among adults acceptable by degrees. They talked outside the doorway, and then Sarah moved to the hearth and sat in the child's rocker for a moment before coming farther into the room. Toby went first to the table behind Dinah's chair and quietly splayed out a collection of coasters, imprinted with various butterflies, which were kept in a box there. At last he came to rest on the arm of Dinah's chair. He stood on one rung of her rocker and bobbed slightly to make it rock. She had to lean to one side to keep from bumping his head with her chin.

"The cartoons are over," he said. "Can we call Daddy now?" She had put her arm around his waist to steady him, and she looked at his pale profile as it swung up and down with the movement of the chair. He was oddly flushed across the cheekbones, and jittery. The skin of his forehead had the dry translucency of parchment. Dinah knew at once the tension and apprehension he must be feeling, and she felt a brief twinge of distaste at her own self-involvement this morning.

"This is a good time to call, I think," Dinah said. "Let's do go call him." And all of them collected napkins and cups and saucers and made their way to the kitchen.

David was sitting at the kitchen table working through the maze on the children's page of the morning newspaper. Isobel began to gather up the breakfast dishes and stack them in the sink, and Buddy went to the coat closet to get their raincoats and Isobel's umbrella. Dinah dialed the number, but she let Toby hold the phone to his ear, so that he could be the first to speak to Martin, since it was his birthday call. Dinah could hear the faint ring of the phone, and she could tell when it ceased, but Toby didn't speak. She looked down at him, and he seemed oddly frozen and rigid, with the phone clasped so tightly that his knuckles were white. "Toby!" she said. "Say something! Say hello!"

Toby looked up at her, mute. Finally, he said, "Hi," not at all like a greeting.

"Toby!" Dinah said, irritated at his unusual reticence. She could hear Martin's voice on the other end of the line, but Toby just stood there wrapped in a quiet and inexplicable terror. She reached down to take the phone from him, and he handed it to her, defeated.

"Martin," she said, "it's Toby. He wants to talk to you before we go to his birthday party. Here, I'll put him on," and she held the phone out to Toby, who didn't lift his hands to take it; he just stared at her in an appeal she couldn't decipher. "Don't you want to talk to Daddy, Toby?" she said in that way of asking that is a command. She was cross; these calls cost money, and the kitchen had become entirely quiet while they all waited to see what Toby would say. She put the phone back to her own ear. "Martin, Toby's feeling shy, I think. How have you been? I almost called the Hofstatters' first. I thought you might be there. How is everyone?" Both of them spoke so carefully across the distance between them that their words were overly enunciated, and Martin's tone seemed peculiarly officious, perhaps because the sound was immediately at her ear, with no time to interpret any inflection. It wasn't at all like talking to Martin, in fact, and she was always bothered by their stilted long-distance conversations.

"I'm fine," he said. "I've been doing a lot of work at home, but I guess everyone's fine. I had planned to call this evening and talk to Toby after the party was over. And I wanted to talk to you, too. How are you?"

Dinah was distracted by the activity in the kitchen, which had resumed somewhat when she took the phone. David was having to hold Sarah away from his work with a hand pressed against her chest and his arm stiff, and she was giggling frantically. Dinah saw that her daughter was too excited, that even her present tentative composure might dissolve any moment. She reached over with one hand to pull Sarah aside. It was mildly distressing to make polite conversation with her own husband. "Is the fall issue almost ready?" she said. "You must be almost done with it."

"Oh, that's going along just fine. I've been working away at it."

"Good," Dinah said, and she stooped to untangle the phone cord from around Sarah, who was in the way wherever she moved. Dinah and Martin talked a little bit about what he had heard about the shop; they talked about Toby's party; and both David and Sarah took a turn. While she stood waiting for them to finish, she realized that she would have liked to have a long conversation with Martin all by herself, so that silences could fall or not. She resented having to perform for all the people in the kitchen. She wished Isobel and Buddy, at least, would leave, but she knew they were only being polite, waiting to make their departure when it wouldn't be an interruption. She took the phone from Sarah.

"Dinah, I'll call you back this evening when Toby won't be so excited. Will you be there or at your mother's?" he said, but Dinah looked down at Toby while Martin spoke, and saw that his face was blurred with tears.

"Oh, well, Martin, wait a second," and she even put her hand out to stop him. "I know Toby wants to talk to you before we hang up." She thought she understood what was bothering Toby, and she turned to the rest of the room while she still held the phone; she pinned it between her raised shoulder and her ear so that she could shoo everyone away with a whisking motion of her hands. "Out! All of you, out! Anyone needs a little privacy just before his birthday party." She heard her own voice sounding crisp rather than conspiratorially jolly as she meant it to, so she turned to smile at Toby, holding Martin there in silence as the room emptied. Isobel and Buddy took this chance to shrug on their raincoats and leave, only after promising the children that they would see them later. David and Sarah were reluctant to go, and Dinah gave them each a gentle shove through the door into the dining room. "Go on! Go on! You can talk to Daddy when he calls tonight. I promise."

"Why do we have to leave?" David said. "I want to finish my maze. *He* heard what we said!"

"Out! Go on! I mean it!" And they left. Toby was still crying silently, and she thought that it must be excitement. She just handed him the phone and made a show of going to the sink to rinse the dishes, so that he would feel free to say whatever he wished.

"Dad . . ." he said, and Dinah could hear sounds of encouragement coming from the other end; Martin was trying to coax Toby out of his discomfort, whatever it was, and Dinah hoped that it would work. Martin and Toby had always understood each other so well. Toby made an effort. "Dad, are you going to come out here?" He glanced around at Dinah, who had stopped moving so that she could hear what he said. She rattled a plate and began to rinse it just before he caught her being so still. She couldn't hear any sounds from the phone now.

Toby turned his shoulder to her, wrapping himself in the cord, and pressed his mouth so closely against the phone that the furtive words were muffled past Martin's understanding. "Dad, I think I might be dying. I think I'm going to die." Dinah understood every syllable, and she gave up any pretense of being busy.

"I said that I'm going to die." Toby's face was entirely wet, though he made no sound of crying. "I'm so sick. I want you to come out here." Dinah turned openly to look at Toby. His face was so tear-covered that it glistened in a grimace of humiliation and fear when he saw that she was staring at him. The pain she felt at his mistrust of her was too vast and too complicated to register entirely just now. For a moment she couldn't act, and they stood there looking at each other with mutual uncertainty. Then she moved over to him and stooped down with her arms around him and the phone. She could hear the alarm in Martin's voice, but not the words. She took the receiver and put it to her own ear. "Don't go anywhere, Martin. I'll call you back in a little while." All she could do now was hang up and embrace Toby entirely, with her arms bent at his waist, so that she could reach up behind him to gather his shoulders to her, and she felt his body go limp against her in a total forfeit of reserve. He was willing to give up his dignity to accept her comfort. She said soothing things and stayed as she was, holding him carefully in the empty kitchen.

She stayed in the kitchen with Toby for a little while and calmed him; then she arranged him on a chair and went to find a thermometer, because, indeed—Buddy had been right—he was very hot. When she returned, she found that he was sitting limply in the chair and that he had vomited everything that could possibly have been in his stomach, and was retching still, with involuntary, shuddering dry heaves of his thin shoulders, so that beneath his shirt she could see all the frail vertebrae down his back as his body arched spasmodically. She picked him up and carried him to the study to put him on the couch. He had become so heavy since she last carried him, and he gagged with such a helpless muscular determination that she was thrown off-balance and bumped her shoulder and his head against the door-jamb.

David and Sarah had come to the door of the living room, but they lagged back with reserved expressions. They had no doubt about what was going on; they respected this illness because it was so apparent, but they were also curious to see what they should do. Dinah called out to them from the study as she settled Toby, "You two go out and play! Toby has a flu or something. You go on out now!" She looked down at Toby where she had put him on the couch, and tried to judge what to do. She couldn't tell what was most the matter with him, but his eyelids were hooded and puffy in that semi-oblivion of children in a fever. She slipped one of his arms out of the sleeve of his shirt and took his temperature under that arm, because it would disturb him least and be reasonably accurate. The thermometer read

104, which she thought was supposed to equal 105 degrees orally, but maybe she had the ratio reversed. This seemed to her, all at once, a real emergency, and the only person she thought to call on for help—to call on without hesitation—was Pam. None of her own family came to mind. Dinah knew instinctively that Pam could handle any sort of encumbrance. Dinah trusted Pam's perception of responsibility, and it was Pam's counsel she would follow, because Dinah was awfully frightened suddenly. She was convinced that a great deal hung in the balance, and she could do no more right now than choose the right advisers. When she left the study to phone Pam, she saw that David and Sarah were still standing about in the hall, and their laggard hesitance annoyed her hugely. "Well, go *on*! Don't hang around in here. Go on outside!"

Sarah just looked at her doubtfully. "It's raining," David said. "We'll go watch television upstairs." So Dinah went to the kitchen to phone Pam, while David and Sarah docilely made their way up the stairs to be out of the way.

"I think you'd better try to give him aspirin," Pam said. "No. No, give him some liquid Tylenol. He's more likely to keep it down. I'm going to try and find Dr. Van Helder and be sure he'll see you. Lawrence will be over in a minute, all right? He can drive you over."

Toby vomited the Tylenol rather matter-of-factly, without complaint or comment. Dinah took it upon herself to get in touch with Isobel. "Come down and stay with David and Sarah," she said, not intending to be brusque, but no one else's pleasure was on her mind. "And call Dad. Rearrange the party." Isobel agreed to do all those things and told Dinah, of course, not to worry.

They wouldn't allow Dinah to go into X ray with Toby, so she could only sit now and wait, and the waiting gave her time to fortify her suspicions of everyone in this foreign place. Dinah sat in an alcove which seemed once to have been a large closet but which now did service as a waiting room. It was entirely yellow, with the exception of a brown flecked rug, because someone had believed that a concentration of yellow would be cheering, she supposed; but the effect was to make the underground, windowless space all the more dismal. She had looked around the small room for distractions, but there was nothing to be found but a stack of magazines she didn't want to read and a frosted sliding partition in the wall that she watched for a little while with the dim expectation that it would open. But, in fact, it never did, and there was nothing to divert her attention. She sat there alone, forced into various considerations and forced, for the time being, to remain more sinning than sinned against.

When Dr. Van Helder had first looked at Toby in the emergency room, he had turned such a masked expression on Dinah that she felt sure she was being harshly judged. "How long has he been limping?" he said to her when Toby moved across the room, with a nurse's help, from the examination table to a wheelchair.

"But that's not why he's here," she said with irritated desperation. Immediately she became more alarmed when she recognized the air of solemnity that was suddenly communicated from the doctor to the nurse. There was a marked lack of the usual bantering joviality going on in the grimly fitted-out room. "It's a flu," Dinah had said. "It started all at once this morning. I thought he was just excited because we were having a party for him, but when he kept vomiting . . . well. He can't even drink water!" But when she saw the look of resigned impatience cross Dr. Van Helder's face, she said with great care, "I would say he's been limping for about three weeks . . . oh, about that. But you see," she went on in low-voiced and studious deliberation, "he's only copying his grandfather, whom he adores. My father has had a limp for years . . ." She came to a forlorn stop. She gave it up entirely, because Dr. Van Helder was only looking back at her with patient but stony toleration. Toby appeared to be too miserable even to have heard what was said.

When she had followed the nurse and Toby through the

corridors to the X-ray department, she felt an overwhelming panic at having to relinquish any one of her children to someone else's expert judgment. When the nurse motioned her to a chair in the waiting room and she saw Toby wheeled through the heavy, wide sliding doors, built to facilitate the transport of people who could not transport themselves, she wondered frantically how she could get him out if she decided this was all a mistake. How could she even find him in the warrenlike passages of the hospital?

The longer she waited, and the more she thought about his conversation with Martin, the clearer it became to her that, in fact, Toby knew what was happening to him. She respected her children; she trusted that they knew what they said they knew. She understood that she should accept Toby's assessment of his own condition. He must have achieved that unusual familiarity with his body that she herself had experienced each time she was pregnant. She had always known long before she missed a period. She firmly believed that, now and then, the body and mind forgo their constant, surreptitious collusion and render up to one's sensibilities some bits of pertinent information regarding the mysterious necessities of the physical being. Sometimes a signal drifted into one's consciousness. She had no doubt that that had happened to Toby now, and she sat there floundering in her own emotions for something with which she could gird herself against the despair that would soon overtake her. She was filled with the bitterest self-loathing and reproach at what she now saw as sentimental facetiousness: the stupid and smug notion that her own perceptiveness in recognizing any possible disaster would ward it off. She rested her elbows on her knees and lowered her head into her hands. For years she had indulged in an absurd kind of emotional self-flagellation. She had believed she would never feel the shock of a misery that she already expected. Maybe part of her constant underlying melancholy was the idea—confirmed now—that there are some things for which one cannot be adequately prepared.

The nurse wheeled Toby back through the sliding doors, and Dinah got up to follow them. They made their way along the same corridors through which they had just come, and Toby was reinstalled on the table in the emergency room. Dinah moved over to him and held his hand, which only hung in her own. He still had the swollen, uncommunicative look of fever, and he lay on the table with a heaviness peculiar to sick children; healthy children are so seldom without animation. The nurse leaned up against the wall with an equally uncommunicative but vacant expression. She tapped her foot abstractedly to a tune in her head. People in hospitals are very good at not being asked questions. All at once she straightened up and left the room as if she had heard her name being called; she just turned briefly to tell Dinah that Dr. Van Helder would be back in a minute, and in fact, he came into the room almost the moment the nurse was gone from sight. He was brisk. He didn't say anything or even acknowledge Dinah, so she stood there looking on silently. The doctor was a fairly short, stocky man with closely cut reddish hair, and Dinah watched him as he bent over Toby, who seemed dark and delicate and refined by contrast. She was filled with a sorrowful and unidentifiable longing that became a metallic taste in her mouth and a long ache and tightness down her throat. The feeling resembled homesickness. It was a need for events to resume a familiar shape.

Toby didn't say anything, but he looked over to be sure his mother was standing there when Dr. Van Helder picked up the clipboard at the end of the bed and consulted it. He began to probe Toby's abdomen with his square fingers while he gazed at the wall in concentration.

"I'm going to set up an IV," he said to Dinah. "I'll be back in a little while." And he, too, left the room. Toby turned his head on the pillow to look at Dinah and see what this meant, although he was too tired to ask and even too tired, it seemed, to be very much afraid. She boosted herself up beside him on the high padded table, and she explained to him what an IV was and that it would only hurt as much as a shot, no more, but all the time she talked about it, the idea of Toby attached to an IV was dawning on her. The picture was forming in her head of how that would be, and she was beginning to think with one part of her mind that the sight would be unendurable. She was finding it dreadful to have been invested with the power of adulthood and now find it had been stripped away. Her authority here was impotent.

She moved away from the table when the doctor and three nurses came back into the room, one nurse wheeling the IV mechanism ahead of her, beaming at Toby as though he were in for a treat. Dinah was frustrated almost to the point of tears at all the stupidity that was rampant in the world. She could scarcely bear it that they would patronize him so. She stood in the doorway watching while they worked over the bed and searched for a vein in his pale limp hand. The nurse took his arm and began slapping it lightly to bring the blood there so it would delineate the elusive network of blood vessels. Dinah even assumed an air of reassurance when Toby turned to look at her in injured inquiry, but she felt such a fury that she was almost dizzy with it. She leaned in as casual an attitude as possible against the wall for support. Never before in her life had she felt a more commanding inclination toward violence. She seethed with the need to do injury to that nurse, to stop her, to hurt her. At the same time, she knew that the nurse was no more than a rather insensitive woman getting on with her job, and Dinah leaned against the cold plaster wall breathless with the drag of civilization on her animal instincts.

"It's all right, Toby," she said, when no one else spoke to him, "they're just trying to find the vein. That nurse is *hitting* you that way," she said with impeccable clarity, "so that it will bring the blood to your arm." She phrased it just like that because she wanted the woman to apologize to Toby—and to her—but the nurse didn't even look up. The doctor looked over at her, though, because he seemed not to have known that she was still in the room; then he bent over Toby again.

"Is your name Toby?" he said, but Toby wisely made no answer, because the doctor didn't care; he was only speaking to distract Toby. "Well, Toby," he said in a slow and meditative voice, mostly to himself, "we're having a lot of trouble with this. Your veins roll. Did you know that?" He and a nurse bent again over Toby to try and insert the IV needle. "This is all your mother's fault," he said by way of conversation, and in the doorway Dinah tightened with astonishment. Of course, she *knew* it must all be her fault, but she still didn't know why or what had happened. When had it started to be her fault? It made her furious that this doctor would reveal her culpability so casually before she even had a chance to assemble her defenses.

"So! You're a Freudian," she said from the doorway, in a weak attempt to appear blasé and in control of some slight humor. She would have to make light of this until she could think of what to say. The doctor looked up blankly at her; then he turned back to his labor over Toby. The nurses fell silent, and there was no conversation at all for a moment.

"You've inherited your mother's fair skin, Toby," Dr. Van Helder said. "That's why it's so hard to find your vein."

While they finished their work and constructed a protective casing around the needle so that it wouldn't be jarred loose, Dinah stood there looking on. She didn't care about trying to explain anything; she knew she couldn't have made herself clear. Besides, she still wanted to know if there was a chance that it was—Toby's entire illness, whatever it might be—all her own fault. Dinah's quiet panic took up so much of her mind that the only other feelings she could accommodate right now were sorrow and responsibility.

Dr. Van Helder went with them while Toby was wheeled on his bed through various corridors and up the invalid's elevator to be installed in the pediatric ward. "He's dehydrated," the doctor said as they walked along. "This will build up his fluid level."

The IV apparatus was guided after them by a nurse's aide. As the bed was wheeled along and maneuvered around corners, Toby began to shudder with dry retching again. Dinah looked down at him as if he were very far away, and then stretched out her cool hand and brushed his forehead to reassure him. The doctor glanced at him but didn't show special alarm or make any comment. The deeper into the hospital their procession progressed, the clearer it became to Dinah that Toby's welfare was beyond her influence. She wondered if he even knew that she had meant to communicate comfort with her brief, fugitive touch. The air was brittle with detachment; she felt that she might be prevented from making such an overt contact with her own son. In this atmosphere the need to hold on to the fragile gestures of humanity seemed excessively sentimental.

"I'll be back in a little while when I get the X rays," Dr. Van Helder said to her before he left the room. In fact, Dinah was in no hurry for him to return. She would gladly have prolonged her ignorance and forfeited the future; it would be better to remain with Toby in this immediate instant than to get on with the truth.

The room had four beds, but Toby was its only occupant, so she switched the remote-control television through all its channels without hesitation. The sound wouldn't disturb anyone, and she hoped the novelty of the machine would interest Toby, but he gazed at the flashing face of the television with apathy, and he didn't want to make conversation either. Finally, she pulled up another chair and put her legs on it, and she curled at an angle, with her cheek against the back of her own chair, so that she could watch Toby and rest, too. But her eye drifted away from Toby and the needle in his hand. Without intending to, she turned her mind to a game show on Toby's television in which two families competed against each other for prizes. She attached her entire consideration to it unwittingly, and when she realized next that time had passed without her awareness of it, she came back to attention with a jolt. The light that summoned the nurse was blinking off and on above Toby's bed, and Dinah fought through a kind of self-induced haze to orient herself. She looked at Toby and realized that he himself had pushed the call button.

"Toby! You aren't playing with that, are you? Sweetie, you should only push that button if there's something you really need!" Even as she said this to him, she saw that she was betraying him once more. She was intimidated by hospitals. She said more easily, "Is there something you need? Are you thirsty or anything?"

Toby looked over at her. "It's leaking," he said, "but no one's come yet."

"What? What do you mean?"

"The tube there." And with his free arm he gestured across his body to the tube running from the suspended bottle of liquid to the hollow needle that fed into the back of his hand. All along the flexible piping were little droplets of fluid, and with horror Dinah looked down to see a substantial pool of liquid on the floor by the bed. She had no idea what was being slowly dripped into Toby's veins—whether or not it was crucial. What would happen if an air bubble made its way through that snaking tube? She had an odd sensation as she leaned over the shiny pool, transfixed; she felt herself blanch. The anger she felt was so absolute and unequivocal, and its summer-long impetus was so great, that its solidification sapped her of any energy directed otherwise. This was someone's fault! She moved from her chair to the corridor with no thought put to the motion; suddenly she was just there, in the hall, looking for someone who could do something. Two nurses were standing outside their glassed-in station, chatting in good humor, and Dinah was very nearly frozen in place by her fury. But in the next moment she walked rapidly down the hall toward them and circled around the nurse whose back was to her, so that she was standing between the two women.

"Don't you *see* that?" she said in a voice that even surprised her, it was so deep with an absolute and vibrating anger. She was pointing over the nurse's shoulder to Toby's light. "Now you just turn around if you're not too busy and see if you can *see* that!" But the nurse was already moving off toward Toby's door as Dinah spoke to her.

Dinah followed her back to Toby's room and stood by the bed while the nurse found the mechanism that controlled the call button and switched it off. Dinah kept her voice carefully level. "You can see it's leaking, there. I don't know how long it's been like that."

The nurse adjusted the clamp on the tube and ran her hands over its length, trying to find the point from which the fluid was escaping. "It's this piggyback bottle that's giving us all this trouble," she murmured. A look of clinical indifference was firmly settled on her face, and Dinah was suddenly tired from her anger; how was *she* to know where responsibility should lie?

"There! That's all taken care of, Toby," the nurse said with repellent heartiness as she finished fiddling with the tubing and the clamp. "Dr. Van Helder will be on the floor in a little while. He'll be in to talk to you." She imparted this information with absolute matter-of-factness, and then she left the room. There was very little injured righteousness for Dinah to muster, anyway, because she had been sitting inattentively right beside Toby when he needed help.

She considered Toby, who was now lying in his bed more alert than before, feeling a little better, it seemed. What she thought was that he had become a masculine presence all at once. He had taken charge without question. When she had been growing up, that had been something that boys did but not girls. Dinah struggled with it still: she still fought her inclination to avoid responsibility—to ask first: Is this all right? Is this allowed?

She looked at Toby with cautious admiration. She had a son who was not a son; he was his own person entirely. By now her emotions had caught up with events, and she was inescapably trapped in the alarming reality. Toby believed he was dying, and he was a competent judge. How would it be? She wasn't trying to gauge the depth of her own sorrow; she knew that she couldn't accurately anticipate that. But how could it happen that the world would not have Toby in it beyond a certain point? What would the world be without Toby in it as an adult? They sat together quietly in the room, and Dinah looked out the window to the parking lot below, where the rain fell steadily, just to keep her bearings. She needed to keep abreast of the fact that time was progressing.

When Dr. Van Helder came in, he paused at the foot of the bed to look over Toby's chart once again, but Dinah knew there wouldn't be any new information on it. She knew that the nurse wouldn't have recorded the incident of the IV, but she would have been happy to have him read the chart forever. She wanted, just for a moment, to become senseless; her body had an impulse to flee, because she didn't even want to suspect it, or to see what manner he would have of imparting the news to make it least uncomfortable to himself. She didn't know this doctor; she wasn't willing to give him the benefit of the doubt. Dinah had straightened herself when she saw him come in, and now he sat down in the chair where she had been resting her legs, so that he and she were almost knee to knee.

Dr. Van Helder crossed his legs and settled back in the chair before he said anything, and it seemed to Dinah that this elaborate arranging of himself took several dreamlike hours. "Well, I think Toby does have a bad flu," he said, conversationally. "But that shouldn't last more than a day or so. He's dehydrated. I'd like to get his fluid level up, as I told you." He paused and looked down at his own crossed knees. Dinah sat very still, because it was clear he had more to say, and she wanted to be able to sit in her chair with composure when she heard what it was. "But I'm worried about that leg," he said in the very deliberate voice doctors cultivate in order to make themselves perfectly clear and yet not cause panic. "Well . . . in fact, it's not his leg at all, really. It's his hip joint. I'm pretty sure he has what's called toxic synivitus. But I don't understand why it's lasted so long. You say almost three weeks?" She nodded. "Well," he went on, "it could be that the muscles around that joint have spasmed in a sympathetic reaction. That's probably why he's still limping." He raised his hands from his lap in an unconscious gesture of calming the waters. "I think it's been aggravated by having gone on for so long." He looked up at Dinah with his face kept blank, and she knew he expected her to explain. But she knew she couldn't have explained to his satisfaction, so she kept quiet. "It's a virus," he said. "No one's ever done much research on it, because, as I say, it usually goes away within a week or so. I think I'd like to keep him in here for a day or two and give that leg a rest and let him get over this flu."

Dinah's gradual relief was so pleasurable that she didn't mind if he thought she had been careless on Toby's behalf. She didn't mind his censure at all now that she knew that Toby only had some virus. Just a virus. Dread still lay solidly in her stomach like a heavy, indigestible food, but she could feel her body reacting just as if her limbs had been numbed and were now coming back to life with a sharp tingle.

"Then he's all right?" she asked.

He looked at her with a puzzled expression, and then he seemed to be really cross. "Well, *no*. You see," he said with considerable patience, as to someone of very slow wits, "he's got something very like an inflamed hip. I think he ought to stay off that leg for some time. He shouldn't walk on it at all."

Dinah looked at him, but she had nothing at all to say. She knew it was not serious. This virus amounted to nothing in the long run. This virus was not death! Her social sense had deserted her, and she didn't respond to his careful explanation of Toby's ailment as solemnly as Dr. Van Helder clearly seemed to expect her to. In fact, to his obvious bewilderment, she could only smile and smile at him in great relief.

CHAPTER TEN

LOST AND
STRAYED

O ver the past few weeks Martin had lost his capacity for enthusiasm, and he was beginning to realize that he was crippled by the loss. His thoughts occupied his head in the same way he now inhabited his own house. He wasn't likely to take much satisfaction in what grace the rooms possessed, but generally he derived a happy serenity from the sturdiness of the tall building itself and the comforting familiarity of it. Now the walls stood high and foreign to him, and the spaces he wandered through were no longer defined by custom; the rooms seemed never to have had a designated function. In the same way, he had lost the habit of organized reflection and contemplation. On the one hand, he was perfectly aware of his aberrant state of mind, but on the other hand, the dismal conclusions that beset him did not seem in the least unreasonable.

One morning he had come awake very early in his own bedroom, because he had forgotten to draw the curtains the night before, and he had been as stunned by the thought awaiting him when he surfaced into consciousness as he was by the heavy sunlight that bore down on his eyelids so that he dared not open them. He was at once overwhelmed by the knowledge that he had lived more than half his life! In this instance, it was simply the brevity of the span of his existence that staggered him and frightened him. What he wished he wanted at that moment was his mother, but in fact, he supposed he must want God. So he just lay still, since it was too late for him to believe in the reassurance of his mother or any God he might evoke. That morning Martin lay completely awake without any solace, but in the days that followed he looked back on that relatively benign realization of his own passing life with an almost affectionate indulgence.

The *universe* became ominous to Martin rather quickly, and he tried to avoid his own perceptions. Sometimes he simply slept deep into the day or got up before dawn and then napped throughout the afternoon. These erratic habits kept him at a distance from the rest of humanity, but paradoxically, he was obsessed with the news broadcasts on television, and whatever times he chose to eat or sleep, he arranged his day around these programs. He watched television in hope of being presented with some fact that would pull him back into a limited and measured view.

For a while he hit upon a comforting spell of fervent organization; he thought he had come upon an arrangement that would help him make a system for his days. Somewhere along the way Dinah had acquired a surgical steel cart her father had salvaged from the hospital when he was in med school. She had used it all through graduate school as a typing table, and it now sat at one end of the kitchen to house all the various portable appliances that they had accumulated over the years but rarely used. The kitchen was a long and narrow room with windows at one end and a glass door at the other. Martin was most comfortable there, and he devoted considerable attention to his solitary meals. For several days, his eye had been caught by the ill-assorted gadgets on the crowded cart. It was an aggravation to his inherent, personal orderliness that transcended even this crisis of philosophy. The little table had become a catchall of sorts and was heavily laden with dust in the spaces between the orange juicer and the ice crusher, and so forth. At last he set himself to clearing it off and sponging and scrubbing the steel surface with boiling water. It glowed with the soft sheen of sterile steel when he was done, and he could make good use of it. He regulated his schedule, and he lived with a certain sense of satisfaction for several days. He prepared his meals with great care and then transferred the food directly to the spotless metal surface of the cart and wheeled his dinner in front of the television. When he finished eating, he sponged down the table itself; there were no plates to be washed. He had made a gesture toward simply getting on with his days, and he was pleased with himself for it.

He sat in front of the news, eating his meals and taking an obscure and chilling comfort in the disasters of the day. His sorrow was there at every moment; in fact, he felt that in its amplitude it encompassed the earth like a mist. But his sorrow and pity were easily attributable. He knew their cause. He watched the numbing ordeal of the Cambodians with despair and with rage. Murders and rapes and fires touched him with impotent horror, as they would any person of even meager imagination, but lurking turbulently beneath these clearly defined disasters and atrocities was a knowledge so devastating to him that he knew there was danger there. He had finally understood the transience of the earth. What awaited him, if he was unable to exhaust his anxiety on immediate concerns, was the knowledge, for instance, of black holes, of a finite sun, of the vast and godless universe.

Martin was even made miserable by his own intelligence. He knew that it was ultimately a threat to his own ego that he was fending off, and yet apathy encroached from all sides. He had hours, sometimes days, when he could not think of a reason to lift a finger, write a word, have a child. If he could not manage to keep his imagination engaged, he drifted off into a nether world of all the consequences of life and growth and change and motion. *This* was the sorrow that held him most securely: the final despair at the idea that, indeed, continuity was the one vision he must abandon.

Martin's little cart, carefully set with his knife and fork and a lamb chop or a bit of roast chicken, was a tentative barrier thrown up against a menacing havoc of ideas, and it worked out very nicely for almost a week. It worked out fine until the evening when he was arranging everything tidily in the cool, high-ceilinged kitchen—he was broiling a hamburger for his supper—and it dawned on him that he could have achieved even greater efficiency by placing the pan of food itself on the impervious metal surface. When this thought occurred to him, the charm of the whole enterprise collapsed like a house of cards. He could have adopted this plan, and it would even have enlarged his menu; he could have soup, salads, spaghetti . . . But Martin replaced all the appliances on the metal cart, rolled it back to its place by the stove, and ate his meals from then on off the everyday china and at the kitchen table. He was gravely depressed that he had expended so much determined thought and energy on such a small and essentially frivolous exercise.

Martin missed the Hofstatters, and he knew that they would welcome him; they were not petty, but he couldn't bring himself to face Ellen's grim disapprobation. Besides, in those moments when he could wrench his thoughts back to earth, he—on his part—felt a certain disapproval of her. He suspected there was something slippery and perturbing beneath the surface of her unique interpretation of morality. The most fearsome thing about Ellen was her unnerving tendency to say exactly what she thought, and in this case she had been unusually strident in her anger.

She had sat waiting for him one day when he emerged from the pond. He had straggled out to see her regarding him with a narrowed, steely look. "I think you ought to know something, Martin," she said as he began to dry himself. "I think you ought to know that you're beginning to disgust me! I wouldn't have thought that you would be unkind. To anyone. But especially not to Dinah."

He was taken aback, because his and Claire's lovemaking had been going on for several weeks, and he hadn't thought

Vic and Ellen cared one way or another. It certainly hadn't made much of an impression on Claire, who went mildly through the days, just as always. It hadn't even made much of an impression on him, although he had never had any sort of affair before. He hadn't, until that moment, even considered it an affair. It seemed far too menacing a description when he thought of it that way. As he tried to towel the murky water out of his hair, he made an attempt to turn and lighten the conversation. "Ellen, I think I'm still a good and proper man." He meant to instill this with enough self-disdain to satisfy her.

"Well," Ellen said, looking straight at him, unnervingly, so that he was aware of a slight roll of flesh over the waist-band of his suit, "I'm just sorry I know what you are. I'm sorry to find out. It's just too bad I know, because you're not much more than ludicrous! In fact, I'm sorry to see that you're almost pitiful."

He became angry now himself. "You sure as hell are righteous today, aren't you?" He still wanted to deflect this confrontation. He just wanted her to back off.

"The thing is," she said, more softly, "you aren't even *thinking* about what you're doing. Dinah couldn't stand it, you know. This is something she just couldn't stand. You ought to know that you're causing real injury." She held up her hand to keep him from protesting. "Even if Dinah *never* knows, you ass!" She had worked up a keen anger once more. "Even if Dinah never knows, she *is* as much what she is in your mind as she is a person in her own right! That's what couples are, you know. And you know what you and Dinah are! You can't ever really be two separate people again." She didn't say anything for a moment, and he had nothing he could say, although he knew that in a little while he would discover some way in which he disagreed with her. Right now she had jumped the gun on him. "Besides," she went on, "you have no right to impose this on us. Vic and I think of you and Dinah together. You just don't have the right to make this our burden, too."

Martin stalked off to the house to get dressed. He didn't

believe that Ellen even liked Dinah very much. After a fairly silent dinner with Vic and Ellen and Katy, he and Claire were sitting alone in the yard while Katy ran around, full of energy. Martin spoke out to Claire and said something he immediately regretted: "I think Ellen's just jealous for her own sake." There was less arrogance in this than there seemed to be, because Martin had an intense knowledge of Ellen's passion for control, but Claire had almost sneered at him when she smiled at that. "Oh, no. No, no. If Ellen wants something, she just about always gets it. She's put off by something else this time," she said.

But Martin didn't believe this entirely. He put Claire's opinion down to the tendency of people to overestimate the influence of their siblings or their parents. Those early battles form an indelible impression of the victor's strength, so that it is easily forgotten that the protagonists are never evenly matched. Martin couldn't imagine that Claire, so much younger and less certain than Ellen, could ever have triumphed.

Since Martin had given up visiting the Hofstatters, Claire and Katy often came by to visit him. Claire was always cheerful and friendly, but since Katy was with her, he and she couldn't have gone upstairs to bed. He didn't care much, and Claire didn't seem even to think of it. When he had made his bed on the long leather couch at the Hofstatters', after the others had gone upstairs for the night, Claire had taken to staying downstairs with him. It had become a matter of course to end up lying there together making love. But Martin didn't know why he made love to Claire; it took on a masturbatory regulation, because it changed nothing in the long run, and neither of them had any intention of changing anything. There was a disturbing sense, too, of never being able to touch Claire at all. It surprised him to make love to someone who seemed to regard it simply as an easy way to bide one's time. He did like Claire very much, but one of them—or perhaps both of them—lacked passion. He felt *some* guilt, of course, because he knew that Ellen was right in one respect. Dinah couldn't have borne being compared to this young girl, and in a sense he did compare them—it was impossible not to. What he never did think of, however, was one as opposed to the other. He noticed the differences in their bodies, but he never considered the question of preference. His guilt was not the slightest bit profound, because there was never any decision to be made about where his affections lay. He felt, as a matter of fact, sorry for himself in some ways, because he knew that Dinah would be baffled and hurt if she ever found out about Claire. He was so bound to his own wife that her sorrow would be intolerable to him. She might experience the sorrow; *he* would really suffer it. As to the sex, he just enjoyed it, without any careful introspection. He had a mild regret, now and then, that he was not sixteen, when he had been almost incessantly interested in the bodies of women—interested in the fact that he might have access to the legs, hips, breasts, arms of women's bodies —but now he was thirty-eight, and he had lost the pervasive intensity of that sweet obsession.

When Claire came to visit him now, in his house, he was glad to have her company. Katy played with some of his children's toys he had found for her, and they sat at the table in the kitchen, where he and Claire drank a beer or instant iced tea. Claire was an undemanding guest; she seemed to be equally content wherever she was or whatever the conversation. She tended to be placid or reserved at the same times that Ellen would have been vocally judgmental. Martin knew now that if he had thought about it early on he would have seen that, inevitably, he would have ended up sleeping with Claire, given the way his summers wound their way out. He suspected, as well, that Ellen had foreseen it, too, and he resented her solicitude for Dinah on *Dinah's* behalf, really. Of all the feelings Dinah might have about his attachment to Claire, surely Ellen's pity would have roused her most bitter reaction. But Martin was glad to see Claire now, because the hours during which he had company kept him busy observing the soothing demands of the social amenities. Any visit was a respite from his new and constant awareness of eventual cosmic grief.

Martin worked over some of the revised articles for the *Review*, but it was just work; he did it because he knew it must be done by a certain time. He didn't do it with even a flicker of ardor or excitement. He wandered around the house, and he diverted his mind a good deal by the physical task of cleaning it up. He had been much surprised one morning when he realized that the living-room floor was still littered with the remnants of the wrappings of Katy's birthday presents from such a long time ago, and he began there, clearing those away, and then moved on to freshening the rooms that were filled with stale heated air and sticky dust from having been closed off for so many weeks.

He had conversations with Dinah on the phone; he thought he had taken to calling her so often because he knew he had betrayed her; he could never think of much to say, but he liked to make the connection. He also had discussions with her in his head, often while he sat in the kitchen eating his meals. He defended himself against her criticism when he sprinkled his scrambled eggs with lemon pepper. In his mind he justified himself to her for liking his lamb chops well done. He agreed with her on the interpretation of almost every national event. For the most part, though, Martin wandered around the rooms or watched television, with a vague hope that he might discover the philosophy he sought. He wished to be dissuaded—or somehow to dissuade himself—from the reality he now perceived.

One afternoon he saw Vic arrive carrying an armful of papers, and Martin was irritable when he greeted him at the door, because he had been comfortably settled on the couch and absorbed in a television documentary on a primitive culture—the first inhabitants of Easter Island— that seemed to be addressing all the issues he feared. But he had only seen the problems laid out; he had to switch it off before he saw them explained away or resolved. In the back of his mind, however, he knew that it was a good sign that he did not want to be caught watching television in the afternoon.

He and Vic sat in the kitchen at the table with the manuscripts between them, and Vic took it upon himself to pour them both a beer. It was a hot and humid day, and the greenery outside the windows was unusually still and without vitality. The landscape had the flat look of a painted stage set. Martin was still thinking of the program he had been watching. "Do you know anything about Easter Island?" he asked Vic while they were still sipping from the froth of their beer and before they began sorting through the manuscripts.

Vic just shook his head and took a long swallow of beer, but he looked up attentively, because he was always willing to have a conversation. It was one of his chief pleasures, Martin had always thought. Martin was quiet a minute, trying to arrange what he would say. The things he had just found out on television seemed momentous to him, and as he had been watching the program, he had been mildly surprised that it had been scheduled at such an obscure hour. But Martin was a modest man, and in everyone's company save Dinah's he tended to skirt gingerly those subjects about which he felt most passionate. Even his academic environment had never convinced him that the display of intellectual passion wasn't really a vanity as base as any other. He despised vanity, but in this case he plunged in, not meaning to be persuasive in any way, but just intending to give Vic information.

"In the pre-Polynesian civilization on Easter Island," he said, "the island was apparently quite lush. It may be the most isolated spot in the world, so the original population didn't have any access to other resources. They only had what the island offered." Martin was sheepish. "This is simply conjecture, of course. Well, there was a program about it on television . . . But what it all comes down to is that they exhausted their timber. Their food supplies dwindled. They took to living in caves. Well, they abandoned their gods, of course. I mean, those gods weren't *working!* And they took up a peculiar religion. They worshipped the bird-man. A man who could fly, you see. Who could escape." There was quite a pause. Vic was leaning back in his chair with his chin on his chest in an attitude of weighty consideration.

"Well," Martin went on, a little hesitantly, "doesn't that put you in mind of the astronauts? Of course, it *does*. But the *outward* quest?" He simply couldn't reveal himself any further, and Vic was nodding agreeably in any case.

"I do remember something about Easter Island," Vic said with what appeared at first to be sober enthusiasm but turned into a kind of glee. "Where did I ever hear this? Easter Island is called the 'navel of the world' by somebody I've read. Now, who? And I've always wondered why. It's a revolting idea! It makes me imagine that the dregs of the earth settle there after the bathwater's drained out." Vic was greatly amused, but the idea had riveted Martin's attention. A sudden image floated through his head of the earth as an aging, withered body, with Easter Island stuck to its belly like a wrinkled raisin on a gingerbread man.

The next few days Martin was disconsolate. He spent his time between the kitchen, simply to eat his meals, and his and Dinah's bedroom. He had strewn his work out on Dinah's desk there, but he couldn't concentrate very well. Now he found that all the articles he had accepted for publication were beside the point and tedious. But his thoughts also veered away from the alarming theories and ideas at the back of his mind, and he tended to think a good deal about his own family. He thought a lot about his wife. One morning an incident came to mind that he hadn't remembered for a long time because it always unsettled him, and it had puzzled him and made him unhappy. He remembered once again what a peculiar state Dinah had been in immediately after she had had David. When she was helped back to her hospital room after the delivery, at which Martin had been present, she began to cry when she discovered that she had missed dinner. Martin had been oddly terrified to see her tears after the ordeal she had just been through, which she had weathered with ominous, guttural moans. Her doctor had sent him a comforting, knowing look across the bed as she lay there with tears flowing down her face, and advised him to go out and get hamburgers for them both. When Martin had returned with the food, she was alone and in a mortified rage.

"I'm just embarrassed!" she said. "I'm embarrassed at the *charade* of it all! It's a barbaric custom! By God, no one but women should be there—no one but women who've had lots of children. Next time, I want to have a baby by myself!" That had hurt his feelings very much, because he was strained and miserable to have seen her in so much pain, and toward the end of the whole thing he had felt guiltily exasperated that any pain could go on so interminably. But he had tried to suffer it as she did; he had tried to be loyal. When she looked up from her hamburger and realized that he didn't understand what she was getting at, it made her cry again. "There's nothing *natural* about 'natural child-birth' when the mother is forced into being a . . . forced into being a *performer!* God," she had said, "the stupid pretense of enthusiasm. Do you know how I really felt after it was over? I felt *tired*. I didn't feel one other thing—not one! Well, yes, I did"—and an odd, sly look came over her face; she wasn't sure whether or not to trust him. "I knew that this was supposed to be what everything is about, and I thought, 'But what's the point?' You see, it will go on and on. I might have more children. My children will have children. But still . . . I'll die. You'll die. We'll still be *dead* someday." She ran down then, like a record player when the power is cut off, and she seemed to decide, anyway, that she couldn't explain.

Now, at last, he saw what she had been talking about. Later, too, she had become quite fierce about the baby. She had found in the baby's existence at least a stopgap to catch her emotions, and she had been in a situation that demanded she function. It was after that, too, that she had forced her energy into the formation of the Guild shop, and simply carried on. She had carried on.

Martin sat gazing idly into their bedroom and formulated questions for her to answer as though he were making up an exam for his students: "If the world is finite, from what corner does one garner motivation? By what method does one fight legitimate torpor?"

He could answer for her, because the question would make her impatient now. She might tell him that it was a perverse egomania to imagine that the permanence or impermanence of the earth had anything at all to do with the leading of one's life. She might know that; that was certainly a thought she might have had. And then, when the phone rang just as he was thinking these thoughts, and he heard Toby's voice husky with a peculiar agony, Martin was flooded with immediate and heartfelt fear, which superseded every other emotion. After he hung up, he no longer sat thoughtfully adrift; he made reservations for a flight to Ohio; he called and arranged to have Lawrence or Buddy pick him up at the airport; and he did all these things without a trace of hesitation. He went into action with efficient dispatch, free, at least for a while, of his enervating listlessness. His fear was astoundingly cleansing.

CHAPTER ELEVEN

FAMILY REUNION

Dinah began to believe that people who were long hospitalized and then died might end up surrounded by friends and relatives who could no longer register grief; they would already have been anesthetized by the tedium of an institutional routine. Everything in a hospital, and even the running of it, seemed to her to be designed to effect a reduction of human emotion. Sitting with Toby hour after hour was wearing. Playing games, watching television, reading aloud—all those things were gratingly dull to her now that there was no danger that might have made her boredom sweet. Even so, when she allowed herself to look at Toby, who seemed unnervingly fragile in the overlarge hospital smock, she begrudged him nothing at all. She redoubled her efforts to entertain him. She became almost frantic, in fact, and persuaded him into more dominoes, another book, or anything else that would distract him. The worst times of the day were those brief periods when he slept propped up against his pillows, with his encumbered right arm rigidly stretched in place beside him. Then she could not help but watch him, to be sure he didn't turn in his sleep and pull the needle loose, and it caused her pain.

She kept the family informed about Toby's condition, so they knew he wasn't in jeopardy, and she called her mother after lunch and found out that Martin was due to arrive any moment. "But, of course," Polly said, "I told Lawrence to bring him right back here. He will have left in such a hurry that he'll be exhausted!" This seemed to Dinah to be a clear case of not having her mother on her own side, but she did not remonstrate; she had used up all her force of objection. A nurse came into the room in midafternoon to tell her that her husband had called, but that Dinah would have to return the call on another phone, because they couldn't tie up the lines at the nurses' station.

She waited until later in the day to call him back, when Toby was distracted by having his dinner brought in. She cut up his meat for him and buttered his bread so that he could manage it all with his left hand, and she asked the girl who had delivered the tray to keep an eye on him in case he needed help. She had to go to the pay phone down the hall to get in touch with Martin. Hospital policy didn't allow any phones in the rooms in Pediatrics, nor did they allow those remote-control devices for adjusting the beds. When Dinah had asked about it, the nurse had looked at her as though the two of them were accomplices. "I can just see that now! You *know* how children are about gadgets!" she said, with a wink at Toby, who turned his glance away in embarrassment. It roused Dinah's ire once again, but she supposed it made a certain sense.

She got Polly first on the phone, and they chatted a moment; Dinah told her how Toby was. "I'll get Martin for you," Polly said. "You must want to talk to him. We've just sat down to eat, but it isn't anything that needs to stay hot." Pam had made a casserole, Polly a salad. To Dinah, standing in the corridor and looking back along the length of greenish linoleum while she waited for Martin to come to the phone, it all sounded attractively cheering and communal.

"Hi, Dinah," he said finally, "I tried to get you earlier. I'm sorry about all this." His voice became muted and confidential. "I meant to come straight on to the hospital, but all these arrangements had been made . . ." He drifted off helplessly, and Dinah knew it was true. Polly could never entirely convince herself that other people were sick or, at least, that other people were sick through no choice of their own. In spite of the fact that her grandson was in the hospital, she would move implacably on through the habitual patterns of hospitality. If Dinah or Martin had attempted to emphasize to her their anxiety on Toby's behalf, their explanations would only serve to direct Polly's nebulous suspicions of melodrama to Toby himself. Both of his parents knew this, though there was no need to say so. "I'll be over just as soon as I can. I'll stay the night with him. I've already got everything packed anyway, and I imagine they'll give me a cot."

Dinah was grateful to Martin for having realized that she would be tired by now, and that she had needed him to be there sooner. He had made every effort to be conciliatory. Nevertheless, she went back to sit with Toby while he ate, and she finished the flaccid meat that he had left untouched on his tray. She ate it with a sullen sense of sacrifice.

When Martin finally came into Toby's room, he hugged his son without reticence or pretension, and Dinah stood up and they embraced, too, as sincerely as they could. Their bodies clasped together just briefly while each of them strained to dredge up the familiarity they remembered. For some reason they met each other after their long separation with an awkwardness tinged with irritation. They were both so tired, and Dinah *was* cross that Martin had not arrived sooner to relieve her. But always at the end of their summer separation they could only simulate, at first, their remembered affection, because, inescapably, there was a trace of shyness between them.

"It's good to see you!" Martin said. "How are you? You must not even have had dinner yet. I tried to get away earlier. I'm sorry it's so late."

"Oh, no. I'm fine. It's wonderful to see you, too." Dinah stood back from him to smile. "I was so glad you could get a flight. I hope you didn't have a long wait at the airport." Martin looked the same, as she had expected he would look, just tired, and there shouldn't have been any reason for her to be slightly watchful and on guard. It was always like this, she assured herself, after such a long time. She saw him take in the IV apparatus and *not* react, because they both instinctively pretended to Toby that nothing could be more natural than to have a needle stuck in your vein and fluid feeding through it. Dinah had no idea why they pretended this; Toby clearly thought it was decidedly unnatural and unpleasant and he had asked all day when it would be removed.

Now, in the hospital room, both parents began to bristle. Their sudden impatience and unease was due to Toby's circumstance, but there was no one around to hold accountable except each other. Dinah walked around the bed to be on the other side of it from Martin, and she sat on the edge next to Toby.

"Daddy's going to stay with you tonight. Okay, darling?" She brushed his hair back off his forehead. It seemed odd to her that his illness affected even his hair, which looked dirty and lank but shouldn't have; she had washed it last night before he went to bed.

"Okay," said Toby. "Will they take the IV out tonight?"

"I don't *know*, Toby!" she said, not intending to sound so peevish. "Sweetie, I've asked them about it over and over, but the nurses won't tell me. It doesn't hurt, does it? Do you want me to have them come check it?" As it happened, she was as appalled by the contraption as he was.

"It doesn't *hurt*," he said, "but I just don't like it. I don't think I can go to sleep with it. I can't turn over."

"Oh, honey, I'm just so sorry!" She leaned down over the bed to hug him. She was tired, and she was so sad for him that she almost cried. "Maybe they will take it out tonight. Daddy'll talk to Dr. Van Helder when he makes his rounds. *Daddy* will see about it, sweetie." She wanted to hand over some of this burden to Martin; she shot him a cold look over Toby's head, and then she straightened up. "I've got to go now," she said to Toby, "but I'll be back in the morning. Isobel's had David and Sarah all day, and I've got to get home and put them to bed."

"Okay," said Toby, and kissed her back when she bent down to him again. He was worried at seeing her leave.

Martin had only been able to stand there looking on and feeling more and more fearful of being left to fend for his son in this chilling atmosphere. He hated hospitals. Also, it had suddenly seemed to him just now when he met Dinah's glance across Toby's bed that he really did owe it to her to be honest; he felt he must tell her about himself and Claire, right away. He believed that it would be a crisis of valor on his part to make any delay. And, too, he was sure he would have wanted her to be honest with him. He watched her with detachment as she gathered her things together and made ready to depart. She always moved with an air of intimidating self-possession—the more intimidating because she didn't know she had it. She considered herself a person easily unnerved by other people's self-assurance. He followed her out into the hall after assuring Toby, who had turned his attention to the television, that he would be right back.

They stood uneasily in the corridor, moving apart for a moment to allow a man with a floor-cleaning machine to pass between them. "David and Sarah aren't with Isobel," he told her. "They're at Pam's. Isobel and Buddy were going out to some party this evening. Lawrence drove me over. He's waiting for you in the lobby. I couldn't find the keys to our car. I guess you must have them in your purse." Nothing bothered him so much as not being able to find things where they were supposed to be.

Dinah nodded that she did have them, but she didn't offer any apology or explanation. She was thinking in another direction altogether, and somehow, what he had just told her caught her at precisely the wrong moment. She didn't believe that anything had made her as angry today as the fact that Isobel and Buddy would be out being charming, being frivolous, while she went home exhausted, and apart from her husband, to put two tired and cranky children to bed. She didn't say anything at all, but Martin saw her face become rigid as she put on her raincoat.

"Dinah . . ." he began with what even he recognized as an insinuating hesitation. He knew that his face had assumed an expression of martyrdom, but it was involuntary. "Can you wait just a minute?" he went on with that same careful tone, tenderly contrite already. "I want to talk to you if you have a second."

She looked back at him steadfastly and scathingly. Several things clicked in her mind. Odd phone calls, the fact that she could never reach him at their own house when she called him or returned his calls. Somewhere, too, was the knowledge that she had left him alone again, that she had been away from him all summer, and so had his children. But that idea only passed along the outside of her thoughts, the way bacon frizzles at the edges first before it cooks through to the center.

"Martin," she said with fatigued patience, "there's not a whole lot I want to know right now." She just stood there a moment, and then she reached her head up to give him a quick goodbye kiss. She walked away down the hall, and Martin stood there a moment looking after her, then went back into Toby's room.

Dinah walked the whole length of the hospital corridor to the only elevator that serviced Pediatrics. She punched the button and stood looking straight into the face of the elevator door while she heard the machinery bring it to her floor. It opened its doors, hesitated, then closed them and descended again with a rasping pneumatic whine while she stood absently staring straight ahead of her. She turned back and walked down the long hall until she came to Toby's room again, where she only leaned around the door frame.

"Martin," she said, and he looked up with surprise from the book he was reading aloud to Toby, "it's not Ellen, is it? Did you want to tell me something really important?"

Martin was already ashamed of himself, and she saw the remorse that crossed his face; she knew that eventually she would need to know what he was sorry for. What *he* regretted now, however, was his spiteful desire to confess. "Oh, no, Dinah! It's nothing like that. It's just . . . nothing, really. We can talk about it any time. It's about the *Review*.

I just don't know how interested I am in doing it anymore . . . well, I'll tell you about it some other time." He came to the door and kissed her the way they had learned to kiss each other—a gentling of the mouth against the other's—an honest kiss, not striving for anything. Dinah waved again to Toby and walked away, simply settled into weariness this time. She purposely dampened her curiosity.

The kind of fatigue she had developed by sitting for a day in the hospital could not have resolved itself in sleep. The pose of civility she had been forced to maintain in the face of the ebb and flow of nurses and nurses' aides had had the effect of numbing her genuine reactions. She was glad to see Lawrence in the lobby; he was a good and comfortable friend.

When she passed by the gift shop, he got up to meet her, and they walked side by side through the parking lot. The rain had eased into a pale mist. "Pam put David and Sarah in sleeping bags on the sun porch at our house," he said. "She thought you wouldn't mind. They were so excited when Martin came, and just by the whole day, I guess. She thought it would be best to get them calmed down and to sleep."

"She's wonderful to have done that," Dinah said. "She always knows . . ." She had stopped to turn to him and tell him this with a smile of thanks, but all at once she found herself caught up in absurd and heavy sobs. "Well, *she* shouldn't have to do that! Where did Buddy and Isobel go? What about Polly? She's their grandmother!" She was managing to be very loud while continuing to cry. "Even Dad should have had the sense to do *something!*" But Dinah felt an almost delightful resentment clarify itself for her, like the heavy rolling out of steel plate in a mill. Then that very comforting resentment suddenly deserted her, and her crying went far beyond so sure an emotion into tears of appalling loss and sorrow. She felt a sadness large enough to have encompassed the most dire prognosis Dr. Van Helder might have given her. She stood there miserably at a loss for any way to regain control, because she no longer had a fear of Toby's death. What she was left with was the fear that she could never make up having failed him. She knew that fear was justified.

Lawrence was so startled and embarrassed that Dinah managed to subdue herself, and she started moving along again with intermittent, inelegant sobs. She walked along beside Lawrence, wiping the tears from underneath her eyes and tucking up wisps of hair that had fallen loose. She was bedraggled physically and spiritually.

"It's all right, Lawrence. I'm sorry. God! I'm just tired. Would Pam mind if we stopped to get something to eat? Do you think we could just go to Snow's?" She knew Pam wouldn't mind. Pam was without pettiness, without vindictiveness, without that terrible needfulness of which Dinah could not divest herself.

Dinah had asked to stop at Snow's Tavern because she knew it would be very nearly deserted, and she was too tired to make any effort at affability. Snow's had enjoyed a decade of unreasonable popularity—the decade that encompassed Dinah's and Lawrence's adolescence and eventual departures. It had been the place everyone gathered to drink beer or to celebrate after football games. Real romances had begun and ended at Snow's, and the owner must have sent up a prayer of bewildered thanks; he certainly hadn't done much more. The place was as dismal now as it had been then, only now it was no longer enlivened by any promise of excitement or the probability of great fun to be had.

She and Lawrence sat in one of the flimsy orange-stained plywood booths along the wall, and Lawrence went to get her a Scotch sour and a beer for himself. At Snow's there were no waitresses, and it used to be that it took some time to edge up to the bar and retrieve a pitcher of beer and the large paper cups they dispensed for free. There were only a few people here tonight, one other couple, and several men sitting at the bar, each by himself. Someone had started the jukebox, which had long ago been abandoned by or bought from its franchise and was still stocked with the songs of Dinah's own youth. There was a disco in town now, and no one would come to Snow's for the food. Dinah wondered fleetingly why anyone else was here at all; they could be in nicer places.

In fact, while Lawrence waited at the bar for their sandwiches, Dinah looked around at the narrow, dreary room and longed momentarily for the hygienic surroundings of a Wendy's or McDonald's, but she would have found the unfaltering cleanliness and cheer even more oppressive than this glum atmosphere which bordered on squalor. Some places make demands on their patrons by their very nature —Bloomingdale's expects more than Macy's. McDonald's would demand infinitely more from Dinah than Snow's, which, she realized, required no effort of any kind.

Lawrence came back to the table to bring her her drink, and he carried his beer back to the bar to wait for their order. She sipped her drink, which had been made from a powdered mix and was vile, with half the undissolved powder settled into a sludge at the bottom of her glass. She didn't care. She stirred it thoroughly and drank it through her straw, because tonight she wanted this drink very much.

Before she had left adolescence and found out a little more, it had always seemed to her that dancing was far sexier than sex. And she looked around the room now, remembering how much they had danced and how addictive it had been. Dancing was all expectation; dancing was testing sex out; it was the first matching of rhythms. She and Lawrence had been natural partners for dancing—they moved as though they had the same nervous system. They had been surprisingly less successful as lovers, at least from her point of view. Dinah felt awfully mellow all at once, and she sat there waiting for Lawrence and listening to an old recording of Sam Cooke singing "You Send Me." She remembered being on the dance floor, barely moving, held in a paralyzing embrace by some boy, usually Lawrence, while Sam Cooke's soft persuasive voice enshrouded them in the idea of love and sentiment and sensuality. It had been wonderful to be pretty and sought after, and to have ahead of you all the things there were to know just waiting to be found out. The record ended, and another clicked down, getting ready to play, while Dinah ate the pulp from the stingy slice of orange in her drink. All of a sudden, Ray Charles was singing "I Gotta Woman," and when the song began, with that low moan of agony and anticipation, Dinah's whole body prickled with a knowing, cocky intimation of pure physical ecstasy and all its ramifications. That moan was like the preamble of sex, a teasing, whining, clamant music that filled her with the same amorphous eroticism it had engendered in her when she was fifteen. Lawrence brought their sandwiches, and they sat together eating for a few minutes.

"You know," she said, "now that I think back on it, it doesn't seem to me that it was so bad to be young. Well, I worry about my children. David's ten! It's horrible to think of all the things they'll have to go through. I mean, they will have to suffer a lot, but . . . well, it's exciting. It *is!* To be that age." They both knew what age she meant—not ten, but somewhere between thirteen and twenty.

Lawrence was chewing his sandwich, so there was a pause, and a look of wistfulness became very plain on his face. "I don't think there ever was a time—or ever will be—better than that, better than when we were in high school."

She hadn't meant anything like that. She hadn't had any notion so absolute. She thought of a word in its French pronunciation—*sévère*. She was appalled. "Lawrence! That's not true! I didn't mean that at all. You aren't remembering it very clearly." But she thought of Lawrence's life, wending its way through all the hours in his own childhood house, now refurbished and rejuvenated by his own wife and his own child, but what she recognized in that image was predictability. His life, to a degree, *was* predictable, but, after all, predictability can be a comfort; once they had longed for it. Twenty years ago, though, the final arrangement of their lives had been open-ended. Perhaps it was a maudlin indulgence now to bemoan this apparent finality; perhaps it was arrogance to believe things were settled; perhaps it was tempting fate. And yet they both were convinced of the truth of it. The events that might astonish them now—the only things that could not be foreseen—were the *unpleasant* surprises.

Lawrence offered to get her another drink, and even though she had finished eating, and they could have gone home, she nodded. She was too tired to go home to the house that would be entirely empty, because in the uninhabited rooms her ragged sensibilities would overtake her. She sat in the booth waiting for Lawrence and subsided warily into nostalgia. She knew that tonight she was unusually susceptible to a yearning for the past, a yearning to be without responsibility, and she went on longing for it even though she knew it had never existed for her. Her life had always been more complicated than that.

On the weekends, when Dinah was fifteen or sixteen, it wasn't uncommon for her friends to gather at her house and spend the day in her room, sitting cross-legged on the floor discussing that night's dates with an edge of protective scorn in their voices. An awkward moment could develop if any girl made it clear to the rest of them how much all this might matter to her, how much she might care about some boy. They gathered at Dinah's because no limits were put on their behavior there. The girls could sit and light each other's cigarettes one off the other, in a jaded and sophisticated manner. If they slept over, there was no curfew to obey; no one noticed if they came in drunk or disarrayed. They were treated dangerously like adults. Polly was simply uninterested, for the most part. She wandered around the house, halfheartedly doing one thing or another. Generally she spent the weekends stretched out on the long chaise in her bedroom, reading.

But Dinah did remember one afternoon, when Polly had knocked on the bedroom door and entered with a silver tray of delicately made triangular sandwiches, carefully trimmed of crusts, and glasses of iced tea with mint in it. She passed these around to all the girls, then sat among them eating, too, and her face had about it that fey, abstracted look that was, in fact, enchanting. One wanted to pull toward oneself the fine and gossamer attention that was so seldom captured. The girls regaled her with more and more daring, more intimate stories of their lives. Polly exclaimed and nodded and smiled dreamily. Dinah thought, now, that she and her friends—who had they been, those girls?—had been alert to Polly's air of lazy reverie because she remained so mysterious. If Polly had some secret, that had been a moment she might reveal it. She *had* said, all of a sudden that afternoon, and right into the conversation the girls were carrying on, "You know," with an imploring gesture—listen with pity, she signified—"I think the very best thing about dates . . . oh, at Wellesley and even at Emma Willard when we were allowed out . . . the most wonderful part of it all was the endless . . . *preparation*. It was so lovely," she had gone on, "to be getting ready! It could take days, you know. Planning what to wear, what to say. Would we have a wonderful time? Would it be awful? And the worst—would it be dull?"

The girls in Dinah's bedroom, and Dinah herself, gazed at Polly and saw her beauty and excitement as it must have been. So much had she transformed herself into that same anticipatory girl that when she was gone from the room they were left to look ahead to their own evenings with less hope. Their own expectations seemed flatter, less animate, by comparison to all the things Polly had once felt were ahead of her.

But now that Dinah remembered it, she thought that Polly had been right. In the late afternoon all the girls—whoever happened to be around—would get into one of their cars and go out for hamburgers somewhere, all of them with their hair wound on pastel plastic rollers and their bangs and side curls molded into place and plastered to their skin with Scotch tape. Each girl tied a silky scarf over her rollers, so that Dr. Briggs said that from the rear a car full of them looked like a bunch of balloons. "Why don't you just all grow up to be hairdressers?" he asked. He was elaborately, flatteringly disdainful of the effort they took on behalf of beauty. He would talk about the natural beauty of unadorned youth. He was very charming. He didn't want them to waste their time, and the implication there, of course, was that their time was valuable. If Polly happened into the room during one of these bantering little lectures, she would only smile with a touch of derision.

When all the girls were in the car together at the Monument Drive-In, where they ordered their dinner from one of the microphones at each parking place, those girls felt their own power. The boys cruising around and around in their cars could see that *these* girls were not available to anyone but those they chose to see. Their elaborate, cocooned heads in their colored scarves were signals of their desirability. They had to hurry. They needed their hamburgers, their french fries, and their lemon Cokes right away. They had to hurry, because they had to go right home and get dressed.

But when their dates arrived, the boys were usually kept waiting while the girls had one last cigarette, settled back on Dinah's bed, or changed clothes once again—swapping a skirt or a blouse; they traded off with one another. Finally, they did leave, but they went off into the evening with a faint air of regret.

When Isobel was home, the tempo changed. She would be seeing Buddy; she was eager to get away. She dressed in a flash and never did more than brush her straight thick hair back and secure it with a tortoiseshell barrette or a plain ribbon. She had no patience with the knowing, leisurely, confidential atmosphere of Dinah's bedroom full of girls. In fact, she hardly ever joined them there; she usually dressed next door at her own house, but she would sometimes come over to wait for Buddy and smoke a cigarette. She was like a needle, slipping in and out of the room, putting on lipstick, teasing Dinah's father, or drawing Polly into animated conversation.

"Oh, I'm getting married tonight, Dr. Briggs. I'm eloping."

"Then I'll greet you in the morning as a daughter-in-law, I guess," he would say. Not really taking up the game, since it wasn't especially amusing, but catering to Isobel because he admired her so. She had gone away to school; she was planning on a career—many of them. She was getting out into the world. He had never understood his own children's reluctance to leave home, to go to a *good* school, nor had they. They had only known not to leave these two parents together; they knew it would be perilous to leave them isolated in this house by themselves with no go-between. Buddy and Dinah had never said this to each other; each of them had instinctively come to feel this, independently of the other.

Dinah sat looking around Snow's and remembered Isobel's influence in her life; she remembered the envy she had felt for Isobel's possession of dull and predictable parents, and she also saw that even Isobel had been young and fatuous, simply on a different level. For a long time Dinah had been made miserable by the idea that Isobel could so easily command more of her mother's attention, her father's approval, and her brother's affection than Dinah could attain through a sustained and everlasting effort. It was still true, and it was still painful.

Her father had never attempted to hide his admiration for Isobel. She had always been able to amuse him in a way that Dinah could not, and would not have been able even to attempt. In fact, it was Dinah's father around whom the girls, their dates, the gossip, the latest news, all orbited. He was exotic. The things he deplored! All the things he wanted them to know!

"You girls, you girls! Don't give up your lives to these boys. Use your *minds!*"

They were so interested to hear this exhortation. They were so vain, and they had an insatiable craving for their own reflections thrown back at them through someone else's eyes. When their dates arrived, the boys sat with Dr. Briggs to wait for whomever it was they had come to get, and they sat there intimidated. Dinah's father would sit in his study sipping a drink, leaning back in his chair, casually dressed on the weekends, but impeccable in chino pants and Sperry Top-Siders—"I grew fond of them in med school, in the operating room. If there was much blood on the tile, they would always keep you from slipping." He would explain how the treads were minutely cross-hatched. He would sit in his house and gently harass these vulnerable young men; he would whittle away at them with a mild, sardonic tone. "But Nixon? You ought to look at his face when he speaks. What do you *really* think?" He would lean back in contemplation. He would try to pin them down in other ways. What did they think, he wanted to know. "Now, take God. Whichever one"—and he would wave his hand to suggest their choices—"do you think He's up in the heavens with his tally sheet? Right this minute?" What could they say, these young Republican Methodists and Episcopalians? They had never thought anything through in their lives, and they met his inviting smile apprehensively. They stammered out and grappled with the few ideas in which they thought they had invested. In the end, of course, all the girls could see that none of these boys was in any way superior.

Dinah looked across the table at Lawrence. He had spent hours in that study. Over the years he must have developed a certain leeriness of her father; he could be a terrible man. "Was my father . . . well"—she wasn't sure exactly what she meant to ask him—"what did you think of him?"

Lawrence looked straight at her, but she could see that he was embarrassed, and it surprised her. "I tell you, Dinah," he began, rather ponderously, and Dinah wondered if she really cared what he thought of her father one way or another, "I guess that in spite of the whole mess I really do feel sorry for him." He seemed to think that this was a magnanimous attitude, and Dinah was mystified, but she also realized that they were both getting a little drunk. She peered at Lawrence and bridled at the smug look of pity that he had assumed in relation to her own father. She didn't say anything, however, because she was curious.

"Of course," Lawrence continued, "he hasn't ever been the same since that whole thing out there at the motel, but —well!—it must have been humiliating! I mean, to have been in his position." Lawrence didn't seem dreadfully sorry about it. "I wouldn't have believed it at all, I guess, if my father hadn't been handling the whole business for him. The legal side, anyway. Well, in the end it didn't come to much, but it could have gotten pretty ugly. You know, that man was going to *sue!*" This struck him as incredible, and Dinah just stared at him while she tried to puzzle this out and regain her balance. "Even though he'd already *shot* your dad. He didn't have a permit for that gun, either, so he could have been backed down, I imagine, if it had come to that. No one else *saw* your father at the window, either, so that was a break. But for a while that woman swore she was going to testify. I'll tell you! She was mad! And they probably thought they could collect a bundle. She could have crucified him, of course. Lord, it was a real mess!" Lawrence sipped his beer, and Dinah took a swallow of her drink. She wanted to be very quiet. "She finally just dropped out of the picture," Lawrence said. "The thing was wrangled around so much and went on for so long that she just left town."

Dinah reached across and put her hand on Lawrence's arm before he could raise the beer glass again. She wanted to stop his attention from going in any other direction. "What do you mean, Lawrence?" she said. "Are you saying . . . Do you mean to tell me that that man shot Dad because Dad was looking in the *window?* Now wait . . ." She drew her hand back and laid it palm down on the table. "Do you mean that he was just a *voyeur?*"

Lawrence looked back at her blankly, due in part to the amount of beer he'd drunk and in part to real surprise. "Well, yeah"—his voice inflected upward in puzzled apology. "What did *you* think he was shot for?"

"God, Lawrence." She could only make a vague gesture and smile at him without any meaning or intention in the world. "I never thought it out, I guess. No one said. It was all so mysterious that I thought it was something much more . . . well, I just thought it would be something more than that."

Dinah had traveled the route between Enfield and Fort Lyman well over three thousand times in her life. The road was imprinted on her nervous system, every hill, every sudden turn and dip, and the final long, upward climb, the shifting down of gears, had always been a moment to assemble herself in one way or another. When she was young, and if she had been to town with a date, it was the moment to be sure her blouse was tucked in neatly, and to put on fresh lipstick. This is what girls did then: they perched on the edge of the car seat and turned the rearview mirror so that it would reflect their own face, and they would dart a small, flip, conspiratorial smile at whatever boy had made this repair necessary. With one sure sweep— if this was a popular girl, sure of herself—she would repaint her mouth and give that same boy one more arch look as she dropped the lipstick back into her purse. It was one of many small ways of making a kind of claim. Dinah had done it many times on this same drive.

These days she usually made this trip with children in the car; she ferried them back and forth. When she shifted into low to begin the winding, wooded ascent to the village of Enfield, she called orders back to them. She told them to get their bathing suits and sandals together, or to throw away the sticky stems of the lollipops they had been given at the bank—"in the ashtray!" She got them settled apart from each other, with their belongings collected so that she could drop them at their separate houses without too much rearranging.

Tonight, though, she remained slumped against the car seat while Lawrence drove the car up that same hill. She was engaged in frenetic reassessments, and yet she was so weary that she couldn't get anything sorted out. All of a sudden she felt a little as though her history had come unstuck. She kept thinking of an aunt she had visited now and then as a child, and of whom she had always believed she was very fond. This woman would invariably stoop down, upon catching her first glimpse of Dinah after a long interval, and say to her, "Oh, Dinah! How lovely to see you! Why, I've know you since you were a baby!" That had been the most seductive of all assertions. Dinah thought that those words alone must have convinced her of her affection for that woman. Dinah was very sad tonight, and she supposed, tiredly, that the gratification she had felt upon hearing that she had been known since she was born was no more than another example of the endless racketing around of the ego in constant search of recognition.

When Lawrence parked his car in front of the Hortons' house, Dinah simply didn't respond. She only sat there, delaying the moment when she must move, until he got out of the car and came around to open her door for her. She assumed he would do that, if she sat there long enough, despite whatever progress had been made in Enfield regarding equality between the sexes. But he sat on, too, behind the steering wheel, and they didn't say anything to each other for a while.

"You know," Lawrence said at last, and with rather a slowing of his speech, "I always thought you and I would get married. I mean, when we were growing up." This was only a statement; it didn't have the sound of any sort of plea. "And then, when I didn't marry you, I thought you wouldn't get married at all, the way your father felt about it. But when you finally did marry Martin, I thought, 'Well, Dinah and I know each other so well. We could always make love. It wouldn't matter where we met or how old we got. Even if we were walking down a street in some city and just happened to pass by each other by accident, we could still go off to bed together and never feel strange about it. We've known each other for so long!' "

He was still sitting away from her on his side of the car behind the wheel, and she was awfully glad he hadn't moved over to her or even reached out a hand to touch her. When she cast her eye over the dark house where no one was waiting for her, she was tempted to take Lawrence inside with her. All those early-morning hours they had spent drinking coffee in the heat and talking quietly must have been leading up to something. She knew that they had both believed that it *was* leading up to something. They had been on the edge of this all summer, but she wondered now what Lawrence really hoped for. He knew that Martin was in close proximity now; why hadn't he approached her sooner? Why hadn't she made the invitation clearer? Perhaps he had only meant to stay there, on the verge of something. She thought that must have been her *own* intention, but nothing that came to her tired mind right now was articulate enough to prevent her from doing whatever she wanted to do most, and she just sat there a moment, considering. She looked again at the Hortons' house, which tonight seemed more than ever to belong to strangers, and she spoke before she knew what she was going to say.

"You know what, Lawrence? I think I want to get David and Sarah from your house and put them to sleep in their own beds."

He looked at her to see if she meant it. Not much weight had ridden on his vague and hesitant proposition; they *did* know each other well enough so that there wasn't any embarrassment between them, but he didn't approve at all of this plan. "That's silly, Dinah! You'll just wake them up. They're perfectly comfortable. In fact, they were delighted to be able to sleep in sleeping bags."

"Oh, I know that. But it won't bother them all that much if I get them up. I won't be going back to the hospital until Toby's had his breakfast and Martin's seen Dr. Van Helder, so they can sleep late. I won't be leaving until sometime after ten."

They retrieved Dinah's children. Pam didn't protest at all, and she seemed even to have expected them. She had David's and Sarah's belongings gathered together in a shopping bag all ready to be taken along. At the Hortons', Lawrence carried Sarah upstairs to her room; she was sound asleep. David had awakened, and he made his own way to bed. When the children were settled, Lawrence gave Dinah a quick kiss on the cheek and took his leave.

Dinah changed her clothes and went to her bedroom and lay in bed in her gown and heavy robe. The rain had stopped earlier, but the cool damp air lingered on. There were no lights in her father's house across the way, and she stared out the window at the quiet street, which was gently illuminated by the streetlights as they beamed down in rainbow circles through the mist. Here she came every summer, back to this town where everyone said they had known her all her life. It seemed reasonable that among those people she would find peace and security. But she was thinking of Martin when he had first come into the hospital that evening and asked Toby how he was feeling.

"Oh, I don't know," Toby had said, as Martin had hugged him in greeting. Toby had turned his head away slightly, with a smile.

Almost at once, Martin had turned to Dinah, even before he had given her a quick embrace, and said with pleasure, "He looked so much like you, just then." He had said that with a voice full of delight and a smug satisfaction. She had been absorbed by other things then, but now Dinah was overwhelmed in the dark, thinking about it. All at once, she felt that the only people she *did* know, and the only people who had, in fact, known her all her life, were Martin and her own three children.

CHAPTER TWELVE

TAKING LEAVE

Dinah and Martin didn't get to spend a night together until Toby was out of the hospital, because in spite of the assurances of everyone on the Pediatrics floor that Toby would be perfectly well looked after, his parents didn't believe it for a minute. There was never any question in their minds that they should be there. They had noticed that the hospital was an unhealthy place for sick people, and especially for children and old people, who weren't listened to and couldn't fend for themselves. The nurses crept in at night, meaning to administer a shot to Toby without awakening him first and giving him a warning. Dinah knew they thought he would cause them more trouble awake than asleep, although she had noticed with a pathetic and mis-directed pride that on Toby's chart, which was clipped to the door, he was checked off as a "good" patient. Toby was a stoic patient; he didn't argue with whatever he realized was inevitable. But Dinah insisted they wake him, and Martin was even angrier at such a self-serving trick on the part of those very tired nurses.

The two of them did leave him alone for an hour or so during his lunch while they went together to the snack bar to get sandwiches and drinks from the machines. But for five days they saw each other only in the company of other people. They unwrapped their sandwiches at one of the round white plastic tables in the concession area and sat trying to make conversation. There was no lack of tenderness between them, and there was no more irritation, but they had scarcely even touched each other, and it was a little as though they were still speaking over a distance of a thousand miles on the phone. They were very polite and fond and considerate, and that was all they could be.

Toby was not terribly ill, and so he had become restless and querulous. He was homesick and made to feel lonely, since no matter which parent was with him, *he* was the only one subject to the imperiousness of the regimental order of the hospital. He was still in the hospital now just to keep him entirely off his leg. The IV had been removed the morning of the second day of his stay, and the reason for his ever having had it was entirely too vague from Dinah's point of view. But she didn't argue with anyone. She didn't intend to alienate Toby's doctor. After all, Toby was entirely in his power.

Toby had recovered from his flu, although at home Sarah and David both came down with it simultaneously. This made for an exhausting and demoralizing several days for Martin and Dinah. There was no real rest to be had at the hospital, because one always had to be on guard against the bureaucracy. And at home there was no leisure at all. When the other two children were not actively sick, either Dinah or Martin had to make an attempt to beat back the disorder that built up when their normal routine was so violently interrupted. Laundry, dishes, shopping, garbage. But the two of them got through those tiresome days without any keenness of mind. It was a good thing to be a trifle anesthetized; they didn't fall into the frenzied irritability that might have overtaken them. By the time Toby came home, the household was relatively serene, and the weather had hit that wonderful spate of glory before the days begin seriously to promise the coming of fall. The sun shone all day, but the humidity was so low that Dinah's hair crackled when she brushed it, and the temperature stayed in the seventies. It was the best weather possible; it was the weather that, in the deepest part of winter, Dinah always remembered as the essence of summer.

When Martin brought Toby back to Enfield after lunch one day for his first evening at home, the late afternoon was very nice, in part because they prized this familial euphoria that couldn't last. David and Sarah had made signs to hang on the door, welcoming Toby, and for that first evening the three children were so glad to have normalcy restored that Toby's celebrity was acceptable enough.

Martin and Dinah exchanged glances now and then, because they knew that in the next week various resentments and jealousies would break out. But each of them found it pleasant to be a benevolent conspirator once again; they were so glad to find themselves realigned.

Toby had to be carried wherever he went, until his hip improved. Martin placed him on the chaise longue outside on the grass, under the trees, and he was content while the rest of the family went about their business. The sky that had hung low in the summer heat now soared in a cloudless pale-blue sphere so high above them that the lush lawns of Enfield looked blue-green, and the green leaves of the trees and shrubs, thoroughly washed by several days of rain, glistened blackly. The buildings, too, were washed clean, and in the clarified air their precision of line arrested the eye. The atmosphere was pure and sweet. Toby sat quietly on his lawn chair, almost drowsy from the wash of fresh air.

Martin was grilling hamburgers for dinner, and Dinah was in and out of the house with plates and salad. She was boiling water on the stove for corn on the cob. Sarah and David sat beside Toby for a while, talking with him with a rather unctuous kindness; they meant well. They had missed their brother, but the novelty of exhibiting such ostentatious goodwill soon wore off, and David went to ride his bike with some other boys on the street, while Sarah rode her Big Wheels up and down the sidewalk in front of the house. Toby seemed glad to be able to sit quietly, and Dinah noticed that in just five days he had lost weight and developed shadows under his eyes. She knew that in the next few weeks his temporary decrepitude would turn into crankiness while his body devoted its full energy to restoration.

She knew she would find herself having to remember that he was in some pain in order to be patient with him, but this evening everything contributed to their communal but quiet exhilaration. They had a lovely meal out under the trees; the clear air that had moved over the region had absolved them personally, it seemed, from the pressure of their own anxieties.

When the children were in bed, Dinah and Martin sat up drinking wine in the study, with the television turned on to the news, which Martin was watching alertly, leaning slightly forward toward the screen. Dinah meant to attend to it; she would have liked to move from all the immediate concerns that kept her poor brain busy with a circling around of reassessments and reevaluations, but tonight she couldn't redirect her attention. Now that she was un-occupied with dinner and the children, she was repossessed by all her minute and petty worries. She longed for them to evaporate.

Martin, on the other hand, was uncomfortable with his own absorption in these events he watched with depressing fascination. The short evening with his family had held him fast in the moment, but now his thoughts soared again, bounding out into the terrifying universe. Even in the hospital with Toby, he had kept careful track of current events; his summer fears had not been allayed. Tonight, both Dinah and Martin were too tired to rechannel the currents of their thinking. They had no choice but to be washed along with their separate thoughts.

But later, when they finally settled themselves in the same bed, they were both made easier by their instinctive inclination to turn toward the other. Each one had expected that the other would be too tired to make love. In fact, they made love with a gentle and slow pleasure, because their energy was not great. Their passion was not ragged or in-sistent, and Dinah was glad that her body was allowing her this great enjoyment; she wasn't hindered by vanity and self-evaluation; she was not being judged. The two of them were such good and comfortable partners; their instincts were always reliable, so that they lay in bed after making love, satisfied and no longer needful in any way, for the time being. Dinah was thinking that sex can be the sweetest, kindest way finally to overcome reticence. They both felt at ease at last, and in the morning they were fond and affectionate with each other and with the children. Their physical isolation from the other had made them forget how to be familiar, and now they remembered.

The Howells' summer residence became a way station of sorts now that Toby was immobile and required attention, if not for his own sake, then for the sake of social custom. The weather held in its clear, translucent beneficence, and the doors stayed open all day. People came and went with such frequency that it was soon a habit—to drop in, to have some coffee, to chat with Toby and lean against the walls talking with whoever else came by. The days after Toby's homecoming took on the quality of a running celebration.

Isobel was a great treat. She was most beguiling in her role as Toby's godmother, and she brought great style to the playing out of it. Dinah thought this was unusually generous, because Isobel wasn't particularly interested in, and certainly was not entranced by, children. She seemed to like Dinah's children, but Dinah had already found out that it really isn't possible for most people to be devoted to any children but their own. Isobel made a good job of whatever attachment she did feel. She arrived daily with treats and presents; she whirled in and out, but the children had the impression, because of her intense charm, that she spent a great deal of time with them. One day she brought sacks tied with ribbon—one for each child—filled with every imaginable forbidden fruit of her own and Dinah's childhood. There were handfuls of bubble gum, whistles, harmonicas, jujubes and malt balls, grotesque wax lips and teeth that could be either worn or chewed for their sickly-sweet flavoring. She had even found some castanets, which she and Dinah had longed for, and which were sold, for some reason, at the Fort Lyman Trailways bus station along with other Mexican souvenirs—hammered metal ashtrays, beaded belts, and so forth. She had packed Slinkys in each sack, and Silly Putty. Dinah was just as pleased as the children for a while; she was flattered that Isobel remembered these things, too.

One afternoon Isobel brought Toby a magnificent marionette, and she spent longer than usual with him, explaining the working of it, but it was so intricate that as soon as she left, it became hopelessly tangled, and several days later Dinah cut off all the strings and gave it back to Toby to use as a jointed wooden doll.

Isobel was irresistible, but when she took her leave the children were left with an expectation of even more excitement, more stimulating and inventive ideas and diversions. They retained a jagged feeling of anticipation that couldn't be satisfied. Of all the guests, Pam was the best. She knew exactly what would be the most useful entertainment for Toby. She never brought dramatic gifts; in fact, she never brought gifts at all. But she arrived most afternoons, just in the nick of time, when Dinah and Martin's good intentions of the morning were showing themselves to be impracticable. She came calmly into the house, trailed by her son, Mark, who was a docile little boy, and settled down with all the children to devote two hours or so to playing with them. She would come in and play a game of Sorry, or help them put together a jigsaw puzzle, and this was the most therapeutic sort of kindness—extended to the whole family, really. It gave Dinah and Martin a respite, and they had regained their good nature by the time she left.

With all this, though, Dinah was bothered by the fact that she was not fonder of Pam. Pam possessed such a genuine charity of intention, and yet Dinah only admired her. Dinah puzzled over this and finally came to a hesitant conclusion. She decided that it was because she could never possess even a trifle of Pam. In little ways, it seemed to Dinah, people need to cling to each other, and Pam, in her self-possession and perfect assurance, didn't offer a hand-hold. When Dinah proffered a little of herself—"I can't stand the children another minute! Lord, I need an hour!" —she really meant to be presented with some desperation of Pam's in return. But Pam would say, "Of course you do, Dinah. Look, why don't I take all the kids to get an ice-cream cone." Then Dinah would feel unworthy of being the mother of her own children, and she would spend those free moments lurking in the kitchen, not pleasantly, eating something unhealthy, and being no less irritable when the children were returned. It came down to the fact that Pam needed nothing from Dinah, nothing at all. If there had been any aid to Pam that Dinah could have supplied, she might have liked Pam very much.

One afternoon Dinah's father rang the bell, although the door stood open. He had not been a visitor since Toby's return, so he didn't enter casually. He had done no more than briefly speak to Martin and shake hands with him in a formal greeting in one of the times they had passed in the village. Dinah let him in, and he was accompanied by one of the many workmen who loitered about his yard digging idly at a plant here or there. The man was carrying a sizable box, and Dr. Briggs asked Dinah if she would mind calling the other two children into the house.

They all gathered in the small study where Toby spent his days lying on the couch, watching television or looking out the window at the pale sky. Martin and Dinah hung back at the doorway, because neither of them felt that they had been invited in. Dr. Briggs opened the box with elaborate and dramatic heedfulness; inside were three Siamese kittens, who cocked their batlike ears and began bleating in their piercing voices the moment they perceived a crack of light. The children were awed and surprisingly quiet.

"Now, Toby gets first choice, since this is what I had planned for his birthday present," her father said, and Dinah watched with an immense welling-up of ill-defined sorrow when he lifted each cat from the high-sided box with such caution. Their legs straggled over the large palm of his hand, because they had reached that ugly-duckling stage through which Siamese cats pass before they become their sinuous, swanlike selves. His affection for these animals was so apparent that the children caught on to it right away. They reached out to pet the kittens, but they didn't pick them up. Dinah remembered all the cats her family had had over the years, dozens of cats trailing through Polly's house, sitting on windowsills, and she remembered, of course, Jimmy, the most recent Briggs's cat. All at once, too, she remembered her father saying on some occasion during her childhood, "It was the hardest part of medical school—those experiments on cats. You see, they had all been done before a thousand times. We all knew there was no reason for them. There's great contempt for cats, you know."

The kittens stalked tentatively across the couch, where her father had put them, and they glanced around fearfully with their protruding blue eyes. The three children were familiar enough with animals so that they still knew not to pick them up.

"I want that one. That tall one," Toby said, in a voice of command that he had recently developed and that was grating, but that was probably the result of being expected to infuse eternal gratitude into his every exchange with well-wishers and visitors. He had come to know how much people needed in return for small favors. Nevertheless, Dinah didn't forgive him immediately for this transgression, though she kept quiet about it for the time being.

"Well, you go on and pick, Sarah," David said, standing away from the others; his encroaching adolescence caused him many complications lately. "I don't care which one I have, but I do want to call mine Jimmy, so I want to have a boy."

Dinah felt immense gratitude toward her son for this gesture. She was delighted with him. Once again, of course, she remained entirely still, as though she was not part of this occasion—indeed, she was not. Her father turned to David with pleased surprise, although it was likely he had expected some such homage, but he would have expected it from Toby. Dinah was briefly sorry for Toby in his naïve and insensitive youth. His stoicism had made him seem so much older than he was, but now he had resumed his social age.

Martin was as moved by this tableau as Dinah was. The state of disquietude that encased him these days like a transparent wrap was rent apart by this little scene as though his black anxiety had been speared by a shard of glass. When Dinah suggested that the three of them sit out in the yard and leave the children alone with the kittens, Martin followed along absently; he was thinking he might like to talk to this man at some length. He imagined that Dinah's father must have some of the answers or solutions to all the questions that unsettled him.

When Martin had first met Dinah's family, he had not been at an especially contemplative age. He had arrived in the Midwest expecting that he would like her parents; he hadn't listened with great care when she had talked about them. Any nuances that were there to be caught had passed him by. In fact, it hadn't mattered much to him *what* he thought of them, and so, when he met them, he had simply acknowledged to himself that they were nice and intelligent and attractive people. But being intellectually undemonstrative, he had been hugely uncomfortable when Dinah's father would settle himself in his library and attempt to engage Martin in the elaborate wordplay he so enjoyed. Dr. Briggs relished philosophical disagreement, and Martin had noticed that he would argue either side of a proposition, depending upon the persuasion of his adversary.

Martin had been unnerved by Dinah's father, and he remembered one incident very clearly. He had thought of it often, and even upon reexamination he could not see what had been required of him, and what he should have done.

"They're making great strides in the understanding of human nature through the study of dolphins," Dr. Briggs had suddenly announced to Martin over the top of a newspaper one evening while they sat together in the library when Dinah was late coming down.

"Is that right?" Martin said.

"What do you think of that?" Dr. Briggs had asked him then, insistently, leaning forward to point a finger at him.

"Well, I don't know. I don't really think anything much about it. I don't know anything about it at all." In those days Martin enjoyed the innocent cockiness of bright graduate students.

At first, Dr. Briggs leaned his head back as though this were an affront, but then he launched into an imperative discourse on dolphins, their language, their songs, the size of their brains, their intelligence, etc. "Now, imagine this," he had said, spreading his hands, "here are all these young men—brilliant scientists—standing around these great glassed-in tanks. Or maybe they stand on a cement apron, peering down into an enclosed marina. They monitor every little thing about those dolphins, you see, in hopes of finding out why New York City has become dangerous at night, or maybe they will find a cure for melancholia—well! The possibilities! They have such machines! They take every measurement. Heartbeat, pulse rate, well . . . Now, here are all these young men, with their brittle elbows and bony knees hidden inside their crisp white lab coats, watching every move made by those sleek, slippery animals. They move without effort, you know, in the water," he said in an aside, very softly. "Of course, the animals are aware they're being watched; in fact, they rarely mate in those conditions. Who could blame them?" He smiled bleakly. "Those men are very serious about the whole thing, with their pads and recorders and their pasty, dull faces." He looked at Martin very long, seeking collaboration, then, of some opinion he had drawn about all this, but Martin was taken aback, and since he was mostly just waiting for Dinah, he simply nodded.

"Well?" Dr. Briggs had suddenly become brusque and gotten up from his chair all at once. "Suppose those *dolphins* are studying those very clever young men?" he said with a persistent rage, and started toward the library door. "We'll look to be a sorry species, won't we?" He left Martin alone in the room, because clearly Martin had not been a worthy conversationalist. Martin had concluded then, not profoundly, that Dinah's father was an angry man. Eventually, Dr. Briggs's anger had become so large, and his disapproval so all-encompassing, that he and Dinah stayed apart. Dinah had drawn away to protect herself, Martin had always thought.

Now Martin saw that Dinah and her father had come to some sort of reconciliation, and he was pleased; he thought this might make Dinah's life more pleasant. In fact, she wouldn't have to think so often about her father at all; she could let it rest. Right now, however, Martin wanted some word from Dr. Briggs, whose intelligence Martin had always considered eccentric, but which he now perceived—in his own new state of revelation—to be incisive. Martin had the feeling that he could broach any subject at all with him and be taken seriously.

Dinah and Martin and Dr. Briggs went through the kitchen and out the back door to sit in the yard. The flowers had waned and dropped their heads, but now that the air was so mild the heavy scent of decay was not trapped over the garden. The season was ending, but all the foliage was still intensely green.

Dinah brought out wine and cheese and crackers, and the three of them sat in a triangle around the low metal table on which she placed the tray.

"The kittens were the nicest thing you could have done, Dad," she said. "It was very smart of you to get three, and not just one for Toby." She seemed maudlin, Martin thought, almost teary.

"They won't really belong to anybody, you know. Those cats won't be owned by any of the children," her father pointed out, matter-of-factly. Any idea of sentiment seemed to have left him. Dinah looked up quickly, and then her mood changed, too, and she laughed. "Oh, yes, they will. As much as cats do belong to people, they'll belong to me! Litter box, cat food, and all! I'm pretty sure of that."

Her father gravely sipped his wine and nodded.

"You know," Martin said to him, "did you ever see patients who you knew would never improve? Well, I mean, just suppose they perceive *ultimate* hopelessness." Martin spoke in a soft and pleasant voice, without any timbre of desperation to it, but Dinah watched him with surprised curiosity. "Suppose they *were* able to comprehend the universe—and beyond that, too. Well, what becomes of those people?"

Now Dinah was suddenly wary for her husband, and she was hurt. He could have asked me first, she thought. But his face was open and vulnerable. Her father laughed shortly and leaned back so that he could turn in his stiff way to look at Martin directly. "Well," he said, "you know how to tell the difference between the patients and the doctors in any asylum, don't you?"

Martin shook his head, annoyed at what seemed to be an insider's joke, a med student's grisly riddle. His attention began to wander again, until Dr. Briggs leaned forward with his hands on his knees. "The doctors are the ones who are *talking! They* ask all the questions!" he said with startling vehemence. "The patients, you see, already *know!*"

Dinah looked at her husband to see that he was absolutely stricken, as though he had no breath. She was infuriated with these two men; she was far too irritated to stay in their company. She wouldn't have helped out either one, at the moment. "I'm going in to check on the kittens," she said, "and set up the cat box." She had heard her father tell this little tale time and again, with the same attempt at drama, and at last he had found his audience. She went back to the house as agitated and angry now as she had been sympathetic and soothed a short while ago. She had thought that, if nothing else, her father could never be accused of hypocrisy. But there he sat, in the beautiful day, embracing and encouraging a bitterly luxurious nihilism, when he disproved it himself by being as subject as the next man to the sordid, paltry, futile pleasure-seeking of the human race. Whatever pose it assumed, that search for the gratification of some desire at least bespoke hopefulness, hopefulness at its lowest point.

Toby's birthday party was held the day before the Howells left Enfield for the summer, so it was intended as a goodbye party as well, but Toby clung to the idea of its being his celebration, much to the dismay of David and Sarah. They were tired of Toby's illness, and they didn't entirely believe in it anymore, since they couldn't see anything wrong, even though Toby was still not allowed to walk very much on his own and often had to be carried. Dinah had never been inside her father's new house, and she was impressed but unaffected by the beautiful rooms. She was glad it was a pretty house and so handsomely fitted out, but this was the house of her father, and she was ill at ease that there was nothing of her childhood there. She stared into the long living room, and her eye took in the lovely dark floors and white woven carpets. Her mother had done this, of course; she had decorated this house, and it suited the client. The lines of the furniture were tall and clean and spare. Books were everywhere, and the colors were absolute—not beige, but heavy tan walls, for instance, the color of grocery bags. The woodwork in the house was a brittle, glossy white. They moved past the living room and dining room to the kitchen at the back of the house.

Dinah and Martin had spent the week packing, and Martin was still distracted and inattentive to details. Dinah felt compelled, each summer, to leave the Hortons' house in the same good order in which she found it, but this year Martin had not been at all exact about the replacement of the Hortons' objects which he and Dinah had put away for the summer. She had taken on the house this time, and left him to do the packing of the car, which he went about with an irritating and melancholy slowness. But when they crossed the street to attend this celebration, everything was ready; and Dinah and the three children were in that tiresome state of simultaneous regret and anticipation at the idea of leaving.

Martin carried Toby across the street and into the house, where he put him down on a couch in a beautiful brick-floored room that Polly had designed and Dr. Briggs had built out from the kitchen. A long, narrow, white-tiled counter separated the cooking area from this retreat, where the family and Pam and Lawrence were all gathered. Dinah's father was fixing drinks there, and all along the spotless white surface were meticulously arranged trays and plates of crudités and hors d'oeuvres. Dinah was surprised at all the trouble her father had taken, and she thanked him for it when he handed her a drink with a slight Old World flourish of courtliness. But the children almost immediately grew uneasy and whiny when they sensed the formality and intention of the setting. Dinah tried to put together plates of things she thought they might eat from this exotic collection, and by looking balefully at them on the sly, she tried to instill in them the proper sense of gratitude, but she didn't think it boded well, all this lovely elegance.

She supplied Toby with a plate of smoked salmon, tiny Norwegian sardines, and various sizes of crackers. She spread each cracker with the parsley-flecked mayonnaise her father had made himself. "Well, you *like* fish," she said when Toby sullenly fingered the food on his plate.

Buddy and Isobel were both there, but they seemed less a couple in her father's presence. In fact, Isobel was somewhat stark in her attitude of bristling independence. Her determination hardened her features almost past beauty. Buddy joked with Sarah and David, who gravitated toward him as always. Martin meant to be polite, and he fixed his drink and moved around the room talking to everyone and then sat down alone, just looking tired.

Dinah began to move across the room to go and talk to Polly, who in these surroundings had no more impact than a child of Sarah's age. When Dinah had caught sight of her across the room, she was very nearly alarmed by the ineffectualness of her mother's bearing. It seemed to Dinah that her mother looked afraid. But Lawrence reached out a long arm and detained Dinah with a great hug around her waist and a kiss on her cheek. Pam smiled at him placidly, and Dinah knew that he had had several drinks—she and her family had been caught up in last-minute packing and had arrived about an hour late. Suddenly Isobel was there, too, almost incandescent with the energy of her odd, high-strung restlessness.

"Ah, Dinah!" she said. "You're not buying *that*, are you? That's the jogger's hug, you know. The crunchy-granola, health-food hug!" She moved around their small group gracefully, but she ended up at its center. "Now, in the office we call that the 'it's-perfectly-healthy-to-have-a-quick-lay-with-someone-you-trust' hug. You have to beware of those, Dinah!" Only Isobel could say these things, because her pointed face took on a smile of self-mockery. There was nothing that could not become a source of amusement for Isobel. Parties were her métier, and she could move from group to group, rustling through their conversations like an unexpected breeze. She would move on to the next group, having made an impression, having unsettled the people she left, unpleasantly or not. But Dinah looked at Isobel this afternoon with rare discernment. Old friends are just like creatures from dreams. They are so elusive because they are made up of memory that isn't always reminiscent of reality but only of one's past ambitions, hopes, and necessities. Dinah could look and look at Isobel, and still she would not quite know the essence of what she meant to find.

Dinah hugged Lawrence back and leaned over to give Pam a light kiss. "Thank you both for all the help you've been," she said. She didn't pause to banter back and forth with Isobel. Dinah's day of packing had made her too tired to be proficient, right now, at party conversation. Isobel's almost visible outflow of energy heightened the pitch of the party, but it affected Dinah no more than the buzzing of a gnat. For once, Dinah, in Isobel's presence, was the final arbiter of her own behavior.

Dinah came up to Polly and stood beside her, and Polly turned and gestured around the beautifully laid-out room. Her face was tense and silvery in the light. "Now isn't this lovely?" she said earnestly. "You see how the intense color washes out toward this end of the room. You see, I didn't want anything to compete with the garden. What a lovely room! It always surprises me." However, Polly wasn't looking at the room, she was facing the garden, which hadn't many blooms left. "I can *make* these places. You know, I'm really talented at putting these rooms together. I have a client in Columbus, now . . . well, I wish you could see the house. It would have been so ordinary. I can *design* beautiful places, but I can't live in them." She said this in a soft, puzzled voice. "I've often thought that if your father had married someone else . . . if I could have been different. Well, look at this"—and she swept her arm back to indicate the house, the whole interior—"*I* created it, but I would never be able to . . . serve it well."

Dinah had seen her mother just this sad all too often, and once again she felt she would cry for her mother's despair, but at the same time she resented the spasm of sympathy that shot through her. It was a sickening sensation, approaching nausea. Dinah knew that Polly herself was well aware of her father's ability to make one feel that his failings were one's own fault. It was usually Polly who pointed out that very thing. And who was to judge this, in any case? Dinah would always have her grudges on both sides, and she would not try again to bolster her mother's self-esteem. She was caught once more in that double bind of misery on behalf of both parents, but this time there was nothing left for her to say. She stood there beside her mother, looking out the window and considering all the ways their lives could have been different, given this action or that. She could hear David and Sarah making too much noise, and from the corner of her eye she could see them bounding around the room unheeded. Buddy called to them to settle down, but Martin still sat in some trance, oblivious.

"I picked up a cake for Toby at the bakery. Do you think Dad would care if we had it now? It might pacify the children a little," she said to her mother.

Everyone had to stop what they were doing and gather for this ceremony, and they came to Toby where Martin had put him, on the white couch, which commanded a view of the room and the garden. Dinah put the cake, with its candles all lit, on the coffee table in front of him. The adults began to sing along when David and Sarah began "Happy Birthday," but suddenly Toby let out a shriek of pure fury and turned his face against the cushion of the couch. "You stop it, David! You *stop* it!" he said. And Dinah alone knew what had happened; everyone else paused in surprise. David and Sarah had been singing the birthday song they had learned at camp:

Happy Birtle Daytle toodle yoodle,
Happy Birtle Daytle toodle yoodle,
Happy Birtle Daytle toodle yoodle doodle,
Happy Birtle Daytle toodle yoodle.

The two of them clasped each other in giggles, and Dinah, and now Martin, too, were horrified at them.

"We'll start the song over, Toby," Dinah said as sooth-ingly as possible, but she felt the boredom of the adults radiating around the little circle, and it was with forced enthusiasm that they began again. Everyone had had enough to drink so that they didn't want to divert their attention from their party, although they certainly wished Toby well. David and Sarah began the song again:

Happy Birtle Daytle toodle yoodle,
Happy Birtle Daytle toodle yoodle . . .

Toby turned his head once more into the cushions of the soft white couch, sobbing, and then he threw up all the sardines and smoked salmon he had eaten over the space of the afternoon. The party came to an absolute halt, and Martin held David's and Sarah's arms in grips that whitened the skin under his hand. Their faces had gone just as pale.

"Oh, that's too bad, Toby," Pam said, kindly—with such kindness that Dinah felt her chin quiver in tearful gratitude. Everyone else stood silent. "Come on," Pam said, "let's move into the living room. I'll help Dinah get this cleaned up." The whole group was grateful for this suggestion, and Dinah could do no more than signal to Pam, with a motion of waving her off, that she could handle this mess.

She found the paper towels in a cupboard and some sponges underneath the sink, and she set to work trying to rectify the damage. She moved Toby to the other end of the couch—he didn't say anything; he was limp all over—and went about sponging up the stain from the Haitian cotton upholstery with soap and water. She wondered if she could use bleach. *Why* did her father have white furniture? What a thing to have! She believed there was a fearful arrogance in the possession of white furniture. It was such a clear announcement of what was expected of any guest. She went back and forth through the long room to the sink to rinse the sponge she was working with, and she realized that she was crying, with fatigue, she thought. She put the sponge down on the counter finally and poured some wine out for herself. She didn't think she could get the couch any cleaner, and Toby seemed to have fallen sound asleep in the exact position in which she had put him down.

Her father came in to mix more drinks for his guests, and for a minute neither of them said anything. Dinah was sitting on a kitchen stool drinking her wine.

"Is Toby all right?" he asked her. "I'm sorry about that. David and Sarah went outside to play."

Dinah couldn't answer right away; her thoughts were so much wider, just now, than the moment.

"You know," she said at last, "it seems to me that you could have spared us so much pain." She was really almost musing; her voice held a faint note of discovery. "Really, you could have made life so much easier. We suffered so much for your integrity. Buddy and I—we could have had easier lives. Maybe Polly, too." She was all at once anxious to make him know this. "You do such damage! You do such terrible damage!" Even as she said exactly what she meant to say, she was filled with dismay and fear at speaking. Her father went on mixing drinks and placing them on the tray. He didn't turn around to look at her, and she was glad, because tears were slipping down her face again.

"Well . . ." he said slowly, standing still over the full glasses, "I never had anything but the best wishes—all the highest hopes for your life." His own voice was oddly defeated. "But I never thought your life would be easy, Dinah. I knew you were bound to be unhappy. You were always like that. You don't make clear distinctions. Buddy can, but you never could. I think Buddy's life hasn't been so hard." He didn't go on for a minute; he began to fold cocktail napkins into triangles and place them next to the drinks. "But it's not easy, either, to know that you can't love your children the way they want to be loved. You can only love people however you happen to love them. I *did* always know that you weren't happy and that it would be hard for you, but I always thought that you understood that I don't . . . *enjoy* life either. I hoped you'd give me credit for my own misery. And I hoped you'd know that I wished you well."

Her father was still arranging things on the tray, and Dinah looked past him at Toby, who was beginning to stir. She didn't feel tears anymore; she felt still all through herself.

"Oh, Lord, Dad." She was very tired. "Well, no, you're wrong about me. No, my life is very good. Dad, I'm as happy as I *can* be." All her energy had drained away, and if she was to be burdened with pity for her father, she would realize it later. But she knew that her father had just said to her what she would someday long to say to her own children: God knows what cruelties you may have suffered at my hands, but this is how I meant to love you: without reservation. Dinah also knew that there would never be a child who could believe that.

In the morning the air was warmer, and as the Howells drove away from Enfield, the interior of the car was comfortable in the dry heat. Dinah was sitting sideways in the front seat looking past Martin through the windows at the rolling fields, which were now dry and tan and used up. The children were excited and agitated in the back seat, laughing too loudly, so that the fun in the laughter might dissipate in an instant. The three kittens were miaowing pitifully in their travel case under Dinah's feet, but she thought that they would calm down in a little while. Martin looked over at Dinah to see if she was going to settle the children down, but when he realized that she was lost in a sort of pleasurable listlessness, he turned back to the children himself. "Why don't you sing some songs, or something? Or play Going to California. You three take it easy back there!"

"Okay, okay," David answered, in an overexcited tone. "We'll sing!" He began loudly:

Happy Birtle Daytle toodle yoodle . . .

And both parents tensed and came to attention. Dinah looked back to see Toby's face go rigid for one instant, and then he, too, joined the song. They all sang too loudly and with too much vigor—they had a two-day drive ahead—but Martin and Dinah relaxed in the front seat, and went back to thinking their own thoughts. Dinah continued to look out at the countryside, but she could see the children, too, and when she glanced back at them she realized that each one of them might remember this exact moment for the rest of their lives. Each one might always have an image of this leave-taking. It might be profoundly thought of, or it might never cross their minds again. She knew, though, that each child's perception of a moment of his or her history —each unique version of one moment mutually shared— would be the true version. Each one of her children would be able to—would have to—create his or her own separate and individual history, and that was a frightening idea in the warm day. She would have liked to think that she could insure their memories, render them safe and absolute.

Dinah let the passing view fill her mind with its color and variety, and she settled herself comfortably in her corner, easing her thoughts into a gentler territory. The road ran on and on, and she listened to the children's songs and wondered what they were going to do with the kittens when they stopped for lunch.

Martin was watching the landscape, too, and with the children in the back seat and his wife beside him, he realized with wonder and relief that he was happy. He was thinking of Mies van der Rohe. He was thinking that Mies van der Rohe had said that God hides in the details. Somewhere along the way as an undergraduate Martin had picked up that fact; somewhere he had discussed it on an exam. He was surprised that this thought had come back to him now, and that now he knew what it meant. Martin could never have seen it in stone; Martin's God was hiding in the instant. It was only in the detail of the moment that he could find God. Martin's ultimate comfort was the adhesive intricacy of this domestic life. Each moment was a clear, glutinous cell of experience, and an affirmation of his own existence that kept him tethered safely to the earth.